Also by Alretha Thomas

Daughter Denied

Dancing Her Dreams Away

A NOVEL

ALRETHA THOMAS

Diverse Arts Collective

Published by Diverse Arts Collective, Inc.

First Edition

ISBN-13: 978-0615958675 (Diverse Arts Collective)
ISBN-10: 0615958672

First Printing February 2014

www.Alrethathomas.com.

ACKNOWLEDGMENTS – THANK YOU, LORD!!!

I want to extend my sincerest gratitude to all of my readers everywhere and to all of the book clubs who have supported me since the launch of my debut novel "Daughter Denied" in 2008! Special thanks to Angel Book Club, Diva Readers Book Club, My Sister's Secret Book Club, Reader's Paradise Book Club, Say What?? Book Club, Sistah Girl Reading Club, and Sistahs Read Too Book Club. Your support and encouragement are sincerely appreciated.

A heartfelt thanks goes to Conversations Book Club and Cyrus A. Webb for his longtime support, encouragement, and recognition. Yolanda Oliver, thank you for being my friend and incredible beta reader. Your opinion means the world to me and your unwavering support brings joy to my heart. Selatha Smith of Circle of Friends Book Club, you have been with me from the beginning and I treasure your friendship and loyalty. Ruth Bridges of Literary Sisters, your support has been above and beyond what I ever expected. Bless you! Adai Lamar of KJLH Radio, hugs and kisses for being there for me when it truly counted! A shout out to my gym girlfriend Margaret Stayman. She has the body of a twenty year old! Thank you for reading my work.

A shout out and bear hugs to my agent—Stacey Donaghy! Thank you for being "THE ONE."

Much love to my church family, Monique Bacon, Susan Bacon, Shelley Brown, Damita Ford, Gaylon Griffen, Carolyn Johnson, Alice Jones, Dorothy Samuels, Linda Thomas, Gwendolyn Tolbert, and so many more. Much love and thanks to my girlfriends, Mary Ghorbani, Vanessa Hawkins, Veronica Hendricks, Carolyn Johnson, Veda Johnson, Erika Keys, LaTonya Lindsey, Alisha M. Simko, Angela Williams, Leticia Williams, and Belecia Wilson.

And family, you are last but not least. Love, hugs, and kisses to my husband Audesah Leroy Thomas. Much love to my siblings, aunts, uncles, cousins, nieces, nephews, and in-laws. You mean the world to me! God bless you all.

This book is dedicated to:

My loving mother Elizabeth A. Baker (1939-1975).
My darling husband Audesah L. Thomas.
My siblings Vivian, Levertie, Malik, Farah, and Louis.

Prologue

Good afternoon, my name is Sabrina Brown, and I'd like to officially welcome you to my party, or better yet, my celebration. Maybe send-off would be more appropriate, or as my dear mother would say—my Homegoing. Okay, enough with the euphemisms, welcome to my funeral.

Who knew? I should have. I was the smartest person in high school. They called me Braniac Brown. I was Bradshaw High School's class of 1993 Valedictorian. I graduated top of my class at Spelman and sailed through medical school *and* my residency. I knew it all. So two years ago when one of my new patients asked me if I was expecting, I looked at her askance, hissed, and replied with an unequivocal, "No!"

After soothing my bruised ego, I wondered if she was

onto something. My stomach *was* quite large, but I hadn't been eating a lot. In fact, I didn't have much of an appetite, and I *wasn't* having regular bowel movements. And on more than one occasion I found myself short of breath. Those thoughts sent chills through me. Barely able to think straight, I made an appointment with my gynecologist, hoping that *I was* pregnant. How could I have been so neglectful? But when you're a busy doctor, running your own practice in the hood, it's hard to stop and smell the symptoms. After meeting with my gynecologist and undergoing numerous tests, I learned that my belly wasn't full with my husband Walter's baby. It was full of cancer. And that cancer had wrapped around part of my bowel. The news was paralyzing. I felt like an imbecile, a hypocrite. I couldn't help but think about my female patients and how I had scolded them incessantly about regular check-ups and preventive medicine. And there I was, unbeknownst to me, at death's front door.

As much as I wanted to, I had no time to sit on the pity-pot. My doctor, Walter, and parents were determined to get me well, so they lashed out at the cancer as vigorously as it had attacked me. Time didn't fly, it moved at warped speed. Before I could blink back crocodile tears, I had had a radical hysterectomy, which included the removal of my uterus, ovaries, and fallopian tubes. To my utter disgust and dismay, I also had to have a colostomy. Then there was chemo, hair loss, depression, and sometimes hope. But instead of getting better, in spite of a change in diet, alternative medicine, meditation, and endless rounds of acupuncture, I got worse, and at the advice of my therapist, I decided to stop fighting the inevitable. I took a break from all the debilitating treatments and assessed my life—I took an objective look at who I had been, who I was now, and how I wanted to be remembered.

At the beginning of year two, the final year, Walter told

me he couldn't handle it anymore. He said he couldn't sit around watching me die. I'd be lying if I said I was surprised. When I had opened my clinic eight years ago, I needed a plumber. I got on the Internet, did a search, and *Walter Brown's Perfect Plumbing* was listed as a reliable business on Angie's List. I clicked on the website and Walter's handsome smiling face was looking back at me. He was on time, clean, and smelled good, just like the plumber in that annoying commercial. He said he was impressed with me, and through quivering, beautiful full lips, asked me on a date. The poster child for workaholics, I hadn't had a real date since high school. So I went and we hit it off immediately.

Soon thereafter, he asked my father for my hand in marriage. My father liked Walter and he liked that he shared our surname. And then we started our life together. Unfortunately, each year my practice grew, Walter's business shrank. He began to stay out late, disrespect me, and at one point, I suspected he was cheating on me. That all stopped when I was diagnosed with the Big C. Walter was my knight in shining armor—at least he tried to be, but like my medical degree, the cancer intimidated him and he began to come up missing on important days. And when he did show up for my chemo, you'd think he was the one who was sick.

Before he took off for good, I had started going to chemo by myself. My parents wanted to go, but I wouldn't let them. I wanted to be alone, so I made them wait in the car or go to lunch or even shopping, anything but sit and look at me like I was dying. Okay, I was, but I didn't need to be reminded. I just needed to be alone. My mother couldn't understand that. She wanted me to have someone there and she begged me to call my girls—my Bffs. But they didn't know I was sick. I hadn't told them and I felt guilty for shutting them out, but I didn't want to be pitied and to be honest, I was pissed at them—angry with them for all the years they had wasted.

It's something about being diagnosed with a terminal illness that gives you new found respect and appreciation for life. And every time I thought about how close we all were in middle and high school, before that one unfortunate incident that led to the dissolution of The Fresh Five, I would get furious.

They won't talk to or see one another. Over the years, they've all been there for me, but neither of them would ever let me talk about or mention the others. I couldn't even invite them to my wedding. They opted to celebrate with me one-on-one afterwards. I finally had the upper hand. I decided to use my illness and pending death as a way to get them to come back together. At one point I thought about putting my demands in a will, but that seemed weird. Then I had planned on having my mother send each of them a letter announcing that I had died, that I wanted them to come to my funeral, and that I wanted them to reconcile. But that all just seemed too forced. I knew I had to trust God to answer my prayers. I had to believe that they would come to my funeral, see me in my casket, and have a change of heart. And if none of that happened, then it just wasn't meant to be and our friendship was only meant for a reason and a season, but not a lifetime.

So far, part of my prayer has been answered. They all showed up today—Sheridan, Faye, Victoria, and Danielle. All probably wondering what the hell happened and why I didn't tell them I was dying. Well, get over it, bitches! This is your wake-up call.

Today reminds me of what I had heard a preacher say during a sermon. "One day my friends and I will get dressed up to go to a funeral and when it's over, my friends will go home." I hope my four friends don't just go home. I hope they fulfill the second part of my dying wish—forgive one another and rekindle the love we all once shared. I truly hope they see the light, because life is…oh…okay…here I go…they're putting the casket into the ground now. This is it. Put on your seatbelts, your life jackets, your parachutes, because you're in for a…."

Chapter 1

Sheridan

I hate this part. Let me get the hell out of here. Why in the crap did I come to the cemetery anyway? The service was bad enough with all the sobbing, screaming, and people falling out. I'm just a freakin' glutton for punishment and I have a black eye to prove it. I shove the sunglasses I bought at the carwash up the bridge of my nose, while Sabrina's casket is being lowered into the ground. I stand on my long shaky legs, smooth my wrinkled black dress I got from the Swap Meet yesterday, and pray I don't run into "The Others." That's what I call them now — Faye, Victoria, and Danielle. They're "The Others." Hell, it's been twenty years.

I probably wouldn't even recognize them. And I'm damn sure they ain't gonna recognize me. Truth be told, there are times when I look in the mirror and I scare myself. Time is a mother!

"Excuse me?"

Startled, I turn at the sound of the whiny-sounding voice and give the dimpled-faced woman the once over, wondering how she got the drop on me. The burial ceremony ended thirty minutes ago and the people with good sense have already paid their respects to Sabrina's family and are headed to the parking lot.

"I think you dropped your cigarettes," she says, reaching for my Menthol Kools splayed out across a patch of grass. She scoops the two loose ones up and grabs the pack. She thrusts the tobacco my way, while staring at me with bloodshot eyes and smeared makeup. I take my smokes and give her a slight nod. She gives me a faint smile while she rifles through her small black clutch. She pulls out a crumpled handkerchief, covered in dried mascara and dabs at her face. Must be one of Sabrina's relatives. She looks like she took it hard. I cried too—inside.

"Thanks," I say. I pause when my eyes lock on the ring on her finger. I notice 93 and Bradshaw. "Did you go to Bradshaw?" I ask.

She stops wiping her tears, squints and says, "Yeah, I did. I graduated in 93."

"I did, too," I say, stuffing my Kools into my purse. "How do you know Sabri—"

"Sheridan!" she screams, cutting me off. "Sheridan Hawkins? Lord, have mercy. Good Lord Almighty. Is that you?"

I stand there dumbfounded, wondering how I didn't recognize Faye "Dimples" Johnson. She was known for her big dimples and whiny voice. I'm even more mystified that she's being so cordial, acting like we're Bffs, acting like all the ratchet stuff that went down back in the day never happened. "Yeah, it's me."

"Sheridan, I'm Faye…Dimples…remember, the preacher's kid?"

"I know it's you…I mean I didn't at first, but how could I have not known. You still have that whin…voice of yours and those pretty dimples. You haven't aged at all!"

"Well, you know what they say, 'black don't crack.'"

Bitch please. She just had to go there. "And white ain't tight?"

"Sheridan, you look good for a —"

"Almost middle-aged white woman?" I ask, snatching off my shades.

"Lordy no…you look good period. Look at your pretty blue eyes. And you still have all that pretty long blonde hair. You know you were the prettiest girl in high school. Every guy and male teacher wanted a piece of Miss Sheridan. It's no wonder Gary… "

We share knowing looks and tension-filled silence sucks up all the oxygen. I clear my dry throat and we both look at the cemetery workers repositioning the large wreath stand near Sabrina's burial ground.

"Are you going to the repast?" she asks, interrupting the quiet.

"I hadn't planned to," I say, now desperate for a cigarette. "What about you?"

"Of course. You know my husband did the eulogy and New Hope is our church," she says with a look of pride.

"No, I didn't know that. I didn't know you were married."

"Yeah, I am," she says, glancing at the class ring on her wedding ring finger. "I just wore this today in honor of Sabrina. I can't believe she's gone. My, Lord, she was such a beautiful person inside and out."

"I can't believe it either. I guess *I will* be going to the repast."

"Oh...okay, I'll see you over there. I can't — " The sound of a horn brings our conversation to a halt. Faye wipes the sweat from her arched brow and swivels her long neck toward the parking lot. "That's my husband Mark. I better go. I can't wait to catch-up. It's been a long time. By the way, do you still paint?"

"Rarely," I say. "Do you still make those dolls?" I ask.

She nods, the horn sounds again, and she takes off, looking over her shoulder one last time. I watch her sway her narrow hips in her long black dress while she picks up speed. Her shoulder length weave moves like it's really her hair. I wonder where the other two are. I wonder if they were here and I just didn't recognize or see them. Not everybody came to the cemetery. Maybe they were no-shows. They were probably at the church and I just missed them. Now I wish I would have let Sabrina give me the 411 on the others. She tried, but I wasn't hearing it. I didn't wanna know nothin' 'bout Faye, Victoria, or Danielle. They were non-mother...let me chill.

I take one last look at Sabrina's burial site before I head to my car. Why didn't she tell me? Why didn't she tell me she was dying? Two years ago was the last time we had spoken to one another. I called, emailed, sent text messages and came by a whole bunch of times, and I always got the same response. "She's out of town." "She's not home." "I'll tell her you called." Her mother would always be the one to answer her cell phone, her house phone, and her front door. It didn't take me long to get the message. Sabrina was done. I knew she was pissed that I wouldn't fix things with the others, but I didn't know she would go totally left. I wonder did the others know.

I get out of my head and walk toward the parking lot. I can't wait to get out of this black dress. It's one of those scorching hot October days in the city of angels. I look up and squint as the sun's rays stretch over the clear blue sky. Blinded, I look away and zoom in on a large oak tree just in time to see an orange butterfly with specs of gold and green land on a thin branch. I get a kick in my gut. Sabrina loved butterflies. Butterflies are free and now she is, too, from her pain and this hell masquerading as life.

As I near my car, I grin. I'm happy I got it washed. It doesn't look so bad next to the Mercedes in front of it. I remember when I had a Mercedes and a Lexus. And Gary had a Porsche. I remember when we had it all. I stop thinking about what I used to have and get behind the wheel of my silver Honda. I turn and stare at Sabrina's obituary on the passenger seat. Her cat shaped eyes seem to look right through me. I remember this picture of her when she first opened her clinic. She was complaining about her freckles. I snatch the obituary and scream, "Damn! Damn! Damn!" Now I know how Florida felt on "Good Times" when her husband James died.

I toss the obituary to the side, grab my cigarettes from my purse, and light up. I take a drag, praying that I don't get cancer, too. I need to quit, but I need something to take the edge off while I try to get through the repast and my life. I don't know why I told Faye I'd go. I guess because she said she was going. I don't want it to look like she cared about Sabrina more than I did. She already out cried me. I suck hard and let the smoke calm my nerves. I feel better already. I take another drag, thinking about how beautiful Faye looked. She's right, black doesn't crack. That's probably why I look more like Gary's mother than his wife. We're the same age, but his dark chocolate skin looks as smooth as it did when he played football at Bradshaw. Faye's husband's not a bad looking guy either, and I have to admit he can preach with the best of 'em. Speaking of husbands, I hope Walter's okay. He looked like he was about to past out when the pallbearers lifted Sabrina's casket.

I slip on my shades, put my cigarette out, and start up the car, wondering if Faye has money. That was a big ass church—a megachurch. Shoot, there had to be at least a thousand people at the funeral and the church still looked big. Sabrina took care of a lot of people in the hood for free and they came in droves to show their appreciation. In their eyes she's Saint Sabrina. I have to agree. Out of the five of us, she wasn't only the smartest, but the sweetest—genuine sweet—not that fake sweet Faye dishes out with her church girl act. No, Sabrina was the real deal. One hundred. It's no wonder she was so successful. It looks like Faye didn't do too bad either. That Range Rover she took off in looked new.

I'm not about to be shown up. As far as I'm concerned, I've made it, too. I may be driving a Honda, but my other car's a Lexus! It's in the shop for repairs and Gary and I aren't actually living with his mama in Compton, we're taking care of her—helping her out, while we're waiting for our Beverly Hills mini-mansion to be built. And our daughter Kimberly's a junior at USC. Yeah, that's my story and I sticking to it!

I slowly drive up Sabrina's street looking for a parking space while at the same time eyeing the expensive as hell custom built homes. Ladera Heights is an upper scale neighborhood in Los Angeles. I call it the black Beverly Hills. Cars, ranging from hooptie to luxury, are lined up along the street, bumper to bumper, and people from all walks of life mill about. I notice some still crying and others carrying plates of food, stuffing their faces. If I had gotten here sooner, I'd have a parking space by now, but like a fool, I went to the church thinking the repast was there. It should have been, because this is ridiculous.

A heavyset woman, with a yellow rag on her head, followed by three snotty-nosed kids, runs into the street, making a beeline for Sabrina's house. They probably weren't even at the funeral. They're most likely here to eat and I ain't mad at 'em because Mrs. Brown can throw down. I might pack a few plates myself. I notice an empty parking space at the end of the block and pick up speed, only to be cut off by a late model BMW.

"Excuse you, I was gonna park there!" I yell. The woman wearing a fancy black hat rolls her eyes and shakes her head. "No she didn't!" I say, watching her take the last spot on the block. Okay, let me chill. I'm not trying to set if off at the repast. I circle the block and get lucky. Another spot has opened up. I park and pull the visor down, remove my shades, and touch up my makeup. I wince at the sight of the bruise that can be seen through my foundation. I grab my compact and dab makeup under and around my eye. I put everything away and pop the trunk. Getting out of the car, I crane my neck taking in all the people on Sabrina's lawn. Saint Sabrina would have a fit if she knew they were hanging out on her Saint Augustine. I laugh out loud at my own joke. While I lift the trunk, a smile spreads across my face when I think about the painting I made in her memory. I was gonna mail it, but now that I've decided to actually hang out, I might as well bring it in. I remove it, close the trunk, lock my car, and make my way to the festivities. From a distance I can see the woman who stole my parking space. I should have known she was here for the repast. The black is a dead giveaway, no pun intended. I notice her swaying in her red bottom shoes, barely able to walk. I quickly reach her and then past her. All that rushing and being in a hurry — and I still beat her here.

I pause at the door when I see a butterfly chime hanging from the porch ceiling. I reach up to touch it when a familiar voice gets my attention. "Sheridan! Sheridan! I'm so glad you stayed," Mrs. Brown says, grabbing my extended arm and pulling me into the house. "I want you to make yourself right at home. Sabrina would want that. There's plenty to eat, too," she says, passing her thick hands over an apron with the words *World's Greatest Mom* embroidered on the front. I choke up at the sight of it.

"Thank you, Mother Brown. What can I help you with?"

Her big brown eyes with red rims shift to the package in my hand before she answers. "Do you want me to take that so you can get your food? I'll put it in Sabrina's office," she says, rubbing her flat nose that's sprinkled with red freckles.

"This is for Sabrina," I say, handing her the picture wrapped in brown wrapping paper.

I notice her eyes get misty and she blinks really hard. "Oh, Sheridan this is so sweet of you. You didn't have to."

"What's that?" Sabrina's father asks, joining us in the foyer. Shaking his bald head, he jumps back when a trio of squealing girls brushes past us.

"It's a painting, Jerome."

"A painting?"

"You know Sheridan paints. She won first prize in that art contest at Bradshaw. Remember?"

Mr. Brown knits his bushy salt and pepper brows. "That was a long time ago, Catalina."

"Man, it wasn't that long ago," Mrs. Brown says with a sneer. "Can I open it?"

"Go right ahead," I say.

She moves out of the foyer into the living room, with Mr. Brown and me following. Holding onto the package tightly, she sits in a large orange recliner. I force back tears while I take in the family pictures on the fireplace mantel. Sabrina was so into family. A small group of Sabrina's relatives and neighbors gather around Mrs. Brown while she removes the paper. I feel my face get flushed and my stomach sinks as the portrait of butterflies is revealed. A hush falls over the room and then it's suddenly filled with "oohs" and "ahhs."

"This is just absolutely beautiful," Mrs. Brown says. "Walt, Walter. Where are you?" she asks, stretching her neck.

"I'm right here, Mother Brown," Walter says, from the hallway.

We all turn toward him when he inches his way in. Tall, lanky, and disheveled, he grins with sadness in his doe shaped eyes. He passes his hand over his face and it dawns on me that he's not wearing his wedding ring. My eyes scan the room and the wedding picture that used to hang over the mantel is no longer there. *What's up with that?*

"What is it, Mother Brown?" he asks, looking at me.

"I wanted you to see the painting Sheridan made in memory of Sabrina."

Mr. Brown mumbles what sounds like a few choice words and storms off.

"Jerome! Jerome!" Mrs. Brown shouts. "Never mind him."

Walter averts his eyes and takes the picture from Mrs. Brown. He stares at it and nods. "It's nice," he says, looking me up and down. "Long time no see," he says.

"Yeah...long time," I say, wondering if he was the one who told Sabrina to shut me out. I wouldn't be surprised. The last time I spoke to Sabrina, she thought he was sleeping around on her. I wouldn't put it past him. I never did understand why she settled for a blue collar guy. I told her it wasn't gonna work. The average man can't stand a successful woman. But Sabrina wasn't hearing it. She was in love.

"How you been?" he asks, putting the picture on the coffee table. Then, catching me off guard, he grabs my hand and shakes it.

I snatch it back and say, "Living. But right now I'm...I'm...trying to...to... hold it together. Sabrina was my heart." My eyes sting like crazy and tears pour out of me and onto the floor. *Dammit, I don't want to cry!* My cries turn into sobs and I curl over, shaking and trembling with grief.

Walter and Mrs. Brown grab me and sit me down in the recliner.

"What's wrong with her?" a little girl with braids decorated with beads asks.

"Y'all kids go outside," Mrs. Brown says, shooing the kids away.

The children exchange curious looks and the other adults usher them out of the room. I sit in the recliner with my head down, lost and turned out, thinking about how much Sabrina probably suffered and that I wasn't there to hold her hand. Mrs. Brown sits on the arm of the chair and takes mine. Walter hovers over me with a constipated look on his face.

"It's okay to cry, Sherry," Mrs. Brown says.

"Sherry?" I say, looking up. "That's what Sabrina used to call me in high school." I look in my purse for tissue but I have none. Walter must read my mind because he runs out and returns with a box of Kleenex.

"Thank you," I say, taking a handful of tissue. I blow my nose and look into Mrs. Brown's caring eyes for answers. Walter sits on the sofa wringing his large calloused hands. "Why didn't you tell me she was dying? All the times I called and came over. I would have been here. I should have been here. This is so messed up. How do you think it felt getting that call out of the blue that she was dead?" Surprised at my own rage, I sit back and try to pull it together.

"Baby, I begged Sabrina to get in contact with you girls, but she wouldn't listen to me. You know how headstrong she was."

"But why?"

"She was angry at you girls because you wouldn't talk to each other. She hated the idea that she couldn't have all of you at once. Just bits and pieces of you."

"What do you mean bits and pieces?"

"You know how the two of you would talk and get

together."

I nod.

"She would do the same with Faye, Victoria, and Danielle. Never all together like you all were in high school. She says when she would be with you, she had to act like Faye, Victoria, and Danielle didn't exist and she had to do the same with the others. It was so frustrating for her. She felt like she was in the middle and she didn't like it one bit. She felt like you all were using her."

"Using her?"

"In her mind, as long as you all had her, you didn't have to fix things. You still had a connection to the others."

My bleary eyes meet Walter's, wondering if he's buying any of Mrs. Brown's story. He sits back on the sofa, looking up at the ceiling, tears streaming down his face. "You're not the only one she was pissed at," he says.

"What do you mean?" I ask.

"Sabrina and I aren't together anymore. I mean…not just because she passed away, but a year before she died, I took off. I abandoned her. I couldn't hang. When she needed me the most, I wasn't there for her. Try living with that." He glares at me, rises, and bolts.

Mrs. Brown and I watch him leave.

"Damn…I mean dang. I didn't know."

"So much has happened, Sherry. *I can* tell you this much, Sabrina loved you girls and her last wish was for you all to forgive one another and become friends again. That's all she wanted, all she's ever wanted. You girls have missed out on twenty years. That's a long time. You've done so many things, been so many places, have had so many experiences, separate. You're going to have to get to know one another all over again."

I swallow hard trying to digest everything that Mrs. Brown has said.

"I know that seems like a huge feat, but it's not

impossible. I truly believe deep down you all still love one another. Sometimes pride and ego can get the best of us. Just know that I'm here for you, and I love you all like my own daughters…you, Dimples, Vicky, and Danny!"

I reach over and hug Mrs. Brown. She removes my arms from around her neck and nudges me forward, peering at me. "What's wrong?"

"I should be asking you?" she says.

"Huh?"

"Who's be beating on you, Sherry?" She points to my eye.

"No one. I ran into a door."

"Sheridan Hawkins, don't you —"

"Catalina, Mrs. Franklin from down the street wants to talk to you."

"I'll be right there, Jerome."

"She says it's urgent."

"Okay," Mrs. Brown says. "I'll be right there, and Sherry, don't go anywhere."

I sit there feeling like I'm on detention in the principal's office while I watch Mrs. Brown and Mr. Brown leave the room. I grab my compact and take a look at my face. "Damn!"

Chapter 2

Faye

I sigh while Mark circles Sabrina's block for the fifth time. I told him I don't mind walking. By the time he finds a parking space, the repast will be over.

"*I told* Mrs. Brown she should have had the repast at the church," Mark says, scanning the block. "This is a nightmare," he adds, pointing to all the cars parked on the street and in driveways and people running here and there.

"No, Mark, a nightmare is finding out your best friend had ovarian cancer, suffered for two years, and didn't think you were a good enough friend for her to confide in or be by her side. Then you get a phone call out of the blue telling you she's dead. That's a nightmare," I say, choking up.

"I'm sorry, baby. I'm sorry about what happened with Sabrina, but it's not your fault. You tried to get in touch with her. I was there all the times you called and went by and staked out the house."

"I should have tried harder. I should have demanded to see her! Lord, have mercy. Forgive me, God."

"You're going to have to forgive her *and* yourself Faye."

He looks at me and I turn away. "That's never been one of my virtues, Mark. Forgiveness doesn't come easily for me." I stare wistfully out the window at a group of boys roughhousing on the sidewalk.

"That's what you always say, Faye. How can you ask God to forgive you when you won't forgive your friends? How can you be married to a preacher and not believe in forgiveness? Better yet, how can you call yourself a Christian and not believe in forgiveness?"

"Stop! Stop! That man…over there…he's getting ready to leave," I say, happy to change the subject.

"I told you we would get one," Mark says, pulling up behind the black Escalade. The man gets in his car and pulls off and Mark grabs the spot. He turns off the ignition and peers at me.

"What? What's wrong?" I ask, shifting in my seat.

"You're a piece of work, woman. You need to repent, holding onto something that happened twenty years ago."

"You weren't there, so don't judge. We better head in. I wonder is Sheridan here. She said she was coming, but she's been known to tell a lie or two. I can't believe how much she's aged. And she hasn't done it well either. I'm sure smoking doesn't help. Everyone knows it causes premature wrinkles and if I was seeing straight, it looks like she had a black—"

"Faye!"

"What?"

"Stop it."

"Stop what?"

"Don't you hear yourself? Stop tearing that woman down. You haven't seen her in twenty years. You don't know what's she's been through. Didn't you tell me she grew up in foster care with black parents? Never knew her real parents. That couldn't have been easy."

I take a deep breath and hang my head. Mark is such a better person than I'll ever be. "You're right. I'm sorry. I'm just so out of sorts. Maybe we shouldn't go...or you go...I'll wait in the car."

"We're going in to give the Browns our support," he says, lifting my chin and getting out of the car.

I reach in the backseat for a small package and join him. He locks the car and we make our way to Sabrina's. At a distance, I can see Mrs. Brown in the driveway talking to an elderly woman leaning on a cane. My heart grows heavy when I think about how painful this all must be for her and Mr. Brown. Sabrina was their only child. They say losing a child is one of the worst things that could happen to a person. Sometimes I think not being able to have a child is the worst thing that could happen to a person.

Mark and I have been trying to get pregnant for three years now. We've done it all — prayed, tried artificial insemination, and two rounds of In vitro, to no avail. We've undergone all kinds of tests and a team of doctors swear we should have a ton of kids by now. Mark thinks it's all psychological and that we're trying too hard. Last year he suggested we adopt. The devil is a liar. I'm going to have my own baby. And then there are times when I'm alone and I think about my past — and some of the things I did. Maybe God is punishing me. Maybe that's why I can't get pregnant *this time around.*

Mark grabs my hand, pulls me forward, and plants a kiss on my cheek. God can't be too mad at me to have given me such a loving husband. I wonder how Gary and Sheridan are doing. They were the best-looking couple in high school—prom king and queen. We were all happy for Sheridan nabbing Gary, the captain of the football team— well, everyone except Victoria. She and Sheridan were cheerleaders and she claimed Gary was originally interested in her. That was until he got a whiff of Sheridan. Victoria tolerated their relationship, but she never got over it. In her words, she hated that Gary chose "the white girl," over her. She tried a few times to sabotage their relationship, but things always backfired. I can't blame her for wanting him— *every* girl did. Gary got a full scholarship to USC and I heard he was eventually drafted by the Dallas Enforcers. I never kept up with Sheridan or wanted to after what happened. I couldn't stand to be around any of them after that night. I should have never gone—

"Faye?"

"Huh?"

"Mother Brown was asking you how you're doing."

I look up, wondering when we had made it to the house. I need to focus. "I'm hanging in there," I say.

"I was just telling Mrs. Franklin that we have to trust God. Pierre is missing," Mrs. Brown says.

"He's my baby. All I got. Him and my granddaughter and now she's about to up and get married," Mrs. Franklin says.

"How long has he been missing?" Mark asks.

"Last night was the last time I saw him."

"Have you called the police?"

"I did, but they're not taking it serious. I've put up fliers, too."

"My Lord, how old is your grandson?"

"He's not my grandson, he's my dog."

"Your dog?" Mark asks, trying to stifle a laugh.

As far as I'm concerned he can stay missing.

"Mrs. Brown is right, Mrs. Franklin. God even cares about our pets," Mark says.

Mrs. Franklin rears back and shoots daggers at Mark. "Pierre is not a pet. He's family."

"Excuse me, ma'am. God cares about our family members," Mark says, vainly suppressing the grin that's fighting its way across his face. "Mother Brown, how are you and Mr. Brown doing?"

"As well as can be expected," Mrs. Brown says. "And I want to thank you for that beautiful eulogy."

"It sure was beautiful," Mrs. Franklin says, nodding her head.

"You all hungry? There's plenty of food inside," Mrs. Brown says.

"I can eat," Mark says. "And please don't hesitate to let us know if we can be of help with anything else."

"I sure will and I'll be right in," Mrs. Brown says.

Mark gives Mrs. Brown a warm smile and ushers me into the house. I stop in the foyer, looking around, thinking about the last time I was here. Sabrina and I had lunch on her patio and she was trying to make me feel better about my infertility woes. I remember her lifting her blouse and laughing about how much weight she had gained. She told me a patient of hers asked her if she was pregnant. I never spoke to or saw her again after that day.

"Come on, baby," Mark says.

"I need to use the restroom. Go ahead. I'll be right there. Oh, can you hold this for me?" I ask, giving him my package.

"Okay," he says with a face coated in concern.

I watch my husband disappear into the other part of the house, and I walk toward the guest bathroom. A young couple in the cut sneaks kisses and two teenaged girls fuss over their iPhones. I come to the closed bathroom door and knock. There's no answer, so I turn the knob, but it doesn't open. It seems as if my bladder realizes I'm locked out of the bathroom and suddenly demands to be emptied.

"Do you know if anybody is in here?" I ask the couple.

"I'm not sure," the young woman says, giving me the once over. I want to tell her, I'm happily married and not competing with her, but she turns back to her man. I knock on the door again.

"Just a minute please!" the bathroom hog says.

"Okay, but I have to go."

I shift my weight from foot-to-foot and knock again. "I said give me a minute."

"What's wrong?"

I turn and give Mr. Brown a "help me" look. "I have to go to the restroom really badly and someone is in this restroom and they won't come out."

"Is that all? Follow me. You can use the restroom in the master bedroom."

I remember the way and can get there on my own, but I keep that to myself and try to be gracious. "Thank you, Mr. Brown, bless your heart!"

"How are you doing?"

"Okay. Just trying to be strong."

"That husband of yours is a fine preacher," he says, pressing open the door to Sabrina and Walter's bedroom. I run past him, into the bathroom that's decorated with butterfly wallpaper, and shut the door. "Thank you, again." I lift my dress and do my business.

I hear Mr. Brown's footfalls and then he says, "No problem, I'll see you up front. Oh, by the way, Sherry is here."

Sherry? The last time I heard her called that we were at Bradshaw. Sitting on the toilet, I flash back to my encounter with Sheridan at the cemetery. If I had known it was her, I never would have approached. I had left my handkerchief on the folding chair I had been sitting on and went back to get it when I noticed her sitting out there alone, staring at the casket. She seemed upset and when I saw the cigarettes on the ground, I just felt compelled to reach out to her. The

Sheridan I knew didn't smoke and she was a total looker. Age is something else. I finish up and wash my hands. Looking up at the mirror I gasp. Why didn't Mark tell me my makeup is smeared? I look like a raccoon on crack. I reach in my clutch for my foundation and touch up my makeup, still thinking about *Sheridan*.

"Dimples, are you okay?"

"I'm fine, sweetie. I'll be right out." I put my makeup in my purse and exit the bathroom into Mark's open arms. "What's going on?"

"What do you mean?" he asks, holding me in a tight embrace.

"Calling me Dimples and being all loving."

"I just feel badly about how things went down. Mr. Brown told me you were in here."

I move out of his arms and say, "Yeah. I'll be okay." I gaze at the king sized bed, wondering what Walter is going to do without Sabrina. "Have you seen Walter? He didn't look too well at the funeral." Mark clears his throat and sits on the bed. He pulls me down next to him. "What?"

"Mr. Brown said he and Sabrina got a divorce about a year ago. He says Walt walked out on her. And he says he's 'fit to be tied' that Walter came to the funeral."

"What the hell?" I say, jumping up. "I'd be 'fit to be tied,' too."

"Faye, keep it down."

"I can't believe he had the nerve to show up. Who does that?"

Mark rises, trying to calm me down. "It's not that cut and dry. He was there."

"He was where?"

"He was there the day she passed, but she was unconscious. According to Mother Brown, he came back on his hands and knees, but it was too late. Sabrina never came to."

"I don't think he should be here."

"Mother Brown said Sabrina forgave him before he even came back. And she told Mother Brown that if he wanted to come to the funeral he could."

"That's messed up and when did Mother Brown tell you all of this?" I ask, with my hands planted on my narrow hips.

"When I was in the living room. She told me and Sherry...or Sheridan or whatever her name is."

"You're talking to Sheridan?"

"No, the Browns were talking to both of us."

"Where's Walt now?" I ask.

"He took off."

"Good!" I say. "I can't believe Sabrina agreed to let him come to her funeral after he ran out on her!"

"Faye, not everybody has an unforgiving heart, especially not Sabrina."

"Lord, have mercy. You just had to go there!"

"Baby, you're going to have to let go and let God. It's because of your attitude that Sabrina cut you off two years ago."

"Why are you saying that?" I ask, moving away from him.

"Sheridan tried to fill me in on what Mother Brown told her before we got here. I didn't understand all of it, but it seems as if Sabrina was frustrated with you, Sheridan, Vivian, and Debra not speaking to one another. And because of that she cut you all off. She wanted to teach you a lesson or something like that."

"You mean, me, Sheridan, Victoria, and Danielle," I say.

"Right...sorry...You guys were the Brat Pack...right?"

"No, we were The Fresh Five."

"Whatever you all were called, you need to talk to Mother Brown if you want to hear firsthand why Sabrina didn't tell you she was sick."

"Don't worry, I plan to!" I say, leaving him standing

there with his mouth open.

Chapter 3

Victoria

We need a drink—a real *stiff* drink. No, we need *three* drinks. One for me, one for myself, and one for I! If one more person bangs on this door, I'm going to slit my wrist. This is not the only bathroom in Sabrina's house, people! Okay let me take a chill pill. I wish I had some pills for real so I wouldn't have to feel. I need to calm down. It's going to be okay. Count to ten.

I stand up straight, look in the mirror at the black designer hat on my aching head, and say, "1, 2, 3, 4, 5, 6, 7, 8, 9, 10." There it is. That's better. We can do this. We can go out there and face the Browns and the rest of the good people who are here to show their love for Sabrina. We can even face the ones who are only here to eat, be nosey, or whatever. We can even face Sheridan. Speaking of faces, I can't believe how old she's gotten. I wonder what Gary thinks about his Barbie doll now? I thought I was going to have an orgasm when I successfully stole her parking spot. Now she knows how it feels to have something you desperately want taken from you. I'm surprised she didn't recognize me. I came so close to putting her in check when she ran past me reeking of cheap perfume. But I promised, God, Sabrina, and myself that I would be good today. Loud banging interrupts my thoughts.

"Open this door! Who's in there?"

I flush the toilet and yell, "I'll be out in a minute!"

"No, open this door right now!"

"What?" I ask, wondering who the hell is trying to kick me out of my sanctuary.

"This is Mrs. Brown and I need you to come out right now!"

"Mother Brown?" I creep to the door, open it, and give her the most innocent smile I could muster.

"Vicky! What are you doing in here?" she asks, shoving her way in.

"I was just freshening up," I say, grabbing my makeup bag out of my Louis. I pull out a tube of lipstick and dab at my full lips.

"Mrs. Franklin's granddaughter and her fiancé say you've been in here for over an hour now and that you won't let anyone use the restroom."

"I...uh...that's...the truth. It's the truth."

Mrs. Brown closes and locks the door. "What are you running from?"

"I'm not running. I'm...I'm scared."

"Scared of what?" she asks, removing my hat. "I can't see you with this on your head." She gives my hat a gander and sets it on a wicker hamper next to the shower.

"I'm afraid of who've I've become. Who I am."

"What are you talking about?"

"I should have been there for Sabrina. I didn't even try to see her after she stood me up for lunch. Mother Brown, I never even called to see why she didn't show up at the restaurant. I'm so selfish and self-centered. I'm not right. Look at me now…it's all about me…how I'm feeling. What's going on with me? How are you doing, Mother Brown? How are you holding up? Can I do something for you? Please give me something to do so I can get out of myself. Please, please," I say. Tears pool in my eyes and I swallow hard. I grab tissue and wipe my eyes. "Talk to me, Mother Brown."

"I need to talk to *all* of you. I'm just waiting for Danielle to get here. Her rental car broke down on the way to the cemetery. She should be here soon."

"Danny? I mean, Danielle. I haven't seen her in—"

"Twenty years," Mrs. Brown says with raised brows.

"I wonder what she's doing in a rental."

"Danny lives in New York now. She's a partner at a law firm in Manhattan."

"Oh…I…I didn't know."

"Yeah, she flew all the way out here for the service. Sherry is here, too."

"I know. I saw *Sheridan*."

"As soon as Danielle gets here, we're going to talk. I can't take all this drama. Now I'm trying to be patient with you all, but I just buried my baby today, and I'm trying to be strong, but I don't appreciate people questioning me and blaming me for Sabrina not telling you all she was sick."

"Who's blaming you?"

"Dimples."

"Faye is here?"

"Yeah and you haven't seen her *or* Sherry in twenty years, too."

"Faye needs to go somewhere with her holier than thou

self," I say, ignoring Mrs. Brown's dig.

"She just wants to know why Sabrina did what she did."

"Why did she keep us in the dark?"

"Like I said, I'll talk to you all together. I already told Sherry, and I don't want to have to keep repeating myself."

"I understand, Mother Brown and I'm sorry if I caused you any undue stress. I love you and I loved Sabrina. I just wish I could have been there for her. I just hope she didn't suffer."

Mrs. Brown twists her face and bites on her trembling bottom lip. "What kind of crazy comment is that, Victoria? Of course she suffered. My baby hurt for a long time. What did you think? Did you think having cancer would be pain free?" she asks, weeping. "There was nothing I could do for her. Nothing you could do. I'm just glad God took her so she doesn't have to suffer anymore."

"I'm sorry," I say, sobbing. "I'm sorry for saying what I said. I'm always putting my foot in my mouth. I just feel so guilty. I can't stand it."

Mrs. Brown grabs a guest towel from the rack and dabs at her face and then hands it to me. "Well, you can do something about it now."

I give her a questioning look. "What?"

"Make up with your sisters—your friends. Give Sabrina her dying wish. You girls forgive one another and become a family again. I need my daughters now more than ever."

"But—"

"But nothing. I don't want to hear it. Now get yourself together and come to the living room. And how's Curtis and the kids? Why didn't they come?"

"Uh...uh...they're fine. The kids are sick right now and Curtis stayed home to take care of them. He sends his love."

"Okay, after we work this out, I want to have a big barbeque with all my daughters and their husbands and children. I have faith that this is going to be worked out. Too many years have passed — you girls with your twenty years and Sabrina with her two years. None of it was right. You understand me?"

"Yes, Mother Brown."

I watch her leave, toss the towel, grab my hat, and place it on my head full of curls. Maybe I'll just sneak out before she notices. I put my lipstick in my purse and notice the one year Alcoholics Anonymous chip I got when I took my cake last week staring back at me. I can't believe I've been sober for a year now. I pray I can get through this day without going back out. Next to the chip is my open wallet and I get a glimpse of the Christmas family photo I took with my husband Curtis, our eight-year-old daughter Tangie and our nine-year-old son Matt.

Curtis and I've been separated for a year now and he has custody of the kids. Sabrina loved my kids and she loved Curtis. She thought he was just perfect for me. I didn't have the heart to tell her we had separated and he has custody. I didn't have the heart to tell her I had turned into a drunk and that's why I didn't bother trying to find out why she was a no-show at lunch. Because truth be told, I never showed. I had forgotten all about it. By the time I had come out of my drunken stupor, and remembered we were supposed to get together, it was too late. I called the restaurant and the hostess told me Sabrina had left a message that she wasn't going to be able to make it. I didn't even bother to find out why. What kind of friend does that? What kind of woman loses custody of her own kids? What could a mother possibly do that's so horrible that her babies are removed from her home? Every time I think about what I did to my babies, I want a drink. So I don't think about it. I close my purse, take a deep breath, and head to the living room.

Sitting on the sofa, in Sabrina's living room, I can't seem to take my eyes off of the little vintage doll Faye made in memory of Sabrina. It's sitting next to the gold wrapping paper it came in. Looking at it a certain way, the doll does resemble Sabrina, with its cat eyes and freckles. I can't believe Faye's still making dolls and Sheridan's still painting. I make a mental note to get the plant from my car I picked up from the local nursery. That's my thing—plants, flowers, and gardening. I love getting my hands dirty. At Bradshaw I wanted to take up horticulture, but my mother wanted me to be a cheerleader like she was back in the day. She said it was how she met my father. He was the star of his football team and my mother was the head cheerleader. They eventually got married and he never made it to the pros, but he did make a girl and two boys. "Girl, you have the long legs and the looks," my mother would tell me all fired up. It made me happy to see her happy. So I tried out with Sheridan and we both made the squad. I never saw Sheridan as competition. I didn't even see her color. She was the Teena Marie of Bradshaw. She was blacker than all of us put together. Raised in the system, bounced from one foster home to another. She even lived in the projects at one time. Then she finally settled in with the Greens, a middle-aged black couple who had a huge house off of Avalon. It wasn't until Gary started checking for her, that she became my *archrival*. I've always liked that word. I think I'll make it one of the spelling words for my fifth graders next week.

"Vicky! Vicky! Earth to Vicky!"

"I'm sorry, Mother Brown. What did you say?"

"I asked you why you came in here and didn't speak to anybody."

I take a moment and think about my answer. I force myself to look Sheridan's way. She stares at me while she sucks on a chicken bone. Faye, sitting up under her preacher husband, shakes her head in disapproval. I can't believe two decades has passed. They both look the same—Sheridan a lot older and Faye, just a little older. I can't believe Faye's still rocking a weave.

"I spoke when I came in. You guys were talking and didn't hear me."

"Well, we're not talking now," she says, shifting in the recliner, waiting for me to speak.

"Hello, Sheridan…Faye, Faye's husband."

"Hey," they both say under their breath.

"And by the way, my name is Mark. Hello."

"What time did you say Danielle is going to get here? I'm going to have to get going," I say, ignoring *Mark*.

"She'll be here any minute now," Mrs. Brown says. "Jerome! Jerome!"

"Catalina, why are you doing all that screaming?" Mr. Brown asks, running into the living room.

"Check out front and see if you see Danielle."

"Okay. Okay. Calm down," he says, going toward the front door.

The room grows silent and Mark rises. We all watch him, wondering why he's creeping toward the picture window that's covered with long tan drapes. He puts his thick finger up to his mouth and looks around.

"Mark, what—"

He raises his hand, silencing Faye. With one sudden move, he pulls the drapes back and one of the tiniest dogs I've ever seen comes from behind the curtains, running, skipping, and yelping."

"Pierre? Oh my goodness, it's Pierre!" Mrs. Brown shouts.

"Who's Pierre?" Sheridan and I ask.

"Mrs. Franklin's Dog," Mark says, picking him up.

The dog squirms, barks, and jumps out of Mark's arms. He lands in Faye's lap and she jumps up screaming like she's been hit with the Holy Ghost. The dog nips at her heels while she runs through the house calling on Jesus, Allah, and Buddha. We all roar with laughter. Faye has been afraid of dogs as long as I can remember. It doesn't matter how big or small, she's just afraid.

"Mark, get him. Lord Jesus, help me!" she screams, running back into the living room and jumping onto the sofa. Mark grabs the dog just before he takes a bite out of her toes.

"Gotcha," he says. "What are you doing scaring my wife? Boy, I'll take you to the dog pound scaring my baby like that."

The black dog moves his head from left to right and raises his ears that are white with specks of brown. He looks at Mark as though he understands him and then starts barking again.

We all turn toward Mr. Brown when he enters. "Danielle is not here yet and what's all the commotion? I can hear y'all all the way down the street." Mr. Brown looks up at Faye standing on the sofa and rubs his bald head. "Faye, what's wrong with you?" he asks. She points to the dog. "Oh, yeah right, I see the Lord answered Mrs. Franklin's prayer. Where was he?"

"Behind the drapes," Mrs. Brown says.

"Where does Mrs. Franklin live? I'd love to be the one to deliver her *family* member," Mark says.

"Come with me. She's just four houses over," Mr. Brown says.

"Baby, I'll be right back. You gonna be okay?" Mark asks Faye.

I can't help but admire the way Mark interacts with Faye. Not only is he a powerful preacher, but he's also a looker. He reminds me of a dark complexioned Boris Kodjoe. Yeah...not bad at all. I mean, he's no Gary Hawkins. Speaking of Gary, I wonder why he's not here with Sheridan—standing by *her* side. Maybe they're no longer an item. I stretch my neck a bit to get a look at her left hand. From where I sit, I can't tell if she's wearing a ring. I always wondered if Gary really loved Sheridan or was it Jungle Fever. I mean, *really* cared about her, like Mark seems to care about Faye. I can tell Mark is really into Faye by the way he looks at her. I remember when Curtis would look at me that way. It's the kind of look that makes you feel like you're the only woman in the room and in the world. Unfortunately, the last time Curtis looked at me, he made me feel like I was the worst woman in the world. He was right. I even gave him my three-carat wedding ring back, hoping that would make him forgive me faster.

Faye nods and watches Mark leave with Mr. Brown. She waits until they're completely out of sight before she comes down off of the sofa. We all exchange curious looks and start howling all over again—that is everyone except Faye.

"That's not funny, you guys."

"Oh, yes it is," Sheridan says. "I should have given him this bone to calm his ass...I mean butt down. What kind of dog is that?"

"It's a Boston Terrier," Mrs. Brown says.

"You mean a Boston *Terror!*" Faye shouts.

We all laugh again. It feels good to laugh after a day filled with tears. "Faye, how did you end up being so afraid of dogs anyway?" I ask.

"Yeah, that's a good question," Sheridan says.

"You guys don't remember?"

"No, I just remember you were always afraid of dogs," I say.

"Remember that day we were all gonna meet at Danielle's house?" Faye asks. Sheridan and I share questioning looks. "You guys don't remember the Sadie Hawkins dance?"

"Faye, that was twenty years ago," Sheridan says.

Suddenly the sight of Faye standing in front of Danielle's house with her skirt ripped to shreds flashes in my head. "Wait a minute, I remember," I say. "You got attacked."

"Right...I got attacked by Danielle's neighbor's pitbull," Faye says, shivering. "I can still see him with his ugly-looking self. I could have been killed."

"I don't remember. How did you get away?" Sheridan asks.

"Danielle's brother Richard shot at the dog with his Bebe..." Faye trails off.

We all sit there quiet, staring off into space. I'm hit with a bolt of guilt and am desperate to leave the room. Sheridan's voice stops me.

"Okay, hold up, it's coming back to me now. Didn't Danielle's neighbor try to press charges?"

"Yep, but her father, being a judge, had connections and put a stop to it," I say.

"So can you blame me now for being afraid of dogs?" Faye asks.

I notice Mrs. Brown watching us reminisce about old times with a glint in her big brown eyes. She seems to be really enjoying our company. I'm glad we're still here. Everyone else left hours ago. I find myself thinking about that night. Why did Faye have to bring up that stupid dog incident? 1, 2, 3, 4, 5, 6, 7, 8, 9, 10.

"Catalina! Catalina!"

"What is it, Jerome? And why are you doing all that shouting?"

"Danny's here. She just pulled up."

Complete silence blankets the room and we exchange nervous glances.

Chapter 4

Danielle

"Frankie, I'm fine...The car broke down...I wasn't in an accident...I wasn't jacked. I didn't die. The car broke down...I appreciate your concern...I love you, too. Talk to you later."

I power my phone down and drop it on the passenger seat. Spouses! I appreciate how much Frankie loves and wants to protect me, but give me a break. That's exactly why I made this trip by myself. Danielle does not need the added stress. Danielle is a big girl now. She can do this. I lean back in my seat and wave at Mr. Brown who's standing in the driveway grinning from hairy ear to hairy ear. I wonder who the man is standing next to him. He looks a little like Boris Kodjoe—just a tad bit darker.

Things haven't changed much since I was here two years ago. It's still a nice neighborhood. I have to remember to give the Browns the name of the probate attorney I went to Cornell with. She lives in Marina Del Rey and she's at the top of her game. I can't believe Sabrina didn't have a living trust, but then again I can. She had a one track mind—taking care of everyone's health and everyone's business, but her own. Mrs. Brown told me she and Mr. Brown moved in with Sabrina right after she was diagnosed with cancer and that they're renting out their house in Inglewood. I still can't believe she's gone. And I can't believe she didn't tell me she was sick. I thought we were close. I had a feeling something was up the last time I had spoken to her. I was making plans to spend the summer in L.A. but she kept putting me off. Then when I tried to reach out to her, she wouldn't return my calls or speak to me. Around the time all this was going on, I was trying to make partner and I couldn't get to the bottom of things like I wanted to. Now she's gone. My best friend is gone. My eyes sting and tear up and I feel a cough coming on. I grab my purse and phone and make my way to the house, coughing and choking. Mr. Brown and Boris look at me with concern.

"Are you okay?" Mr. Brown asks.

Shaking my head, I run into the house and make a beeline for the kitchen. I grab a glass out of the cabinet, go to the sink and fill it with filtered water. I take a few gulps and breathe. When I turn around, I have an audience—Mr. and Mrs. Brown, Boris, a middle-aged white woman sporting a black eye and a wrinkled black dress, a woman with a weave that needs tightening, and another woman wearing a gaudy black hat.

"Danny, are you okay?" Mrs. Brown asks, approaching.

"I just had a coughing fit," I say, putting the glass in the dishwasher.

"Look who's here," she says, pointing to the spectators.

I give her a blank stare.

"Danny, stop playing. You don't know who these women are?"

I look closer and my armpits fill with perspiration. I'm glad I listened to Frankie and wore my black Michael Kors suit. "Hey, Danielle," the woman wearing the weave says. The sound of her voice makes me cringe like it did the first time I heard it in middle school. *"Excuuuse meee, is anybody sittiiing here?"* I used to call her "The Whiner" behind her back. "Faye. Hey," I say. She smiles revealing those oh so familiar dimples, but the smile goes no further than her lips. Her eyes say, "I'm under duress."

The woman standing next to Faye removes her hat and her face framed in curls is now recognizable. Victoria. She aged well. She and Faye both have. But—"

"And it's me, Sheridan. Remember?"

"Hi," I say. Sheridan looks like she's been going through it. She was the prettiest girl in high school and everybody wanted to get with her—boys, girl, men, and women. Gary Hawkins was the lucky guy, but as far as I can tell, I'm not so sure Sheridan was the lucky gal.

We all stand in the kitchen, casting furtive glances at one another like we're wondering what to say or do next. Mrs. Brown opens her flabby arms, motioning for us to do a group hug. I stand there waiting to see who's going to make the first move. No one budges. She thrusts her hands into the pockets of her *World's Greatest Mom* apron and says, "Danny, you must be starving. I fixed you a plate. It's right here in the oven. After you eat, we're gonna talk." She gets the plate of food and places it on the table.

Sheridan raises her finger in the air likes she's in church and tiptoes toward the front door.

"Sherry, where are you going?" Mr. Brown asks.

"I'll be outside for just a few minutes," she says.

"Don't you leave without saying anything," Mrs. Brown warns.

Faye grabs Boris's hand and returns to the living room. Mr. Brown joins them, leaving Mrs. Brown, Victoria, and me in the kitchen. Mrs. Brown gives us a sly smile and goes into the living room, leaving us alone. Actually quite famished, I sit at the table and eat. I look up and catch Victoria glowering at me. I stop chewing and ask, "Is there a problem? Danielle is trying to eat in peace. So, if you don't mind, Danielle would like to be alone."

Her curls bounce as she shakes her head and chuckles. "You still do that?"

"Do what?"

"Refer to yourself in the third person."

"And?"

"It's just funny."

"Like your hat is funny?" I ask.

"I see you're still quick on your feet."

"Technically I'm not on my feet, because I'm sitting. You're the one on your feet, because you're standing," I say.

"You definitely went into the right profession."

I give her a questioning look.

"Mother Brown told me you're a partner in a law firm in New York."

"No objections here," I say. "But seriously, it's been a long day, and this food is really good, and Danielle would like to be left alone."

"Sure, no problem," she says, leaving. "I will leave *Danielle* alone, like I've been doing for the past two decades," she says, flouncing out of the kitchen.

Touche! I'll have to give her that one. I chomp on the chicken and follow it up with a forkful of yams and greens. I haven't had a home-cooked meal like this in ages. Putting in the hours I do at the firm, I rely on Frankie to take care of dinner. Unfortunately the only thing Frankie can make are reservations. We eat at high end restaurants, but after a while that really gets old. A tsunami of sadness washes over me when I think about Sabrina never getting to meet Frankie. We met and fell for each other right after I lost contact with Sabrina and we've been married a year now. I noticed I'm not the only one who's tied the knot. Sheridan got hitched right out of high school and based on the fake rock she's wearing; she and Gary may no longer be together. Faye of course, is married—nice...class ring? What's with that? I'm glad to see Vicky, who's sporting a modest band, finally gave up on chasing Gary and got her own man. I don't know what people saw in Gary anyway. He was just another dumb jock as far as I was concerned. So it looks like we're all happily married. *Right!* Fat chance. Well, at least I am.

I finish up the last of my food and head to the refrigerator for something to drink. Mrs. Brown stops me in my tracks before I get there. "You finish?"

I turn and face her, licking my lips. "Thank you, that was scrumptious. You haven't lost your touch. Does Sabrina have anything to drink?"

"There's some punch in there."

"I was thinking more like some wine."

"I'm not sure. Jerome! Jerome!"

"Catalina, why are you always yelling?" Mr. Brown asks, entering the kitchen.

"Does Sabrina have any wine?"

"Did you check the frig?" he asks.

I open the frig, give the inside a gander, and say, "Negative."

"Okay, then I'll go to the wine cellar. She has plenty down there. I could use a drink myself," he says, running off.

"I didn't know Sabrina has a wine cellar."

"She had it built last year. It was on her bucket list," Mrs. Brown says.

My knees buckle upon hearing Mrs. Brown and I fall back onto the refrigerator, thinking about how unbelievable it is that I never got to talk to Sabrina in the end. There were so many things I would have told her. Like how much I loved her red freckles and how much I looked up to her. I was in awe of her brilliance. I wish I could have been there to rub her feet, comb her red frilly hair, just be there to make it all right. Thinking about all of this, the dam brakes and a cascade of tears and snot go everywhere. I sob and sob, unable to stop. I must sound like a mad woman because the others come running in, all except Sheridan and Victoria.

"It's going to be okay," Faye says, helping me to a seat at the table.

"It's not okay and Danielle *isn't* okay. She should have been there."

Mark gives Faye a questioning look. "Who's Danielle? I thought she was Danielle."

"She's talking about herself. She refers to herself in the third person. She's done that since middle school," Faye says. She gets tissue and hands it to me.

"Jerome, hurry up with that wine!" Mrs. Brown shouts.

"I'm coming now," he says, running in with what looks like a bottle of Merlot. "Who wants some?" I raise my hand and Mrs. Brown follows. We look at Faye and Mark waiting for them to respond. "Mark and Faye, do you all want a glass?" Mr. Brown asks. He grabs glasses from the cabinet. "If it was good enough for Jesus, it should be good enough for you," he says.

"We'll have just a little," Mark says. "I'm going to preach at the first service tomorrow."

"Right, just a little," Faye interjects. She looks toward me and says in her whiny voice, no pun intended, "I know how you feel, Danielle. Sabrina didn't tell me either. I had no idea she was sick, Lord Jesus," she says, sitting next to me.

Mr. Brown puts the glasses on the table and fills them. I

grab mine and start to drink, but before the rim of the glass touches my thin lips, Mrs. Brown says, "Why don't we make a toast."

"That's a good idea," Mr. Brown says.

"What about Sheridan and Victoria?" Faye asks.

"Sheridan is outside smoking like a chimney, and I heard Vicky on her phone in the foyer talking to her mother. I can go get them," Mr. Brown says.

"Since when did Sheridan start smoking?" I ask, but no one answers me.

"That's okay, don't bother them right now," Mrs. Brown says. "Let's do the toast and everyone has to say something."

"You know, this reminds me of my 16th birthday party. Remember, Danielle? My mother had made punch and Victoria sneaked and put Wine Cooler in it when my mother wasn't looking."

Listening to Faye, I don't want to remember. I just want to feel the soothing wine go down my throat. But she looks so pitiful and needy, I can't help but go down memory lane with her. I even find myself laughing. "Yeah, I remember and we all got a little tipsy and we couldn't stop laughing. We laughed all night and her—"

"Mother kept telling us to keep it down. She had no idea what was going on," Faye says.

"Sounds like good times," Mark says.

"There were a lot of good times," Mrs. Brown adds.

"Okay, we need to toast now because I'm getting thirsty," Mr. Brown says, raising his bushy pepper and salt brows.

"Here's to my daughters coming home," Mrs. Brown says.

Faye and I exchange wary looks and we clink our glasses with the others.

"Your turn, Faye," Mrs. Brown says.

"Uh…uh, here's to…to…here's to—"

"Forgiving hearts," Mark says, eyeing Faye.

"That's a good one," Mr. Brown says. "What about you, Danny?" he asks.

"Why don't you go first," I say. "Age before beauty."

"Who you callin' old, young lady?" he asks through laughter. "Okay, here's to my daughters coming home," Mr. Brown says.

"That's what I said. You can't steal my toast," Mrs. Brown says.

Mr. Brown rolls his eyes at Mrs. Brown and says, "I can steal your toast, your bacon, and your eggs."

The room fills with laughter.

"Okay, okay, my turn," I say, surprised at my own anxiousness. "Here's to...to...starting over," I say. We all clink glasses and down the Merlot. I tap on my glass for more.

"Do you have a designated driver?" Mr. Brown asks.

The sound of breaking glass startles us. Faye covers her mouth and backs away from the table. "I'm sorry. I'm sorry," she says, bolting.

"Faye, what's wrong?" Mark asks, running after her.

"Did I say something wrong?" Mr. Brown asks.

I avert my eyes and pour myself another glass of wine, while Mr. Brown goes into the living room. Mrs. Brown goes to the utility closet and comes out with a broom and dustpan. She cleans up the mess, washes her hands, and joins me at the table. "I really think you girls should have gotten some therapy after what happened. The therapist who worked with Sabrina is really good. You all need to check her out."

I stop drinking and shut my eyes. I really don't want her to go there. So like the good attorney I am, I attempt to redirect the conversation. "You were going to talk to us about why Sabrina didn't tell us she was sick."

"I already went into all of that with Sherry and Dimples. I wanted to tell you all together. Sabrina was upset with you all for not getting over what had happened. She thought that you all should have forgiven one another a long time ago. She felt you all cheated her out of twenty years of friendship."

"But I *was* her friend. I never stopped being her friend," I say in my defense.

"It just wasn't the same for her. She hated pretending and acting like the others didn't exist when she was with you. So her shutting you out when she found out she was sick was her way of regaining her power. She felt empowered in some strange way and she hoped the shock of it all would bring you all to your senses. It was her last wish."

I sit there listening to Mrs. Brown understanding and not understanding. I guess I never put myself in Sabrina's shoes. In my mind, it was just the two of us. But for her it was all five of us. I never thought about how she felt. It had to have been painful for her. She tried to tell me, but I wouldn't listen. After that night, I just wanted to put Sheridan, Faye, and Victoria out of my mind. Every time I saw them, it brought back the memories of that horrible night. It should have never happened. Now I'm being told Sabrina's dying wish was for us to forgive and forget. How can I ignore that? I know there was a time I would have given my life for these women. There was a time I couldn't even go to the restroom without them. We were inseparable. We were The Fresh Five. Is it possible to get that love back?

"Danny, did you hear what I said. Do you understand?"

"I overstand," I say.

Chapter 5

Sheridan

"I'm outside in front of Sabrina's house having a smoke."

"Alone?"

"Yes, alone. Who do you think I'm having a smoke with?"

"Don't talk to me like I'm crazy, Sher. Men go to funerals, too."

"So you think I'm out here having a smoke with a man? If you had come to the funeral with me, like I asked you to, instead of staying home to watch the game, you wouldn't have to worry about some man checkin' for me."

"Chill, woman. Like I tried to tell you, watching the game wasn't for entertainment purposes. You know I'm hoping to get back with the team. So I was just doin' some research. What time are you coming home? Me and mama are hungry."

"In a minute. And don't worry, I'll bring you guys a plate."

"What did Mother Brown cook?"

"Chicken, rice, greens, yams, macaroni—"

"Shut up. She threw down. She's always been the best cook out of all the mothers. Remember all of us used to hit up her place after school."

"I remember. I better go back inside. Mother Brown wants to talk to us."

"About what?"

"About why Sabrina didn't tell us she was sick. She already told me."

"What did she say?"

"I'm not gonna get into it right now, Gary. I'll tell you when I get home. I gotta go."

"Okay, and remember what I said. Don't be lettin' no thirsty niggas push up on you."

"Ain't nobody gonna do that. Trust me, once they get a look at my big ass ten-carat *cubic zirconia* ring, they'll run for the hills."

"Why you gotta go there? I told you I'm a get your real ring out of the pawn shop when I get my check next week."

"Okay, Gary, I'll talk to you when I get home."

"Love you, Sher."

"Love you, too," I say, hanging up. I drop my phone in my purse and light up another cigarette. I don't know what they're putting in Kools these days, but I can't seem to get enough. I blow circles with the smoke. The white against the dark sky makes me chuckle. I wonder what the others are doing and if Mother Brown has given them the 411. I better head in but I really don't feel like dealing with Victoria or Danielle. Faye, I can stomach somewhat. I saw how Victoria was stretching her wide neck trying to get a look at my hand. Bitch was foolin' nobody. Yeah, as much as you wanted to break me and Gary up, we're still together. And I don't know who Danielle thinks she is, looking at me like I had just crawled out from up under a rock. I don't care if she has a hundred designer suits, she ain't no better than me or anybody else. She always did think her shit didn't stink because her father's a judge. And I don't know why she cut all her hair off. It's definitely not becoming. Let me stop talking about people. I promised God, Sabrina, and myself that I would be decent today.

The sound of the door opening takes me out of my head. I look over my shoulder and my eyes meet Victoria's almond shaped green eyes. They're real, too—not colored contacts like a lot of people in school had thought. She struts past me and my stomach flutters. "Leaving?"

"No, I'm just going to my car," she says, looking straight ahead.

I watch her go to her BMW. I should let her have it for cutting me off and stealing my parking spot, but I decide to keep my promise. I hear two chirps and she opens the back door of her car. She removes a large plant. It looks like a fern, but what do I know. Victoria's always had a thing for plants and all things green. She shuts the door, there's another chirp, and she walks toward the house with the Fern covering most of her face. I wonder where her hat is.

"Nice Fern," I say, when she passes.

She puts the plant on the ground and says, "It's not a Fern, it's a Peace Lily."

"Oh, my bad. It's a nice *Peace* Lily." *How freaking ironic.*

"You know you really should stop smoking. It causes *cancer.*"

"I'm glad you care, Victoria."

"Who said I care?" she asks.

"I'm not going to go there with you, Victoria. Not here and not now. I haven't seen you in twenty years and after tonight, I probably won't see you for another twenty years. And it'll probably be at the next funeral and it'll probably be mine and I'll have cancer, too. Like you said."

She crosses her arms over her flat chest and says, "I'm not trying to go anywhere. I just came to the funeral today to say goodbye to my best friend, and I'm trying to be there for the Browns. This isn't easy for me either, losing my best friend and not knowing she was sick."

"I didn't know either. And she was my best friend, too. She didn't tell any of us. She was mad at us because we couldn't get past what happened twenty years ago. She wanted to show us what it felt like to be shut out," I say.

"Who told you that?" she asks.

"Mother Brown."

"I don't think it was right what Sabrina did."

"And you think it was right for us to have put her in the middle of our mess?"

She gives me a crazy look. "I'm not having this conversation."

"Well, I am, Victoria, and in case you wanted to know, Gary and I *are* still together," I say, flashing my ring in her face.

She blinks wildly and says, "1, 2, 3, 4, 5, 6, 7, 8, 9, 10. Okay, we can do this. Sheridan, I can care less about you and Gary. I have my own man. And I am happily married with two wonderful children."

"I'm glad to hear it because Gary and I are happily married, too. And our daughter Kimberly is at USC with a full scholarship. We're doing quite well!"

"Is that why you have a black eye and are driving a ten-year-old Honda?"

"My Lexus is in the shop. What the fu—?" Before I have a chance to make a comeback, she snatches the plant and disappears into the house. I take a moment, drop my cigarette, and squash it into the ground. Breathing hard, I flip my hair out of my face and march into the house, looking for Queen Victoria. Before I have a chance to let her have it, Mrs. Brown meets me in the hallway.

"There you are. Now that I have you all together, I want to say a few words. I know it's late. Mark has to preach in the morning, and Vicky needs to get home to Curtis and the kids, and Danielle is working on a big discrimination case. So she has some studying to do back at her hotel, and I know Gary is probably waiting at home with bated breath for you."

I force a smile and allow Mrs. Brown to drag me into the living room where the others and Mark and Mr. Brown are seated. I sit on the orange love seat next to Mr. Brown who's nodding off. Danielle, sitting on a wicker chair near the entertainment center, runs her hand through her pixie cut and yawns. She quickly covers her mouth when Faye clears her throat. Faye and Mark are sitting on the orange sofa. Mrs. Brown sits next to them. I scan the room, looking for Victoria. As if on cue, her voice rings out from the kitchen.

"Mother Brown, is there anymore wine?"

"In the cellar downstairs," Mrs. Brown says. "But you can get some wine later. Let's talk so I can let you girls get home."

"That's okay. Never mind. I don't need any," she says, waltzing in. She carries her hat and the plant. She puts the plant on the floor near the mantel and sits on the arm of the sofa next to Mrs. Brown. She places the hat in her lap.

"That's a beautiful plant," Mrs. Brown says. "It's so nice of you girls to have brought gifts."

Faye clears her throat again and Danielle says, "I'm sorry, Mother Brown, I have something back at the hotel."

"You can bring it with you tomorrow."

"Tomorrow?" Danielle asks.

"Yes, I want all of you to go to church with me tomorrow. Mark is going to bring the message. It would be the greatest gift you could give to me and Mr. Brown. Isn't that right, Jerome? Jerome!"

"What...what did you say?" he asks, sitting up straight, wiping the slob off of his sagging chin with his sleeve.

"I said it would be wonderful for the girls to go to New Hope with us tomorrow."

"Right. Right."

I sit there waiting for Mrs. Brown to speak her peace, taking in the faces of the others. My eyes start to burn and I shut and open them. Images of the five of us back in the day flood my head. I think I might have a drink myself. Just a little one before I hit the road. Victoria may not want one, but I really need one. I remember she used to be the life of the party and she drank Wine Coolers like they were Kool Aid—always in the cut though. I remember when she put a Wine Cooler in the punch Faye's mother made when we were celebrating Faye's 16th birthday. And I remember the night...on the real, I thought Victoria would have given up drinking after that night.

"Sherry!"

"I'm sorry, Mrs. Brown, what did you say?"

"I said we're going to start with you."

"Start with me what?"

"Girl, where have you been?" Mrs. Brown asks.

"I was—"

"Never mind. I want each of you girls to tell one another what you've been up to for the past twenty years. Not in a lot of detail. Just talk about your family life, where you work, that kind of thing. I know you all kept Sabrina abreast...but you know...it's just a way to start getting to know one another again." The room fills with sighs and coughs. "Just do it for me, for Sabrina."

"Okay, Mother Brown. For the past twenty-years, I've been a stay-at-home mom and the wife to a football star," I say, looking at Victoria. She passes her hand over her curls and scoffs.

"Now, now," Mrs. Brown warns. "That's wonderful, Sherry. And tell us about Kimberly."

"She's absolutely gorgeous. She's a combination of Gary and me. And she got a full scholarship to USC. She wants to be a doctor like Sabrina. She lives on campus. She was at the funeral today, but she had to leave as soon as it was over. She's preparing for a big exam."

"I know. She came by and spoke to Jerome and me. And are you all still living in Beverly Hills? It's been two years since we've really spoken to you and Gary, with the exception of a few phone calls and surprised visits from you."

"Right now we're living with Gary's mother."

"Doesn't she live in Compton?" Victoria asks.

"We're not actually living there. We're taking care of her while at the same time waiting for our new house to be built."

"In Compton?" Victoria asks.

"No, in Brentwood, I mean Beverly Hills," I say.

"So, I hear your husband played for the Dallas Enforcers," Mark says.

"Right, yeah. He was a running back. He uh, got injured, but he's going to be signing with the uh…the uh…crap, I can't remember the team right now. But he's going to be signing with them soon." I fold my hands and place them in my lap, hoping Mrs. Brown is satisfied.

"Vicky, your turn," Mrs. Brown says.

"I got married to a *wonderful man* named Curtis Williams," she says, looking my way. "I met him when I was getting my *Master's degree* in education at UCLA," she says, now staring at me. "We dated a few times and lost touch. I ran into him again while I was teaching at Bradshaw. The investment bank he worked for came out to meet some of the students for their summer intern program and he was one of the bankers. We started again right where we had left off. When I turned twenty-eight we got married and we've been happily married ever since, for ten whole years, and we have two great kids, Tangie and Matt."

"Are you still teaching at Bradshaw?" Faye asks.

"No, not anymore. I'm at Washington elementary now. High school isn't what it used to be when we were attending. It's really stressful now."

Hmm. I sit there hearing what Vicky is saying, but believing it, I'm not so sure. Why would someone with a master's degree be teaching at an elementary school? Oh, well, that's her business. I get focused, curious about what Faye and Danielle have been up to. Mrs. Brown claps her hands like a baby seal, grins, and juts her chin toward Faye.

"What can I say? I am simply blessed and highly favored," Faye says, looking into Mark's handsome face. "I'm First Lady Faye Davis. I gave up my maiden name…Johnson. Can you blame me," she says, planting a kiss on Mark's cheek. He smiles and if he was lighter you'd probably be able to see him blushing. "Mark and I have a beautiful megachurch in Long Beach, New Hope. You all were there today of course. God has blessed us to have twenty thousand members." Mark cheeses and nods. "Mark and I met at Oral Roberts University. We got married eight years ago and life has been wonderful. Isn't that right, honey?"

"Yes, God has truly been good to us. The only thing missing is a baby. We—"

"He doesn't mean it quite like that. I mean, we're not missing a baby," Faye says, cutting him off. "I mean, we aren't trying to get pregnant yet. But we plan to soon," she adds. Mark gives Faye a questioning look, but she ignores him and rattles on. "Like I said, God has been so good to us. What about you, Danielle? It's your turn," Faye says.

Mrs. Brown scrunches her fast and says, "Yes, go ahead, Danny."

"I guess God has been good to me, too. I'm a

newlywed."

"Oh, my goodness, I didn't even notice your ring," Mrs. Brown says. "You have a band like Vicky's. When did this happen? And, Vicky, what happened to your diamond —"

"I met Frankie two years ago...you know around the time...Sabrina..."

"That's okay," Mrs. Brown says.

"Things are good with us and we're planning on adopting kids."

"You don't want kids of your own?" Faye asks.

"There are so many children in need of a family, we just thought it would be good to adopt."

"Amen!" Mark says.

"I think that's a good thing," Mr. Brown says.

"I made partner two years ago and I'm a discrimination lawyer. I love what I do and I love my life."

"What does your husband do?" Faye asks.

"Frankie's a freelance writer."

"That sounds interesting," Mr. Brown says.

"I'm working a big case right now and I'm going to have to go soon."

"You are coming to church tomorrow, aren't you?" Mrs. Brown asks.

"If I can get a later flight, Mother Brown, I'll come."

"I'm so glad. We're going to the first service. It starts at eight. And I'm so glad we've been able to have this meeting. As I mentioned to most of you, all Sabrina wanted was for you girls to get back together and I think this is a good start. What do you all think?"

We share confused looks and say nothing. Mrs. Brown rubs her eyes and sighs. "Okay, I'm just gonna leave it in God's hands. Sabrina didn't want to force anything and I'm not either. Don't worry about coming to church tomorrow. It's okay, you all go on and live your lives separately like you've done for the past twenty years," she says, leaving the room.

"Cat, wait. Where are you going?" Mr. Brown asks.

"To bed!" she snaps.

We watch the Browns leave and everyone begins to gather their purses. I make my way to the kitchen so I can fix some food to go.

"It was nice meeting you." I turn and look into Mark's face.

"It was nice meeting you, too. I'm sorry it had to be under these circumstances," I add.

"God works in mysterious ways," he says.

"Mark, are you ready?"

"I am, baby," he says.

"It was good seeing you, Sheridan," Faye says.

"You, too. Take care," I say.

"You, too," she says.

They leave and I open the frig and rummage for goodies. I feel a hand on my shoulder and I freeze. "Sheridan?"

"Danielle, what is it?" I ask, turning around and brushing her hand off of me.

"I'm getting ready to take off, but if you need help with anything, let me know. I know a lot of good divorce attorneys."

"Excuse me?"

"I know a battered woman when I see one. And Gary had a reputation at Bradshaw…you know he was suspended once for hitting a girl."

"Are you crazy? I am not a battered woman. Gary and I are doing fine. Thank you very much. I think you need to tend to your own marriage. Like you said, you're a newlywed. Wait 'til you've been married for twenty years and then come and see me."

"Okay, Sheridan, Danielle, is wrong. Danielle will stay out of your business."

"Yes, please tell Danielle to back off."

"Danielle is out," she says, leaving.

I remove the containers from the frig, shaking my head. The nerve of her. Sure, Gary might get upset from time-to-time, but I'm not a battered woman. I ain't no Nicole Simpson by a long shot and he ain't O.J. Forget Danielle. I fix three plates of food and return the almost empty containers to the refrigerator. I pack the plates and make my way to the wine cellar.

Tired, I hold onto the rail and follow the light. This is all new. Sabrina must have had it built right before she passed. I know she used to always talk about having a wine cellar. I make it to the bottom of the stairs and I scream.

"Sorry, I didn't mean to scare you," Victoria says.

"You scared the hell out of me. I thought you were gone."

"Not yet," she says, holding onto a bottle of Merlot like it's the last life jacket on a sinking ship.

"I was just going to have a little before I hit the road, you know...not too much. Are you going to open that?" I ask. She just stares at me. "What's wrong with you, Victoria?"

"Do you still think that what happened that night was my fault?" she asks.

I stand there with sweaty armpits and my heart racing, thinking about that night, not knowing how to answer Queen Victoria.

Chapter 6

Faye

I lower the volume on the car CD player, hoping Mark will talk to me. He hasn't said a word since we left Sabrina's house and we've been driving for twenty minutes. Lord, have mercy. I know he's mad at me. I just hope he remembers Ephesians 4:26: *Be angry and do not sin; do not let the sun go down on your anger.*

"I was listening to that," he says, raising the volume with the button on the steering wheel. You know Marvin Sapp is my boy. Never could have —"

"Are you going to continue to ignore me?" I ask, cutting him off.

We come to a stoplight and he says, "Ignore you? I'm

not ignoring you, Faye."

"You haven't said one word to me since we left Sabrina's."

"I guess I haven't said one word because my word doesn't mean anything to my wife. In fact, a lie means more to my wife than my word or anything that I have to say for that matter."

I pass my hand over my face, not sure how to defend myself. He's right. I did lie, but I just didn't want the others judging me or putting me down. What woman wants the world to know she can't get pregnant...well in my case, pregnant again? Even Hannah in the Bible cried like a drunken woman because she couldn't conceive. "I just didn't want to tell them all my business, Mark. You don't know them like I do."

"Faye, you don't know them like you think you do. It's been twenty years since you've seen those women. You have no idea who they are."

"Some people don't change," I say.

Mark gets on the freeway and turns the CD player off. "I didn't appreciate you contradicting what I said and cutting me off. You made me look like a fool. And what's with you painting this picture perfect life? We're no better than anyone else and we've had ups and downs in our marriage. Granted, more ups than downs, but our union is far from perfect, Faye."

I sit their cringing, feeling like a five-year-old being scolded. Mark and I are the same age, but sometimes when he goes on a tirade, I feel more like his daughter than his wife. "I'm sorry, Mark. I was wrong, but I just couldn't help myself."

"Faye, you've never been pregnant and you may never ever get pregnant. It just may not be God's will for you and you may have to accept that."

Perspiration beads on my upper lip while Mark's

words seep into the depths of my soul. *"Faye, you've never been pregnant."* But I *have* been pregnant. Long before Mark came into my life. It happened in high school. No one but my unborn baby's daddy knows. Not even Sabrina, Sheridan, Victoria, or Danielle. It happened right under their noses. Yeah, church girl Faye wasn't the virgin they thought I was. It all happened so fast. Lord, help. Every time I think about the whole ungodly affair, I want to fall to my knees and beg Mark's forgiveness. I just can't help but think that God is punishing me because of what I did. And I told Mark I was a virgin when we started dating. I know he would leave me if he knew the truth. He *was* a virgin, so he couldn't tell one way or the other, and I made sure to cry and squeal when we made love for the first time on our honeymoon.

"Faye!"

"What…what?"

"Are you getting out? We're home."

"Yeah. Okay." *Wow, I was on one. When did we get home?* I get out of the car and follow Mark into our two-story, nine-thousand square foot Mediterranean home in Belmont Shore. It's an affluent neighborhood in Long Beach, California. We've lived here for five years and we absolutely love our house and neighbors. I just pray one day we'll be able to raise a family here.

Mark disengages the alarm and I head to the bedroom. I'm exhausted and not really feeling up to going to church tomorrow, but as the First Lady, I have to be there. I wonder if the others are going to show up tomorrow. I hope they do. It was actually kind of nice seeing them all today. They've changed in many ways, but in some ways they're still the same. Sheridan is still rough around the edges, Victoria doesn't seem to be as wild as she was, but she's restless as ever, and Danielle chopped all her hair off, but she stills speaks in third person. I wonder if we'll ever get back together. When I think about it, like my marriage, things weren't perfect between us, but it was ride or die until…until that night. God help us all.

I press the double doors to our room open, fall down onto our king sized bed, and kick my slingbacks off. Closing my eyes, I think back to the first time we all met. It was 1988, twenty-five years ago. We were all attending Audubon Middle School and we were in the same math class. It was the first day of the seventh grade and our teacher thought it would be fun to start the class with a math challenge. So she broke us up into groups.

"Sabrina, Sheridan, Faye, Victoria, and Danielle, you'll be group number one."

Mrs. Crowley ran her thin fingers through her red hair and a grin crept over her wrinkled face, as though she knew something about our team that we didn't. The next group was made up of boys and then girls and then boys again. We checked out the other teams and then Sabrina was the first to speak.

"Hey, you guys."

"Hey," we all said, giving each other the once over.

"What elementary school did you guys go to?" Sabrina asked.

"Washington," we all said.

"I did, too," she said. "Hey wanna name our group?" she asked.

I looked into her cat eyes and then started counting her freckles, wondering where she got her courage. She was so outspoken and fearless. I, on the other hand, was shaking in my Adidas, clutching the gold cross my grandmother had given me for my 12th birthday. "Sure," I said.

"Why don't we call ourselves, The Fabulous Five," Sheridan said.

"Gag me on a spoon," Victoria said, rolling her green eyes.

"The hel…heck with you, too," Sheridan said, giving Victoria an icy stare.

"Don't fight you guys," Sabrina urged.

"Danielle has an idea. Let's call ourselves, 'The Fresh Five!'" Danielle said.

"I like that. That's the bomb," Sabrina said. "Do you guys like it?"

We all nodded and she swung her hand forward, palm down, and we instinctively did the same. Then we all shouted, "THE FRESH FIVE!"

We ended up winning the math challenge and were inseparable from that point on. We lived within blocks of one another and once a month had sleepovers, taking turns at one another's houses. Danielle had the nicest house. Her father was a well-known judge. She had an older brother and they both had their own rooms. Sabrina was an only child and got just about everything she wanted. She was smart as a whip and served as the group's tutor. Sheridan lived in a foster home with black parents and a bunch of foster brothers and sisters and Victoria lived in a modest home with her parents and two younger brothers. Like Sabrina, I was an only child and spent most of my time at my father's church. We worked hard and played even harder. We looked forward to each adventurous day and life was wonderful and magical. We dressed alike and even talked alike. Before Victoria could count to ten we were headed to high school.

"Faye!"

"What?"

"You didn't hear me?"

"I'm sorry. What's wrong?"

"I don't want to go to bed with this thing between us," Mark says.

"I said I was sorry," I say, sitting up.

"I'm sorry, too. I'm sorry that I haven't been able to get you pregnant yet, and I'm sorry I haven't been able to give you that perfect life you want."

"Baby, it's not your fault," I say, grabbing him around

his neck. "I love you. You're the best thing that's ever happened to me and I wonder sometimes how I got so lucky. I don't deserve you."

"Yes, you do, Dimples. We deserve each other."

He gazes into my eyes and kisses me on my face softly. When he moves down to my neck and my cleavage, my legs instinctively spread and I grab his hand and place it between my sweaty thighs. I moan when he thrusts his fingers inside me.

"You're so wet," he says, whispering in my ear.

"Take me, Mark. Make love to me."

"Gladly. I'm gonna put my baby inside you tonight. Who's the daddy?" he asks, removing my silk panties.

"You are, baby. Hurry, I want you," I say.

He drops his trousers and boxers and slips his manhood inside me, causing me to cry out in pure ecstasy. He moves in and out of me while I press my nails into his back.

"Dimples, girl, you feel so good. This is my stuff. Daddy's cat. It drives me crazy to know I'm the only man who's ever had you."

I freeze and push Mark off of me.

"Faye, what? What's wrong?" he asks.

"I don't feel well all of a sudden. I think it's the wine."

"But you barely had any," he says, with an exasperated look on his face. "You feel so good, baby. I really want to finish."

I remain still with my legs clamped shut, wishing I was the woman Mark thinks I am. Lordy. Poor thing. He really wants me badly. I slowly open my legs and pull on his tie, drawing him into me. Stiff as an over starched Sunday shirt, he jumps inside me, panting, cursing, and finally exploding. He falls over onto his back, shuddering. "That was incredible. How was it for you, Dimples?"

"Great," I say, hiding my yawn. I get up and go to the

bathroom wincing at the traces of semen sticking to my inner thighs. I take off the rest of my clothes, get in the shower, grab my shower cap, and thrust it onto my head. My next hair appointment is not until next weekend, so I can't afford to get my weave wet. It really needs to be redone. I turn the water on and let it rain on me. It feels good on my skin and I relish the thought of it washing away all my past sins. I grab the liquid soap and my loofah and wash between my legs vigorously. "Please, Lord let me conceive tonight. Please!"

"Is he dead? Please don't let him be dead. Did I kill him? Lord, have mercy. No! No! No!"

"Faye, wake up! Wake up, baby!"

"I slowly open my eyes and remove the cover from off of my face."

"You okay? You were talking in your sleep. Shouting," Mark says, sitting next to me on the bed. I notice that he's fully dressed, wearing his first Sunday suit and tie. "I'm worried about you, baby."

"I must have been dreaming. What time is it?"

"Time for you to get up if you're going to church...Faye, you mentioned something about somebody being killed."

Dread surges up in the pit of my stomach, and I grip the covers. "I...I don't remember what the dream was about. What else did I say?" I ask, hoping I didn't say anything incriminating.

"You just mentioned someone being dead and then you screamed 'no.'"

"Oh...okay. I don't know. Maybe it'll come back to me. I better get my shower and get dressed. That dream was probably just a nightmare."

"Montana has breakfast on, so come down as soon as

you're ready. And Melba's here."

"She's early," I say.

"Remember she took yesterday off, so she's making up for it today."

"Right. Okay, sweetie and I love you."

"I love you, too, Dimples."

I watch Mark leave the room and drag myself out of bed, wondering why I had the dream I did. I've worked hard to bury the memories of that night and Lord knows I don't want to go back there. Maybe seeing all of us together triggered that dream. It's bad enough I have this baby situation; I don't need any more challenges.

When I step into the bathroom, Mrs. Brown's voice echoes in my head. *"And I'm so glad we've been able to have this meeting. As I mentioned to most of you, all Sabrina wanted was for you girls to get back together and I think this is a good start. What do you all think?"*

She seemed so happy last night that we were all together. That was until no one responded to her query. Maybe they'll surprise her and show up at church today and then maybe they won't. Let me get ready and let go and let God.

Mark pulls into his designated parking space at New Hope. He decided to leave the Range Rover at home and drive our Lexus SUV today. I get a glimpse of my ten-carat diamond ring and sigh. Sometimes I feel guilty about our lavish lifestyle, knowing that some of New Hope's members are struggling, but Mark quickly reminds me what Jesus said in John 10:10: *The thief cometh not but to steal and to kill and to destroy. I am come that they might have life, and that they might have it more abundantly.* And if I still express doubt he has me read I Kings 3:13: *And I have also given you what you have not asked: both riches and honor, so that there shall not be anyone like you among the kings all your days.* Mark says that like King Solomon was the ruler of Israel in his day, that he's the ruler of his congregation and that God has blessed us with all of our wealth just like he blessed Solomon. I'm not always sure if that's how the scripture should be interpreted, but I know Mark loves the Lord and he loves the members of New Hope. The way he is before the people, he's the same way at home. He's the real deal, unlike his wife.

I follow Mark to the back entrance and we're greeted by security — a couple of brawny brothers in their twenties and thirties. Rumor has it they used to be Crips gangsters and the six security guards in the front and sides of the church use to be Bloods.

"Good morning, Reverend Davis and First Lady Davis," they say, welcoming us into the building.

"Good morning," Mark and I say.

"You two look like you should be on the cover of Ebony," Lamont, the lighter of the two says.

"Thank you," we say.

Mark looks over his shoulder at me, taking in the baby blue Michael Kors skirt suit and matching pumps I'm wearing, and says, "Lamont, she makes me look good."

"I heard that," Ronnie, the darker brother says.

We all laugh and the men go back to their posts while I join Mark in his office. He opens the blinds and the sun fills the room, exposing a thick layer of dust covering his mahogany desk and bookshelves.

"When was the last time the cleaning lady was through here?" I ask, looking at the numerous awards, city proclamations, and photos with politicians, civic leaders, entertainers, and members, covering the walls.

"I'm not sure," he says, removing his jacket.

"It's filthy in here," I say. I glance at the clock on the wall above the credenza and make a mental note to myself that the first service won't start for another hour. I make my way to the kitchen for paper towels and furniture polish. On the way there, I make a detour to check out the main sanctuary. Sadness takes over when I think about Sabrina's funeral and that her body was just a few feet from where I'm standing now. Wow, it's still so unbelievable. I look out at the sanctuary, that's empty, with the exception of the mass choir going over songs and the ushers making final preparations before the members file in. A group of deacons huddle in a corner praying. I get a feeling we're going to have a beautiful service today — a spirit-filled service. Maybe Sabrina will be watching over us.

Chapter 7

Victoria

"Curtis, you're hogging the blanket. I'm cold," I say, shivering on the floor. *The floor?* I turn over slowly and attempt to sit up, but the sledgehammer in my head knocks me down. I press on my head, trying to quiet the pounding. A foul odor upstages my headache. I sit up and look down at my feet that are covered in repast food — greens, macaroni and cheese...My God, what happened and where am I? I look around the dark space and my eyes lock on rows and rows of wine. My stomach lurches at the sight of the liquor. I'm in the wine cellar at Sabrina's. OMG...I never left. What happened? I slowly rise, grabbing onto a wooden post. My black dress is covered in puke. My heart races at the thought of being found like this. I have to get out of here before the Browns discover me.

"1, 2, 3, 4, 5, 6, 7, 8, 9, 10." I grab my purse from the floor and search for my phone. It's a little after seven in the morning. Mother Brown mentioned she was going to the first service that starts at eight. Maybe they're gone already.

I tuck my purse under my arm and head toward the door. Not able to see too clearly, I stumble over a couple of empty wine bottles. My eyes sting and tear up. I drank again. My God—after a whole year of sobriety, I drank again. What is wrong with me? Suddenly pieces of last night push through my foggy brain. I remember being down here desperate for a drink. Being around the others sent me back to that night and I was wracked with guilt—the kind of guilt that only a drink could wash away. Everyone was heading home. I slipped past them all and thought I was alone until Sheridan showed up. Just the sight of her made me lose all perspective. It appeared she was on edge too, because the moment she saw me she screamed bloody murder.

"Sorry, I didn't mean to scare you," I said.

"You scared the hell out of me. I thought you were gone," she said.

"Not yet," I said, holding a bottle of Merlot in a death grip, thinking she was going to take it. It was a ridiculous thought, considering where I was. But according to my sponsor, alcoholics don't drink or think like normal people.

"I was just going to have a little before I hit the road, you know not too much. Are you going to open that?" she asked.

That was a good question, but I didn't know how to answer her, so I just stared, which led her to ask, "What's wrong with you, Victoria?"

Her penetrating blue eyes seemed to see right through me and then I found myself asking her about that night. "Do you still think that what happened that night was my fault?"

She stood there speechless. "Sheridan, I—"

"I heard your question, Victoria. Why are you asking me something like that after twenty years? What do you think? Was it your fault? Was it your fault for going off on me because I told you guys I was pregnant with Gary's baby? Was it your fault that you had been drinking that night?" she asked. *I think she asked me that.* I press my head trying to remember.

And then...yeah...I said, "A Wine Cooler. I had one Wine Cooler," Sheridan.

"And?" she asked.

"I wasn't drunk."

"What does it matter? He's dead. And you killed him!"

"Don't say that! Stop it!"

"You're a murderer. You killed him. It's your fault. You're damn right it's your fault, bitch! Because of you, I've had to live with his blood on my hands. How do you think it felt having Gary's baby, giving birth to Kimberly, thinking about how we took him out."

"We?"

"No, I meant to say you! You, Victoria."

"You said we...we're all guilty."

"No, you are!" she screamed, lunging at me. *Did she lunge or did she trip and fall. Urgh! Am I remembering this right or did I black out.*

Okay, the bottle fell to the floor, but miraculously it didn't break. *Or did it break?* No there would be glass on the floor. I fell down and we ended up tussling on the floor. I reached for the bottle and tried to knock her in the head, but I missed and she jumped up and ran out. *Maybe I didn't try to hit her in the head, maybe I just wanted to and maybe she didn't actually run. Crap...did all of that happen or did I dream it happened?* I know that whatever happened, I was frantic and I didn't care what was going to happen next. I just knew I needed a drink, and another, and another and after that, I don't remember anything except coming to just now.

I go around the bottles on the floor and wobble to the door leading to the house. The sound of voices gives me pause.

"Hurry up, Jerome, we're going to be late!" Mrs. Brown says.

"Do you want me to see what that noise was or not?" Mr. Brown asks.

"Just hurry. I'll be in the car."

"I'm hurrying. I'm hurrying," he says.

Terrified of being found out, I look around for a hiding place. Sweat sprouts from my forehead when the sound of his footfalls grows closer.

"Hurry, hurry, Jerome," Mr. Brown says, mimicking Mrs. Brown. "That woman is gonna drive me nuts. There ain't nothin' down here."

I hear the door creak open just before I duck behind a stack of wooden crates. I pray he doesn't smell or see the mess. I hold my breath for several seconds and a horn blows.

"Forget it. There's nothing and nobody down here. I'm coming, Cat. Hold your horses!"

I exhale when Mr. Brown leaves and rushes up the stairs. I stay put until I hear their car start and the sound of them driving off.

"Thank God!" I say, rising. My headache reaches new heights. I carefully climb the stairs to the main part of the house. By the time I reach the kitchen, I have to use the restroom.

I make my way to the guest bathroom where I hid yesterday. I should have never let Mother Brown force me out. If I had stayed in there, I'd have 373 days of sobriety. I put my purse on the hamper, fling the medicine cabinet open, grab a bottle of aspirin, and flop down on the toilet. I down three of the pills, hoping that they'll ease the searing pain. I finish my business, wash my hands, and stumble backward at the sight of my image in the mirror. My green eyes are bloodshot and swollen. My face is sprinkled with dried vomit. I'm tempted to strip and take a shower right here and now. I never ever want another drink. Why does that sound so familiar?

Startled at the ringing phone, I pass my hand over my hair. I go to the linen cabinet, grab a couple of towels and a pillowcase, and wash my face. The answering machine picks up just when I finish. I walk toward the living room, curious about who's calling.

"Mother Brown, this is Faye, Dimples…I was just calling to see if you had heard from Sheridan, Vicky, or Danielle. I really hope they can make it. We're going to have a great service today. You might think this is strange, but I felt Sabrina's spirit in the sanctuary this morning. Mother Brown, are you there? Okay, hopefully you and Mr. Brown are on your way here. I'll see you soon. God bless you both."

The answering machine clicks off and I reflect on Faye's message. She really sounds sincere. I wish I could make it to church, but even if I could, I don't know how I would react upon seeing Sheridan. Maybe she won't show.

I go to the bathroom and slip out of my clothes. I turn on the shower and get in, hoping the cold water will shock me back to my senses. I reach for the towel I used to wash my face, and wrap it around the bar of soap I found on the dispenser. Scrubbing myself all over, I fight back tears, tired of crying. I have to get hold of myself, my life. "Sabrina, if you're here, tell me what to do. I wish you were here. You always knew the right thing to say, the right thing to do." I stand still, waiting to hear her voice.

"Hello, is anyone here?" a muffled voice asks.

The hair on the back of my neck rises. "Sabrina?" I've heard of stuff like this…people getting visions and seeing and hearing their dear departed love ones.

"Mother Brown, Mr. Brown, are you all here?"

The voice, now on the other side of the door, makes me shudder with fear. It's definitely not Sabrina's. It's a man's voice. He bangs on the door and the soap slips out of my hand. "Who's there?" I ask.

"It's Walter."

I breathe a huge sigh of relief and say, "The Browns went to church. This is Victoria."

"Oh…Vicky…hey, I didn't know you were here?"

"I'll be out in a minute."

"Okay, I'll be in the living room."

I listen for him to walk away and turn the water off. What is he doing here and how did he get in? He must still have a key. I really don't want to talk to Walter, especially now that I know he walked out on Sabrina. I get out of the shower and dry off, wondering what I'm going to wear. I wrap myself in the towel, grab my soiled clothes, and dump them in the pillowcase. Noticing my shoes near the wastebasket, I grab them and wipe them clean. I gargle with mouthwash, retrieve all my belongings, and head to the master bedroom.

"Vicky?" Walter says, sitting on the bed.

"Walter! You scared me," I say, tightening my grip on my towel. "I thought you were going to be in the living room."

"I was, but…I don't know…I just felt like being near Sabrina." His eyes trace the shape of my body and lock on my nonexistent cleavage.

"I need to get dressed. I'm trying to get over to the church. And I'm late," I say, shifting my eyes toward the clock on the nightstand.

"You stayed the night?"

"Yeah…I uh…didn't want to leave the Browns alone…you know after…after."

"I feel you. That was nice of you. I came by to check on them."

"How did you get in?"

"I live in Westwood now, not far from UCLA, but I still

have my key. Sabrina never changed the locks."

"The Browns need to and they need an alarm, too," I say.

"I'll let you get dressed," he says, leaving.

I shut the door when he exits and toss everything on the bed.

Maybe I will go to church. Lord knows I need prayer. I need to talk to someone about what's going on with me. Maybe AA isn't for me. Maybe I need something else. I go to the walk-in closet and rummage through Sabrina's clothes. She had impeccable taste and we're about the same size — perfect tens. Actually, that was before she gained weight. I freeze when I come to a green and brown dress with a V-neck. Sabrina wore the dress to Matt's kindergarten graduation. I grab the dress and put it up to my frame. My black pumps will have to do. Going to the dresser I sneak a peek in the mirror. My eyes are clearing up, but my hair is a hot mess. And I don't have clean underwear. I see the armoire behind me and attack it, hoping to find a pair of pantyhose. Sabrina always kept extra pairs on hand. Bingo. Just my size and color. I slip them on and then work on my hair. There's still enough curl to make a cute little hairdo.

I dump my purse on the bed and rifle through my makeup. My one year sobriety chip stares back at me. I still can't believe I threw my sobriety away. That's the only thing I had left. Determined not to give up, I put on my makeup and prepare to face the gospel music. I notice the perfume on Sabrina's dresser and spray a little Allure by Chanel behind my ear. I'm actually starting to feel like a part of the human race again. Crap! I have to clean up the mess downstairs. Wow, I should have done that before getting dressed. Okay...calm down..."1, 2, 3, 4, 5, 6, 7, 8, 9, 10. Walter!"

"What's wrong? Are you okay?" he yells from the living room.

"Can you do me a favor?" I ask. I grab my purse and the pillowcase and head his way.

He meets me in the hallway and his mouth drops. "That…that's Sabrina's dress."

"Right. I had to borrow it. I didn't know I was going to spend the night and Mother Brown wants me to go to service this morning at New Hope."

"Right…what do you need?"

"We all stayed late last night and talked about old times…you know…drank a little too much…and a few of us got sick down in the wine cellar. Do you think you can clean it up before the Browns get home? I wouldn't want them to have to deal with that."

"No problem. Of course. Anything to be of help. I'm sure you heard…"

"Yeah, I heard."

"Vicky, I loved Sabrina. No matter what anybody thinks, I did. I just couldn't handle it. The cancer. I was a coward."

"Walter, I'm not going to judge you. I have my own regrets. Thanks for cleaning things up and I'll let the Browns know you came by. Be sure to lock everything up."

"Will do," he says.

"Oh, and the plant in the living room…can you give it some water? It's a *Peace* Lily."

"Sure thing, Vicky. Anything else?"

"No, I think that'll be all," I say. I give him a grateful smile and head out.

The parking lot at New Hope is jammed pack. I grab the first available spot and park. I take one last look in my rearview mirror and make a dash for the sanctuary. I hope I haven't missed too much. This reminds me of how it was back in high school when the five of us would go to a dance on

Saturday night and party too much and too hard. We were allowed to go to the Saturday night parties as long as we made it to church on Sunday. We had all joined Faye's father's church. It was a small church in comparison to New Hope. I'll never forget how we would sit in the back and try to keep one another from falling asleep by telling jokes and passing naughty notes. My spirit is uplifted thinking about those times as I enter the sanctuary.

A greeter welcomes me at the door with a program and a Kool-Aid smile. "Welcome to New Hope, sister." I take the program from her and she nods her head covered in a stylish hat that I would die for—blue with a black bow on the side. *Crap! I left my hat at Mother Browns.*

"I love your hat," I say.

"Thank you."

"I better get inside."

"I hope you enjoy the service, and the Lord sure blessed you with some pretty green eyes," she says.

"Thank you." When I reach the main sanctuary, I rush in, but am stopped short by a woman wearing a white dress with a sash going across her chest that says USHER. She stops me with her hand covered in a white glove.

"One minute please, the Lord's Word is being read."

I nod and wait. My eyes dart around and I observe the staff answering questions and directing traffic so professionally, you'd think this was The White House. The lobby is exquisite with marble floors, recessed lighting, and overhead flat screen televisions broadcasting the service. A group of burly men look my way and then turn and talk amongst themselves. A gust of laughter fills the foyer and the usher who stopped me short rolls her eyes. The men take one look at her and immediately quiet down.

"Okay, it's fine now," she says, letting me pass.

My eyes widen as I take in the luxurious facility. The choir is huge and they sit directly behind Mark. Above them is a stained glass mosaic portrait of a black Jesus on a cross.

The pulpit is large and trimmed in gold. Everything in the church is large. I crane my neck looking for a place to sit. A male usher places his hand on the small of my back and I turn and face him. He motions for me to follow him and he takes me to the front. I want to turn and run. I force my feet to follow him and take a seat in the third row next to an elderly couple and what may be their grandchildren.

I shift in my seat and the woman says, "Good morning."

Glad to see she's friendly, I say, "Good morning to you, too. Have I missed much?"

"They just finished doing the announcements and taking up the first offering, so you're good."

"Perfect," I say. I chuckle to myself thinking about what the woman next to me would think if she could have seen me splayed out in Sabrina's wine cellar. I wonder how many members here today are just coming in from a drinking or drug binge.

Mark's baritone and authoritative voice takes me out of my head. "God is good, church! I said God is good!"

The congregation repeats his mantra and claps enthusiastically. I notice Faye sitting in the front row with the Browns. She looks pretty in her baby blue skirt suit. It looks like Michael Kors. Now I wish I could have gotten here earlier. I really feel a need to connect with them. I'm not sure what it is. Maybe it's Sabrina's spirit still lingering here at New Hope. I don't know what it is, but before I can figure it out, I find myself on my feet going to the front row.

Mark notices me, nods, and shouts, "Praise the Lord!"

The Browns and Faye look up and all three of them give me thousand-watt smiles. They make room for me and I sit between them, soaking in their acceptance and love. An usher thrusts a box of tissue my way. I didn't even realize I was crying. I wipe my tears and let the good spirit permeating the church wash over me. Faye leans over and whispers in my ear.

"I'm glad you came."

"I...I...I am, too."

She places her hand on mine, I smile, and we focus on the service.

Chapter 8

Danielle

"Yes, can you put me on that flight...no, I don't want to go standby. Danielle will pay whatever it costs...*I'm* Danielle...Nothing. Never mind...Yes, please email me the confirmation. Thank you."

I hang up my iPhone and look out the window of my hotel room. I'm staying at the W in Westwood. I don't have the luxury of staying with my parents. They retired and are living in Florida. UCLA is walking distance from here. I almost went there for undergrad, but I got a better offer at Cornell, and I've always wanted to visit New York. I had no idea I would end up living there after obtaining my law degree. Los Angeles is so country compared to Manhattan. When I got here for the funeral, it seemed as if people were moving in slow motion. I can't wait to get home, but I am glad I was able to get a later flight. I really want to be there for the Browns today. But at the rate I'm going, I'll probably miss the entire service. Between working on my brief and doing Face Time on my iPhone with Frankie last night, I barely got any sleep.

I grab my purse, smooth my peach-colored Chanel dress down, and get ready to leave. My ringing phone breaks my stride. "Frankie, I can't talk right now. I'm late for church."

"I thought you weren't going?"

"I wasn't, but I got a later flight and...I really think I need to be there for the Browns. Sabrina would want that."

"What about what I want?"

"I told you when I get back, I'm going to give you my undivided attention," I say with an eye roll, glad Frankie can't see me.

"You promise?"

"I promise," I say, opening the door to my hotel room, determined to make it to the eight o'clock service before it ends.

"You sure you promise?" Frankie asks, standing at the door carrying a Louis Vuitton garment bag.

My phone falls to the floor and I stumble backward, surprised to see Frankie staring back at me. Frankie snatches my phone from the floor and brushes past me into the room. I try to talk, but I'm so stunned, my mouth is glued shut.

Frankie sits on the unmade bed, arms folded, grinning like a love sick puppy. "I missed you, Danny. I know this is a shock, but I had to see you. Aren't you happy to see me? Can you blame me? We're newlyweds. I was thinking we can hang out in L.A. for a while...you know, turn a sad situation into a happy one."

I close the door and stand there trying to get angry, but

the look on Frankie's face makes me curl over in laughter.

"What's so funny?" Frankie asks, handing me my phone.

"You are and I'm mad as hell at you!"

"I don't want Danielle to be mad at me. By the way, Danielle looks absolutely stunning. Peach is definitely your color. And look," Frankie says, pointing to the garment bag, "I brought my favorite Armani suit and tie. You know the one you like. The one that makes me look better than Bradley Cooper and Idris Elba rolled up in one."

"You shouldn't have come," I say.

"But I want to support you. Be here for you."

"You really needed to check with me on this, Frankie. Like I told you, I haven't seen these women in twenty years. It's really complicated."

"That's why you need me—to help sort things out. Hey, I could do a story about The Fresh Five. You know...write about how you all met, the separation, and hopefully the reunion. I have the perfect title, 'Four Ladies Only.' The four would be f-o-u-r...you know...because it's only four of you left."

I put my palm up and say, "Please, this is not 'The Best Man Holiday' and you are not Taye Diggs. There will be no story!"

"Okay, why don't I get dressed and let's go to church," Frankie says.

"No!!! I mean...let's not go to church," I say.

"I'm confused. At first you said you weren't going and then you said you are, and now you're not. Which is it?"

"I just need to be alone right now."

Frankie, with furrowed brows, goes to the window and looks out. "You haven't told them have you?"

"Told them what?" I ask, my eyes boring a hole through Frankie's head, wondering where this line of questioning is going.

"That you're married to me."

"Of course I told them."

"Don't play with me, Danielle."

"I'm not playing with you."

"Did you tell them I'm white?"

"No, why would I tell them that? What does your race have to do with anything? My best friend or former best friend, Sheridan is white. I'm a discrimination attorney and the last thing I'll tolerate from anyone is racism."

"Did you tell them I'm a *woman?*"

It's funny how a little five letter word can bring you to your knees. My lips quiver when Frankie faces forward, looking at me with her accusing grey eyes. She pulls on her silk scrunchie and her thick auburn hair cascades onto her slender shoulders. A few wild strands fall onto her heart shaped face. Whenever she lets her hair down, all bets are off.

"You haven't told them" she says, stepping back.

"I didn't think it was necessary. Not right now," I say, swallowing hard.

"Not necessary. Like you didn't think it was necessary for the partners at your firm to know that you're married to a white woman?"

"Why are you bringing that up again?" I ask.

"Danielle, I can understand you keeping me a secret when it comes to your job."

"You know the partners are right wing repub—"

"Save it. I know your excuse about work. But what about now? These are your friends. You've met all my friends and my family, Danielle."

"I...I just don't want them judging me. And you've met my family, too."

"I know I have, but we're talking about your friends. Why would they judge you?"

I give her a questioning look.

"I get it...they'll think you weren't good

enough…couldn't cut it with a man…couldn't find a man to love you, so you *settled* for a woman. Is that it?"

"No! Stop it. This is all new for me, Frankie. I didn't grow up wanting to trade my Barbie in for G.I. Joe. I played with dolls, I had an Easy Bake Oven, I was as prissy and feminine as a girl could be. In high school I dated boys. Frankie, you've known you were gay since you were five-years-old. That's not my story."

She walks to me and takes my hand. "Okay, Danielle, I get it. You need time to come out of the closet."

I jerk my hand away from her. "I hate that phrase."

"Do you have a better one?"

"I just need time — time to adjust. You're the first and hopefully *last* woman I'll ever be with."

"Hopefully?"

"You know what I mean."

"Danielle, maybe you're not ready for this."

"What do you mean? I married you, for better or worse, for life and I love you."

"I love you, too and I just want to be a part of your life — *all* of your life."

"I know you do."

I go to Frankie and pass my hand over her soft check. She looks up at me with tears in her eyes. "Go to church, Danielle. Go and be there for your friends. I'll be here when you get back."

"Are you sure?"

"Yes."

"Okay, when I get back, we'll go out to dinner. Westwood has some great restaurants."

"I'd like that," Frankie says.

I reach for the gift bag containing a framed photo of the girls and me at Faye's 16th birthday party, with a smile on my face, imagining how excited Mother Brown will be to receive it.

"What's in the bag?" Frankie asks.

"The photo I told you I was going to give Sabrina's mother."

"Right. Okay, you better get going."

Frankie gives me a peck on the lips and I leave her standing there, hoping and praying she truly understands and that she's here when I get back.

I put the pedal to the metal on the rental. If I hurry, I might make the sermon before it's over. I reflect on my encounter with Frankie and am hit with a bolt of supersized guilt. She doesn't deserve to be treated like this—shoved in a box because I literally and figuratively don't have the balls to tell the world I've found the love of my life in a white woman.

I think back to the day we had met. I was on my way to court and was trying to flag down a taxi. It was a miserable day in Manhattan. It had been raining nonstop and the wind was blowing with a vengeance. My umbrella had flown up and the few documents I couldn't fit in my briefcase were getting soaked. The driver took one look at me and tried to take off. I think he mistook me for a black man with my hair cut so short. Frankie jumped in front of the cab and was almost hit. The driver came to a screeching halt and called her everything but a child of God. She went off on him and told him she was going to write an expose' on New York cab drivers refusing to take black fares and that he would be the star of her story. She was like a pitbull. I actually got wet between the legs watching her in action. She opened the passenger door and ushered me into the cab, gave me her card, and told me to be safe. I made it to court on time and couldn't stop thinking about her.

I didn't date much in high school and the few guys I did hook up with bored me. I was a virgin until I was twenty-five. The other girls didn't know that. I always bragged about getting with this guy and that guy, but outside of a lot of kissing and petting, no guy ever made it to home base. Unlike Frankie, I was never turned on by a woman. I mean I experimented with my cousins when we were little girls, but that was the extent of my sexual encounters with the same sex.

After I passed the bar, and landed my position at Lewinsky, James & Melbourne, I started thinking about getting serious with someone. My assistant played cupid and I went on a couple of blind dates. I even joined a few online dating sites. And then I met Mitchell. He was on the fast track to becoming New York's next Assistant D.A. — a hotshot lawyer with a serious pedigree and the looks to go with it. I met him at a conference and we hit if off right away. He was a cross between a younger, taller version of Billy D. Williams — the Billy D. from "Lady Sings the Blues" and I was his Diana Ross. We were a power couple and he was ferocious in bed. I was sprung and after a year, we decided to move in together. That's when I had the misfortune of experiencing his other side.

It was his birthday and I had planned a lavish birthday party with all of our friends. Sabrina even flew in at her own expense. I was so excited. We waited and waited and when he did show up, he walked in and we screamed surprise, but he just mumbled something, threw his hands up, and stormed off to the bedroom. I thought it was a joke. I ran into see what was wrong and he told me he didn't like surprises. A shouting match ensued and our guest left in a hurry. The argument continued and escalated. The next thing I knew, Mitchell had me pinned to the wall with his massive hands around my throat. I pressed charges and he lost all chances at the Assistant D.A. position. I never saw him after that. I was devastated and humiliated. To avoid falling into a serious depression, I drowned myself in work. I didn't come up for air until that rainy day.

Later that night I called Frankie and we talked all night about everything. I really needed someone in my life at that time, because by then Sabrina had shut me out. The next day we had lunch in the courtyard near my firm. I remember it like it was yesterday.

Sitting on a bench, I glance at my phone, wondering if I got the time wrong. Frankie should have been here by now. I look up at the sun, happy there's no rain. My phone vibrates. I look down and there's a text message from her. "Hey you, I'm right behind you." My stomach quivers and I jump up, wondering if she's pulling my leg. I turn around and she's standing there, clutching a picnic basket, beaming brighter than the sun. Yesterday with all the rain, I really didn't get a good look at her. I hadn't realized how stunning she is — shoulder length auburn hair, piercing grey eyes, and an arresting smile. Dressed in a pair of Tommy Hilfiger jeans, a green cashmere sweater, and penny loafers, she makes me feel overdressed in my Armani skirt suit and red bottom shoes. In spite of her casual attire, I notice men of all nationalities doing double takes, but she seems to be oblivious to the attention.

"You are so crazy," I say, extending my arms for a hug. She walks to me and we embrace. Her scent of natural body odor and a sweet smelling perfume brings a smile to my face. "What's in the basket?" I ask.

"Wouldn't you like to know?"

"I sure would, because I'm starving," I say.

"Follow me," she says.

I do so, and she stops at a nice grassy area underneath a tree. "You know I've worked here for the longest and I never knew this was back here. How'd you know?" I ask.

"I staked out the place this morning."

"You're kidding," I say.

"I'm not. I know you only have so much time. I didn't want to waste it."

"And I thought Danielle was an A-type personality."

She giggles and drops the basket on the grass.

"What's funny?"

"It's cute how you refer to yourself in the third person."

I swallow hard and say, "I have my one and only older brother to blame."

Frankie stoops down and takes a blanket out of the basket and spreads it across the grass. She sits and motions for me to join her. I kick my shoes off and flop down next to her. "You were saying?" she says.

"My brother Richard was trying to teach me to spell my name so he would sound it out and make me repeat it and then have me spell it. We would practice around the house and whenever he said my name, I'd have to spell it. 'Danielle is going into the kitchen.' And I would repeat it and then spell my name. It just stuck with me." I choke up a bit and blink back tears before she notices.

"That's fascinating."

I scrunch my face, wondering why she would find that fascinating.

"That's cute, too."

"What?" I ask.

"That funny face you make. If you haven't already guessed, I think everything about you is cute," she says in a tone that makes the hair on the back of my neck rise.

"What's in the basket I?" I ask, changing the subject.

She reaches in and pulls out sandwiches, fruit, and chips. I grab a sandwich and start to eat. I feel her staring at me and say, "Aren't you going to have one?"

"Sure," she says. "But I need to tell you something."

"What?" I ask, chowing down on my sandwich.

"I know we talked about a lot of things last night, but there's one thing I didn't mention," she says.

Still eating, I give her a questioning look.

"Danielle, I'm a lesbian."

I nearly choke on my sandwich.

"Are you okay?"

She reaches into the basket and hands me some bottled water. I take it and guzzle. "I'm fine. I thought I heard you say you were a lesbian."

"You heard right. Does that bother you?"

"Of course not, I've had gay friends, I have gay friends."

She smiles and takes my hand. "I have gay friends, too, Danielle. I don't need any more friends, and I'm not looking for friends. I'm looking for 'The One.'"

"The One?" I ask, pulling my hand out of her grasp.

"Yes, that person I can eventually share my life with and raise a family with."

"Good luck with that. Been there done that and —"

"I'm not Mitchell, Danielle. I would never hurt you. I'd only love you."

My throat constricts and I want to jump up and run. I've never met a man or woman who's as straight forward as Frankie. It's just a little too much to take and I guess my face shows it.

"I'm sorry, Danielle. I didn't mean to be so forward, but I've never been a bullshitter and I go after what I want and I want you. I knew it the moment I laid eyes on you and after we talked, I was certain. If you want to get up and run, you can. If you never want to talk to me again in life, I'd understand."

"But, I'm not gay, Frankie. I've never made love to or loved another woman in that way."

"I'm not asking you to be gay. I'm just asking you to give me a chance to get to know you, to become your friend. I'm just asking you to be open. If things never progress, then they just don't. I won't disrespect you or come on to you in any way. We can just be friends. See what happens."

"Frankie, I just met you and I like you a lot, but I can't promise you anything, and I can't promise you I won't date men. I can promise you this; we can be friends as long as you respect my boundaries."

"I can live with that," she says. "Now let's eat, girl."

Six months after that, we had moved in with each other and a week after that we made love for the first time. It was beyond anything I had ever experienced with a man. On my birthday, she proposed to me in Central Park and we've been married for a year now. I never have sorted out whether I'm gay or not, I just know I'm madly in love with Francine Renee Wiley.

I pull myself off of memory lane and pull into an empty parking space at New Hope. The lot is full but I still might have a chance to make it in before the sermon is over. I check myself out in the mirror and head for the entrance, wondering if the others showed up.

Chapter 9

Sheridan

In our bedroom, putting the final touches on my makeup, I watch Gary primping in our standalone mirror. He sucks in his gut that makes him appear to be nine months pregnant. Gone is his six-pack from back in the day. The only time six-pack and Gary can be used in the same sentence is when he's asking for his beer. Sweating and cursing, he tries to fasten his pants, but it's not happening. In the past year he's put on about twenty-five pounds. All he does is eat, crap, screw, and fantasize about playing football again. In his mind he has a shot, but at thirty-eight, overweight, with a bunch of injuries, he has as much a chance of getting another NFL contract as I do winning "America's Next Top Model."

"Where are my other pants, Sher? That cleaners is shrinking my pants. These slacks didn't fit me like this the last time I wore them," he says, letting his trousers fall to the floor.

"I told you, you don't have to go to church with me. We've probably missed most of the service." If truth be told, I don't want him to go. The last time the others saw Gary, he was serious eye candy. He could make a nun drop her drawers. Compared to Faye's husband Mark and Vicky's husband Curtis, Gary looks tore up from the floor up.

"Okay, yesterday you acted a fool because I wouldn't go to the funeral with you, and now that I wanna go to church with you, you act like you could give a flying rat's patoot. Who's at the church, Sher?"

"What do you mean who's at the church?"

"Am I speaking a foreign language here? I asked what nigga is meeting you at the church."

Sick and tired of being sick and tired of his accusations, I throw my lipstick at him and flop down on the bed and cover my face with my hands.

"What's your problem?" he asks, stepping out of his pants.

I peek at him through my splayed fingers and burst out laughing. He's a sight to behold in his red boxers, nylon socks, and chicken legs.

"Woman, you must be crazy, throwing stuff at me and now laughing like you done lost your mind. What's funny?"

"You are and stop accusing me of gettin' with every Tyrone, Devon, and Hakeem in the neighborhood. Nobody's checkin' for a tore down middle-age white woman."

Gary sits next to me on the bed. He turns my face toward him. "Stop talkin' 'bout my wife like that. To me you're as pretty as the day I saw you at the cheerleader tryouts. Why you think it makes me crazy to think about you being with another man."

"Gary, I've never been with another man since we got together. Now can you say the same?"

"Of course I can. I've never been with another man since we got together either."

Shaking my head and laughing, I grab the pillow off of the bed and hit him with it. "You know what I mean."

"No, I don't. We're gonna miss church."

"Wear your blue suit," I say.

"I can't find it," he says, picking his pants up off of the floor.

I brush past him and go into the walk-in closet we share. I remember when we had separate walk-in closets—when we lived in our mini-mansion in Dallas. I go through his clothes and find the blue suit wedged between a bunch of sweatshirts and football jerseys. A wave of sadness overtakes me when I think about how much Gary loves football and the injuries, depression, drinking, and drugging that took him out the game.

"You find it?" he asks.

"I got it, babe," I say, coming out of the closet.

He takes the suit and kisses me on the cheek. "You're such a good woman, Sher and I'm sorry again for losing my temper the other day. If I hadn't been going off, you probably wouldn't have run into the door."

"I should have been watching where I was going. You know I've always been on the clumsy side. Remember in high school when I fell down in the cafeteria?"

"Yep, maybe I need to start taking anger management classes again." He looks at me with a questioning look—the look he always give me when he wants my opinion—eyes wide, mouth slightly parted. "Most of the guys in those classes have hit their women. I mean, I've never laid a hand on you or any woman for that matter. Now there was this girl at Brad that accused me of hitting her, but it was a straight up lie. But I know there's more to it than physical abuse, there's emotional abuse."

"You've come a long ways, sweetie, but I guess It wouldn't hurt to sit in on some more sessions. Speaking of classes, have you ever thought about using your degree?"

"What am I going to do with a communications degree?" he asks, getting dressed.

"I don't know. Maybe you can coach."

"Sher, I was born to do one thing, and one thing only, and that's play football, and if I can't do that, I don't want to do anything."

I bite my tongue, not wanting to get him going. He looks in the mirror and smiles at his image. "Now that's what I'm talking 'bout," he says, admiring himself. "No wonder all those broads were after me at Bradshaw. Hell, I still got it. You know you were the lucky one, Sher. I could have gotten any one of those Bradshaw beauties I wanted, but I chose you. You know Vicky was stone crazy about me. She was too through when she found out we were an item."

"You're preaching to the choir, Gary. I know all about Vicky. Speaking of Vicky, we had a little run-in at the Browns last night."

"What kind of run-in?"

"I went down to the wine cellar at Sabrina's to get me a little drink."

"I didn't know Sabrina had a wine cellar," he says, straightening his red tie.

"I didn't either. Mother Brown says it was on her bucket list."

"Damn!" Gary says.

"When I got down there —"

"Let's go, Sher. You can talk on the way out," he says, grabbing my purse and handing it to me.

We leave the bedroom and stop off in the kitchen where Geraldine, Gary's mother, is washing dishes. "Ma, we're heading to church," Gary says.

"Bye, ma," I say. "And please stop doing the dishes and rest yourself. I'll do those when we get back."

"But you cooked breakfast, Sher. I can at least do the dishes."

"I got it, ma."

"I sure wish I could go with y'all, but I'm just not feeling up to it this morning," she says, rubbing her arm.

"Is your arthritis still acting up?" Gary asks.

"My arthritis and everything else."

"Take it easy, ma," Gary says.

A smile spreads across her thin dark face and she winks at Gary with dark eyes filled with sadness and regret. I'm not sure if her sadness is because of how her life turned out or how her only son's life turned out. "I will. Y'all pray for me."

"We will," I say, following Gary to the driveway. "You driving?" I ask.

"You wanna get there on time and in one piece, then you need to let me drive. Where's the church?" he asks, getting in the driver's seat.

"Long Beach off of—"

"I see the address right here," he says, picking up Sabrina's obituary off of the floor. "I can't believe she's gone. She was good, people, Sher."

I get in the passenger seat, he hands me the obituary, and backs out of the driveway. "Put your seatbelt on," I say, putting on mine.

He buckles up and then asks, "So what happened with Vicky? Is she still cute? And what about Faye? Hmm…Miss Bible Girl. Is Danielle still a stuck up dyke?"

"Hold up. What do you mean is Vicky still cute?" I ask.

"I'm just messin' with you, woman."

"And why are you calling Danielle a dyke?" I ask.

"Any girl going to Bradshaw that wasn't checkin' for me had to be gay."

"So just because Danielle wasn't all over you back in

the day, she's gay? Wow, you never cease to amaze me. And why are you so interested in everybody now? I tried to give you the 411 last night and you didn't have time for me."

"You got home so late, I was too tired," he says, heading toward the freeway.

"That's what I was trying to tell you. Why I got home so late. I got into it with Vicky. She was down in the wine cellar holding onto this bottle of wine real tight like she was an alcoholic or something. She scared the crap out of me when I first came down there. She was looking all glassy-eyed. Then she asked me if I still blamed her for what happened."

"Shut up! What did you say?"

"I didn't know what to say. At that point I just needed a drink. So we had a drink together. Sabrina has all these glasses down there on a rack. It's really classy. So after we had a couple more drinks, Vicky started talking about her husband Curtis. She showed me his picture and the picture of her kids at Christmas and then she said something about them being molested and how guilty she felt and she asked me was it her fault about the kids. The more she drank, the crazier she sounded. I started getting a little freaked out and I was trying to leave, but she started pulling on me and I fell down and hit my head on a wooden post. I didn't hit it hard or anything. Then she started crying and trying to touch my head. It was surreal. I ran out of there."

"So you just left her like that?"

"I guess I shouldn't have. I hope she's okay. Hopefully, she'll be at church."

"You know, all of you should get back together."

I give Gary a crazy look.

"Don't look at me like that. You girls were tight back in the day and now that Sabrina's gone, y'all need to make up. What if God has put a curse on you guys and he's taking you out one-by-one until you make up with one another.

Maybe Sabrina's the first one and then somebody else will be next. Like in that movie...uh...I can't think of it."

"You're talking about 'Final Destination.'"

"Right, that's the one. What if it's like that?"

"Gary, please. It's not like that at all."

"You don't know. Y'all need to work it out."

"The freeway is coming up," I say, pointing.

"I see it," he says, getting on the freeway. "Stop trying to change the subject."

"I'm not. We've been doing fine for the past twenty years without one another. I think we should leave well enough alone."

"What about Sabrina's dying wish? That doesn't mean anything to you? Sabrina has been there for you. If it wasn't for her helping out with Kimberly's tuition she would have had to drop out of school a long time ago. And she wouldn't be living on campus either. Not to mention all the times she let you work part time at the clinic. Sabrina had your back. You need to take heed to her wishes."

I sit there fidgeting in my seat, wishing Gary would pipe down. He's right about Sabrina being there for us. And I guess if nothing else, I should try to be cordial. Maybe we can all exchange phone numbers and emails and stay in contact that way. I guess it wouldn't be too bad. Danielle doesn't even live in California anymore and Vicky...I'm not sure about her, but I can see hanging out with Faye. Yeah, Faye and I could be besties. I always was a little closer to her than the others being that she didn't grow up with a mother. Her mother died of lupus when Faye was only five. I know what it's like not to have a mother. My mother left me at a fire station when I was six and I never knew my father. I was bounced around in the system after that. I came close to getting adopted, but it never happened. I think people were more interested in newborns. Faye could become my new Sabrina. I grin and find myself chuckling.

"What's so funny?" Gary asks, getting off of the

freeway.

"Nothing. The church is over there," I say, pointing.

"I see it."

Gary enters the church parking lot and we exchange wary looks when we see all the cars. A parking attendant motions and Gary follows him to a spot in the rear. "Dang, it's gonna take forever to get out of here. We should park on the street," he says.

"Where on the street? Didn't you see all the cars?" I ask.

"Whatever."

He parks and we get out and walk to the sanctuary. I take a moment and size him up. Actually, he doesn't look too bad in his blue suit. He looks kinda good. I reach for his hand and he takes mine and kisses it. I get a tingle in my choochie and snuggle up next to him. It's moments like these that remind me why I fell in love with him twenty years ago. I guess a part of me feels like he's the father I never had. I mean I've had foster care fathers, but they were getting paid to care about me. Gary loved me unconditionally and he was so protective. I felt safe with him. As we stroll hand-in-hand through the parking lot, I briefly think about the first time I laid eyes on him.

It was the first week of high school and all five us were beyond excited and nervous. We had been dreaming about attending Bradshaw the whole time we were in middle school. All the cool people went to Brad. That's what we used to call it. The Fresh Five were going to be the freshest freshmen Bradshaw had ever seen. We wore our jean suits with Converse All Stars that day and our hair in ponytails. I remember we were all having lunch and a group of boys were sitting at a table across from ours. Sabrina noticed them first.

"Psst. Psst," Sabrina said.

"What?" we all asked.

"Over there."

"Where?" Faye asked, looking around, swooshing her fake ponytail.

"Don't look!" Sabrina squealed.

"You guys are trippin' for real," I said, pointing to the table where the boys sat.

"Sherry, don't!"

Danielle shook her head and rolled her eyes. "You guys are whack. You act like you've never seen a boy before."

"They're not just any boys, there on the football team," Sabrina announced. She sipped on her punch and winked at Vicky.

Vicky started cheesing and swinging her curly ponytail. Before we could say anything, she had gotten up from our table and was walking toward the cafeteria vending machine, switching her narrow hips the entire way.

The boys all looked as she walked by and one of them said, "Her eyes are so pretty." Something about the way he said it made me jealous. So I got up and walked over to the vending machine, too. On the way there one of the boys stuck his foot out and I was so busy shaking my tail feather that I tripped on his foot and fell flat on my face. A sea of laughter filled the cafeteria and I could feel my face turn red. I was afraid to even get up. I was so embarrassed. The next thing I saw was this large hand reaching down for me. I grabbed it, stood up, and brushed myself off.

"You okay?" my savior asked.

I took one look at him and went mute. He was the most beautiful human being I had ever seen. He wasn't at the table with the other guys, he had just walked in. He looked to be about six-feet, which was tall for a freshman. He had long lashes, curly hair, and the darkest smoothest skin I had ever seen. I was in love.

"I asked you if you were okay."

I breathed and forced out, "Yeah. I'm okay. Thanks...uh..."

"Gary. Gary Hawkins. I'm on the football team. I just

made the team and I'm stoked."

"Well...uh...uh...congratulations."

"Thanks."

"What's your name?"

"Victoria!"

Gary dropped my hand and turned toward Victoria. She had been standing there the entire time. I stood there, not sure what to do, so I went back to the table while Victoria chatted up Gary. The others at the table shook their heads and we watched Victoria and Gary until the bell finally rang. I don't know what they were discussing, but Gary never gave me the time of day again until I tried out for the cheerleading squad three years later during my junior year. I don't think he even remembered who I was. By then my breasts had really developed and my foster mother had made me an outfit that was all that and a bag of chips as the girls used to say. The little brown skirt showed off my shapely legs and the gold mid drift top with tassels showed off my flat stomach. I remember Gary and a few of the guys from the football team were watching the tryouts and Gary couldn't keep his eyes off of me. I made the squad and that same day Gary asked me for my phone number. We started dating and then in my senior year I got pregnant and shortly after that all hell broke loose.

"Come on, Gary says, entering New Hope. "We're already late."

"Coming," I say, bringing myself back to the present.

Chapter 10

Faye

"...The poet Alexander Pope in his Essay on Criticism said, 'To err is human, to forgive, divine.' My brothers and sisters, you see, in order to forgive you must have a mind like God — a Christ-like mind. Peter asked Jesus in Matthew 18:1 how many times did he have to forgive his brother. Now don't get it twisted, as the young folk would say, brother includes sister."

The sanctuary fills with laughter and I groan. I have a funny suspicion my husband's message today is for my benefit.

"Do you know what Jesus told Peter, Saints when he asked him how many times he has to forgive his brother?

One time? Two? Three? Seventy times seven! That's a lot of forgiving. So if your brother or sister sins against you, you must forgive them seventy times seven."

The congregation is stone quiet. I glance around and notice members squirming in their seats. I can see Victoria in my peripheral vision staring straight ahead, focused on Mark's every word like her life depends on it.

"Now some of us, and I'm not going to name names, would have a hard time with that. Some of us are ready to set it off if somebody steps on our toe and please don't back into someone's car on the parking lot—I'm talking World War Three."

Sister Green, sitting behind me shouts, "Amen!" Last Sunday she accidentally backed into a senior deacon's brand new Mercedes and it took two security guards to calm him down.

"Some of you come to church with a *list*. You know which *list* I'm talking about. The one that has the names of the people you aren't going to speak to or sit next to, and it's been so long since you fell out with the person, you can't even remember why you're mad at them. Sound familiar?"

The church fills with the sound of the members mumbling, rustling in their seats, and laughing with recognition.

"We have a hard time forgiving. But when it comes time to *be* forgiven, we're the first ones in line. *Please, please, please*, Lord, forgive me. How do you expect God to forgive you when you won't even forgive your brother or your sister? We have to do better saints."

I feel Victoria looking at me and I turn and face her. She gives me a weak smile. "He's really good, Faye."

"Thanks," I say.

"He's telling the truth about how we want to be forgiven, but we aren't willing to forgive others."

"Right," I say, turning back toward Mark, thinking about all I've done, the life I've led, the sins I've committed. How could God even think about forgiving me for what I did? Maybe that's why I can't forgive Sheridan, Victoria, and Danielle. Maybe it's because I haven't been able to forgive myself. Lord have mercy on my dark soul. I need to come clean about everything. But what if Mark won't forgive me? I'll lose everything and I can't risk that.

"Are you okay?" Mrs. Brown asks, patting me on the hand.

"I'm fine, Mother Brown."

"You looked like you were in pain. Your face was all twisted."

"No, I'm okay."

Mark concludes his sermon and asks those who want to accept Christ to come forward. He also asks those who want to forgive and be forgiven to come forward. I look around at the people rushing to the front of the church, wanting to join them, but afraid of what the members might think. I'm the First Lady of this church. I'm supposed to be perfect.

Victoria taps me and says, "I'm going up."

My heart races upon hearing her and a wave of fear passes through my trembling body. I want to join her, but my butt is glued to my seat. I give her a nod of approval, wondering what she's going to ask God to forgive her for. Is she going to ask him to forgive her for being drunk that night? What other dastardly deeds has she done? I think to myself while she walks to the altar wearing…Sabrina's dress?

"Why don't you go up and support, Vicky?" Mrs. Brown asks.

"But…but—"

"But nothing! Go ahead."

Raised to respect my elders, I do as I'm told and head to the altar, sweat beading on my upper lip, feeling like I'm on death row walking to the electric chair. I can feel all eyes on me and I imagine the members gossiping among themselves. *What did she do? Lord, I knew it. Too good to be true that a woman that pretty could be faithful. So she's a sinner just like the rest of us.* Yeah, I can just hear my haters chopping me up into tiny pieces. I'm loved at New Hope, but not by everybody. I reach Victoria and I gently take her hand. It's wet and clammy. I fight the urge to snatch my hand back and wipe it with my handkerchief. I couldn't if I wanted to, because my handkerchief is in my purse and my purse is on my seat.

"Glad to see you here," Victoria whispers.

"Mother Brown thought I should give *you* some support," I say, hoping she understands that I'm not there for myself.

She widens her green eyes and says, "Must be nice to be free of guilt or sin or..."

I swallow hard and take a moment before I speak. "I never said I was perfect, Victoria. I've sinned just like everyone else. I need forgiveness just like everyone else."

"And you need to forgive, just like everyone else."

Stumped, I stare at her and then look away. Mark begins praying over us and I shut my eyes tight, fighting back tears. The sound of soft prayers can be heard throughout the sanctuary. I listen intently to the voices of those around me begging God for forgiveness. The prayer that gives me pause is Victoria's.

"Lord, please forgive me for hurting my kids. God, I didn't mean it. I was..."

She trails off and then becomes silent. I notice her lips moving, but she's inaudible. I wonder what she did to her kids. She's lucky to have kids. If my baby had lived it would be nineteen going on twenty — the same age as Sheridan and Gary's daughter, Kimberly. I call my baby "It." I don't know if *it* was a boy or a girl. I didn't want to know. All I know is that I had to get rid of *it*. I couldn't bring shame on my father. He was a well-respected preacher. What would people think? What would they say? I'm so sick and tired of living my life for others. I want to be free. Tears stream down my face and I drop to my knees, forgetting about those around me, not caring about what anyone has to say. I go deep within myself and focus on God and his unconditional love and I talk to him within my soul.

Lord, I don't know where to begin. I've done so much wrong. God, I'm a fake and a fraud. I always have been, but I'm sure I'm not telling you anything you don't already know. In school I tried to be perfect. I wanted people to think I was the perfect little church girl – my daddy's girl. But the real me was anything but perfect. When I got to high school my hormones were raging and I wanted to be like the other girls. I wanted to know what it was like to kiss a boy and what it was like to be touched down there. Sheridan used to tell me about the things she would do with Gary, and Vicky had a boyfriend, too. Danielle didn't date much, but I knew she had been kissed and touched before. And Sabrina had at least one boyfriend. I was the only one who didn't have anyone.

And then one night during Bible Study I noticed Gary sitting in the back of the church. I was shocked that he was there. I didn't even know he knew where our church was. After the meeting, he spoke to me and told me he needed prayer because the championship game was coming up. I asked him where Sheridan was and he told me not to worry about her.

I could barely control myself talking to Gary. He was so handsome that he was beautiful. The way he spoke, moved, everything about him. God, you really out did yourself when you created Gary. The next thing I knew, I was in his car and we were driving – where to, I didn't know. He started telling me how pretty I was and how sweet I was, all the while reaching over and touching my leg. I felt moisture materialize between my legs. Sheridan told me that happens when you're turned on by a man. One part of me wanted him to stop and another part of me wanted to just go with the flow. I was nervous because I knew he was Sheridan's boyfriend and I knew I shouldn't have been in his car. What would my father do if he knew I had left church with Gary?

After about thirty minutes he pulled up to an abandoned house in the hood. I started getting scared. He held me and told me not to worry. He told me that this is what all the girls did when they became a senior. It was like an initiation. I was so naïve and horny I believed him. He took me inside. The house was empty with the exception of a dirty mattress on the floor. He took his letterman jacket off and put it down and then motioned for me to lie down. At that point I wanted to run, but there was something about Gary that made me feel safe. There's no way someone as beautiful as he was could be bad.

He sat next to me and just talked to me and told me how nice I was. He said my dimples were my best feature. And then he told me to sit up. I frowned, wondering what was going on, why he wasn't touching me, making love to me.

"What's wrong?" I asked.

"Do you know where you are?" he asked.

I looked around and said, "No."

"Faye, right now I could do anything to you. I could rape you, kill you, anything, and who would know?"

My eyes started to water and I jumped up. "What are you saying?"

"I'm not saying anything. I'm teaching. Teaching you a lesson! Don't ever, ever, get in a car with a boy. I don't care if you know him or not and don't ever let him take you someplace that you're not familiar with."

"Why...why...are you doing this?"

"Because Sherry asked me to."

"What? Why...what?" I said, stammering.

"She's worried about you."

"Why?"

"Because there's a bet going on at Brad. There's a bet going on with some of the guys on the football team. They're going to try to see who can have sex with you first. That's why, Faye. And you're gullible. They want to brag that they screwed a preacher's daughter. You don't want to lose your virginity that way. It should be special."

"Why didn't you guys just tell me? Why take me here and take me through all of this?"

"We wanted to drive the point home!"

"But...now Sherry will know I was going to be with you. She's my friend. She'll hate me."

"Faye, please. Can't no woman resist me. Sherry knows that."

"Oh..." I said, smoothing my dress down.

"I better get you home," he said, grabbing his jacket and walking toward the door.

I stood there feeling like an idiot. And then anger started to rise within me. I wanted to strike back somehow. I knew Sherry called herself looking out for me, but it pissed me off. One more time I felt like they had one over on me. So I walked to Gary and I started rubbing his groin. He pushed me away and I flung myself at him. Surprised, he stumbled backward and fell onto the mattress. I unzipped his pants before he had a chance to stop me and I did the unthinkable. He kept saying no, but I didn't stop and after a while he stopped protesting and gave in and had sex with me. It wasn't anything like I had fantasized. I didn't feel anything, but pain. I didn't have the "Big O" that Sheridan bragged about. Afterwards we both felt lousy and we swore to each other that we would keep what we had done a secret.

Gary took me home and there was a message waiting for me that Sheridan had called. My father asked me where I had been and I told him that I had been with a few girls from church. I ran to my room, nervous, shaking, and bleeding a bit. Showering, I thought about what had happened and how it had happened. My father knocked on the door and I jumped so high, I hit my head on the shower rack. He told me Sheridan was on the phone. I got out of the shower and braced myself.

Sheridan confessed that she had Gary set me up just like he told me she had, and I thanked her for the lesson and quickly hung up. I thought it was all over. But the following month I didn't get my period. I took five home pregnancy tests and they all came back positive. Then I dropped the bomb on Gary. He told me he would help me get rid of it. By the time I was supposed to meet with him,

I was rethinking the whole thing. I had spent two weeks fantasizing about what our baby would look like and Gary having a change of heart and asking me to keep our baby and marry him. I got a rude awakening when he told me Sheridan was pregnant, too. I asked him if he was going to help Sheridan get rid of her baby and he just looked at me. I already knew the answer before I had asked the question.

I shut down after that and let him take me to the "doctor." It was over just as fast as he had plunged himself inside me, breaking my virginity and my heart. I put the whole sordid event out of my mind and tried to act as if it never had happened. "God, I never once asked you to forgive me for aborting my baby, for having sex with my best friend's boyfriend, for committing fornication, for lying to my father and my friends. And now I can't have children because of what I've done. I'm sorry, God. I'm sorry," I say, sobbing.

"Faye, Faye, baby. It's okay. It's okay."

I get hold of myself and look into Mark's tear-stained face, realizing that what started out as a silent prayer ended with an all-out confession. I pull away from him, embarrassed, humiliated, shamed, and I run. I ignore the murmuring and the voices calling out to me. I fight off the security guards trying to stop me. I make it pass the ushers and onto the foyer where through bleary eyes I see Vicky, Danielle, and Sheridan who's holding a strange man's hand. I brush past them and make my way to the parking lot.

I come to our car and quickly get inside.

"Faye! Faye!" Mark screams, running toward me.

I get in the car and lock the doors. He bangs on the window. Lamont, the security guard, runs up to the car with an extra set of keys. He unlocks the door and Mark gets in the passenger seat. I cover my face with my hands. "Leave me alone, Mark. I'm no good. I lied to you. I lied to everybody. I had an abortion. I was pregnant before. That's why I can't get pregnant."

"I know, Dimples, I heard the end of your prayer."

"You called me Dimples."

"Aren't you my Dimples?"

"But what I did and now the church knows."

"They don't know, sweetie. I only heard you because I had come down from the pulpit when you fell to your knees. You were crying and praying so hard I was worried about you."

"But I've shamed you. I've shamed us."

"No, you shamed the devil!"

"Huh?"

"He's been holding this secret over your head for twenty-years. And now that you've confessed and ask God to forgive you, he doesn't have anything on you anymore."

"But God isn't going to forgive me. I murdered my own baby."

"Faye, God forgave you the moment you asked him to. Why do you think Jesus went to the cross? He bore our sins on that cross."

"God forgave me?"

"Yes."

"What about you, Mark? I lied to you. I made you think I was a virgin. I'm the reason — "

"Sshh! I forgive you, baby. Stop it. What you did in your past and who you did it with is none of my business. All I know is that all the things you did in the past and the experiences you had in the past, make you the woman you are today — the woman who I love."

I look into my husband's kind face with deep felt gratitude. Maybe God gave me a loving man like Mark because he took my mother away from me when I was only five. Maybe this is his way of making up for that devastating loss.

"Now, I want you to do something," Mark says.

"What?" I ask.

"Forgive yourself."

"But—"

"Are you better than God?"

"No."

"Repeat after me," he says. "I First Lady Faye Dimples Davis."

"I First Lady Faye Dimples Davis."

"Forgive myself."

"Forgive myself."

"For all the sins that I have ever committed."

"For all the sins that I have...have...ever committed."

"I First Lady Faye Dimples Davis forgive Sheridan, Vicky, and Danielle."

"Huh?"

"Do you want to be free?"

"Yes."

"Then say it."

"I First Lady Faye Dimples Davis forgive Sheridan, Vicky, and Danielle."

"In Jesus name, Amen!"

"In Jesus name, Amen!"

"Now I want you to come back inside."

"Oh...gosh...no, I can't face the church. I can't ever."

"Faye, you are a light. You have a testimony. For every young girl who has ever gone through what you have, you have to face the church."

"But—"

"Do you want to be free, baby?"

"Yes!"

"Take my hand," he says.

I grab his hand and he helps me out of the car. We make our way back to the sanctuary. I hold my head down and he lifts it. When we reach the foyer, Vicky, the Browns, Danielle, and Sheridan are there. I do a double take when I get another look at the man holding Sheridan's hand. He's dark, with a receding hairline, overweight, and wearing a blue suit one size two small. That can't possibly be Gary. The Browns approach us and shower us with smiles and hugs. When we enter, the congregation rises to their feet and applauds. Tears pour out of my eyes and I hold my head high and walk to the front of the church.

An usher hands me a mic. I stand there not knowing what to say. Mark takes the mic. "Saints, thank you for showing my wife so much love. She, like all of us, has sinned, but we serve a forgiving God and she is forgiven. The congregation applauds. Now we need your help. We've been trying to get pregnant for three years now. We need you all to pray for us that God will bless First Lady Faye's womb."

"It's done!!!" a woman shouts from the rear. Then more people repeat her mantra. I hug Mark, believing that God has forgiven me, and for the first time, I'm hopeful that we will be parents one day.

"We receive that," Mark says.

He takes my hand and we walk out of the sanctuary with the members showering us with smiles and words of encouragement. In that moment I feel like I have been released from a lifetime prison sentence. And then all my joy dissipates when I remember that night—not the night with Gary, but the night that changed The Fresh Five forever.

Chapter 11

Victoria

Talk about drama! Wow! The cheers and shouts from the sanctuary spill over into the lobby. When Faye and Mark approach, I exchange looks with the Browns, Danielle, Sheridan, and the strange man masquerading as Gary. The Browns and Sheridan embrace the couple and the rest of us look on. I'm not sure what happened at the altar because I came out to the lobby shortly after my prayer to get some fresh air. I remember opening my eyes and being surprised when I got a glimpse of Faye on her knees with her eyes shut and her lips quavering. I was even more surprised to find Sheridan, Gary, and Danielle waiting in the wings. If you arrive after the sermon starts, you have to go to the overflow room and apparently the overflow room was full today as well, so they had to watch the service from the television screens in the lobby.

I kept my distance, not sure what to say to Sheridan. I waited for her to say something, but she kept her eyes glued to the large screen television and when she wasn't watching the television, she was fussing over Gary who I barely recognized. He's put on about fifty pounds, is going bald, and walks with a slight limp. I can't believe he's the boy from Bradshaw that every girl in school was competing for. Danielle kept to herself as well, and after our little kitchen episode last night, I decided to give her some space. Then I thought about my prayer and that I had asked God to forgive me for what had happened with my kids and my hardened heart started to melt. I made up my mind that I would tell Danielle that her peach dress complements her light complexion. Then I was going to go over and apologize to Sheridan and pay her a compliment about her hair that she's wearing up today. Finally, I had planned to tell Gary that he looked great in his blue suit and that the extra pounds were becoming. But before I had a chance to play nice, my thoughts were interrupted by shouts, screams, and the sanctuary doors flying open. Faye, with her weave going every which way, but the right way, ran past us, crying harder than she did at the funeral. Mark was right behind her. Then a security guard ran past with keys in his hand and finally the Browns joined us.

Before I could ask them what had occurred, Mark and Faye waltzed back into the church like nothing had ever happened. Then Mark told the congregation that Faye was a sinner like everybody else and that she's been forgiven. The most surprising announcement was that they've been trying to get pregnant for three years. I had no idea, and of course Sabrina never mentioned it, and if she had tried to, I would have stopped her, and Faye tried to downplay it at the repast. Faye, like the rest of us, is thirty-eight and at that age, her eggs would be somewhat compromised. I remember there was a rumor going around Brad that Faye had gotten pregnant and had an abortion, but we all knew that was impossible. Faye's father was as strict as they come and when Faye wasn't with us, she was at church. Just the thought of her being with someone back then made us all laugh. She was so green.

I get out of my head while Mark, Faye, Sheridan, and the Browns talk. Gary stands off to the side with his head down, like he's just an observer. Danielle looks my way and gives me a slight smile. My stomach flips and I get an urge to connect like I did this morning when I saw the Browns and Faye. I follow my instincts and approach her. She takes a couple of steps back and I hesitate, but force myself to keep going.

"You know that dress really looks good on you. You should wear peach all the time."

"Thanks, Victoria," she says, looking me up and down. "Isn't that Sabrina's dress?"

"Yeah…it is. I ended up spending the night at the Browns, and I didn't want to wear the dress I wore to the funeral."

"Right…uh…is that…is that Gary?"

"I look over my shoulder to make sure she's referring to the right person. Church is over and the lobby is filling up quickly. "Yeah, it is."

"Wow…time is something else. He doesn't look anything like he did back in the day," Danielle says.

"I know."

"And Sheridan looks like she's been going through it, too. Did you see her black eye?"

"Yeah, I did. Do you think Gary hit her?"

"Is the sky blue? Yes, Danielle thinks he hit her. Remember when he got suspended for hitting that girl back at Brad?"

"I know, but the truth came out and she was lying."

"Then why would Sheridan have a black eye?"

"Your guess is as good as mine," I say.

"Girl, it's a lot going on. And could you believe what Faye's husband said about them trying to have a baby for three years."

"I know. That wasn't her story last night."

"Girl, what is going on with us?"

"I don't know, but it looks like you have it together," I say, glancing at her wedding band.

"Danielle is happy," she says. "And I'm so glad you got over Gary, and I'm sure after seeing him today, you're glad, too."

We exchange mischievous looks and break into laughter. My eyes sting and tear up and I begin to cry. Not sure why. Maybe because after twenty years Danielle and I are talking…okay, more like gossiping, but we're actually talking. I can't believe it and in this moment I realize just how much I've missed her.

"What's wrong, Victoria?" she asks, awkwardly putting her arms around me.

"I missed you. I missed all of you. I can't believe I let twenty years go by and I miss Sabrina, too."

"Aww, don't cry. Count to ten…come on…do your counting."

"1, 2, 3, 4, 5, 6, 7, 8, 9, 10."

She looks at me and says, "Better?"

I nod and hug her. "Thanks, Danielle."

"And stop calling me Danielle. Call me Danny, like you used to."

"Okay, Danny. And you stop calling me Victoria and call me Vicky like you used to."

"Okay, Vicky," she says, laughing.

"You're still beautiful even with your hair cut short."

She takes a long breath and her face reddens.

"What's wrong I ask."

"I just never imagined we'd be talking like this and you're beautiful, too, and I've always loved your curly hair."

"Girl, that's why The Fresh Five was all that and a bag of chips. We were the cutest girls in middle and high school. Sabrina with her frilly red hair, cat eyes, freckles, and light skin, Sheridan with her crystal blue eyes and long blonde hair, Faye with her dimples and chocolate complexion, you with your flawless light skin, and me with—"

"Beautiful curly hair, pretty green eyes, and a honey brown skin," Danielle says.

"Thanks, Danny...what happened to us? I know what happened was horrible, but why did we let it destroy us?"

Danielle's eyes well up with tears and she turns away. "It still hurts. I miss him."

I rub her back and try to soothe her. "I'm sorry, Danny. I know I've said it a million times, but I truly am. Please, please for—"

"Danny, Vicky...what's wrong? What's wrong, with Danny?" Mrs. Brown asks.

"She'll be okay," I say.

"Hi, Mother Brown. I'm okay," Danielle says.

"I hope you're both hungry because Faye and Mark have invited us all to their house for lunch."

"Are you cooking?" Danielle and I ask at the same time. "No."

"Well...I'm not sure...Faye can't boil water," I say.

"I think I'm going to pass, too," Danielle says, dabbing at her tears with tissue. "I have to meet a friend for dinner."

"Faye is not cooking. Her chef is cooking."

"Chef?" we both ask.

"She has a chef *and* a maid."

"Get out!" we say.

Mrs. Brown laughs.

"What's so funny?" I ask.

"This reminds me of when you all were in high school.

You would talk at the same time and finish each other's sentences — "

"Are they coming?" Mr. Brown asks.

"They better be coming," Mrs. Brown says.

Danielle and I shrug and follow the Browns, Mark, Faye, Gary, and Sheridan to the parking lot.

I park my BMW behind Danielle's rental and get out of the car with my eyes bulging and my mouth watering. Faye's house is beyond incredible. It looks to be about ten thousand square feet and on one side there's nothing but water. Danielle, holding a gift bag, gets out of her rental, shaking her head, seemingly just as amazed as I am. I point to the large windows and balcony in the front and am transfixed by the lush landscape. Boy, I'd like to get my hands in Faye's dirt. We follow Mark, Faye, the Browns, Sheridan, and Gary to the front of the house. I step back, looking in awe at the tall arched glass door. Mark opens it and calls out to someone named Melba. A middle-aged Hispanic woman appears wearing a maid's outfit. She smiles and nods.

"Melba, where's Montana?" Mark asks.

"She got your message and she's almost done with lunch. She's in the kitchen."

"Wonderful," Mark says, pressing his hands together. "Melba, I want to introduce you to our friends. You know the Browns."

"Yes, so good to see you again and I'm so, so, sorry about Sabrina. She was such a lovely young woman."

"Thank you, Melba," Mr. and Mrs. Brown says.

"Melba, this is Gary and Sheridan Hawkins. They are also Sabrina's good friends."

"So nice to meet you," she says, shaking their hands.

"And this is Victoria and Danielle. They're also friends

of Sabrina's."

She shakes Danielle's and my hand and then says, "Sabrina has so many friends. She was such a good person."

We all nod in agreement.

"Melba, Sabrina and I went to school with Sheridan, Danielle, and Victoria," Faye says. "We were called The Fresh Five."

Melba laughs and her almond shaped eyes light up. "I like that name. Who came up with that?" she asks.

"Danielle did," Danielle says.

"Who's Danielle?" Melba asks.

"I'm...I'm Danielle."

"Oh...right...right," Melba says.

"I wanted us to be called The Fabulous Five," Sheridan adds.

"You are fresh and fabulous," Melba says, grinning broadly, revealing a gap in her front teeth. "It's so nice to meet you all, but I have work to do."

"Thank you, Melba," Mark and Faye say.

Melba leaves and I stand there pinching myself, wondering if this is all a dream. When we were coming up, I never could imagine Faye living this large.

"Why don't you give them a tour," Mrs. Brown suggests

"Do you guys want to see the house?" Faye asks.

"I'd love too," Gary says. "Mark...uh...I know you're a man of God and all, but would you happen to have some beer?"

"Yes, I do. I don't have a problem with drinking, as long as it's done in moderation."

My stomach drops listening to Mark and Gary talk about alcohol. I pray God answers my prayer and helps me not to drink.

"Why don't we start in the kitchen, then," Mark says.

"Mark, Faye, we're gonna go out to the patio," Mrs.

Brown says.

"Okay, we'll meet you out there," Mark says.

"Oh, Mother Brown, this is for you," Danielle says, handing Mrs. Brown the gift bag she had taken out of her car.

"Thanks, Danny," Mrs. Brown says. She and Mr. Brown leave.

The rest of us follow Mark and Faye to the kitchen. I almost trip, looking up at the vaulted ceilings. I force my eyes down and I stop in my tracks at the sight of the rich brown hardwood floors. The house is amazing. Apparently I'm not the only one who thinks so. Sheridan, Gary, and Danielle, "ooh" and "ahh" right along with me.

I look over my shoulder at the curved stairway and notice a wedding portrait of Mark and Faye. They do have it all and I hope God blesses them with children. They deserve it. Even though their home is massive, you can feel the love bouncing off of the walls that are decorated with expensive paintings and family portraits. I also love how Mark treated Melba — with respect. Now I know some people don't quite believe in mega preachers and all the money they rake in, but there's a lot of work that goes into building a ministry and if you have the education, talent, and charisma to lead, I don't think there's anything wrong with being compensated for that. And from what I can tell, Mark loves people and is a good man.

We come to the gourmet kitchen and it's just as breathtaking as the rest of the house. It's completely white with built-in appliances. There's a breakfast nook/island in the middle of the floor flanked by tall wooden chairs. A white woman in a chef's uniform is putting the finishing touches on what looks like salmon with rice and asparagus covered in cheese.

"Montana, how are you?" Mark asks.

"Almost done."

"Thanks for taking care of this with such short notice,"

Faye says.

"It's more than my pleasure," she says.

Glancing out the large window that's above the triple bowl sink, I notice a few of the security guards that were at the church milling around back.

"This is our kitchen," Faye says.

"How many rooms does this house have?" Sheridan asks.

Mark pokes his chest out and says, "Six bedrooms, eight bathrooms, an office, a home theatre, and two guest rooms. The Grand hallway has twenty-two foot ceilings and domed skylights. There's a library and great room with a view of the bay."

"Damn...I mean, dang," Sheridan says.

"You're livin' better than most star athletes," Gary says. "We had a nice crib in Dallas, but it wasn't anything like this."

"Where are you living now?" Mark asks.

"With my moms in Compton," Gary says.

Sheridan's face turns blood red. "We're really just there helping her out...you know...just until our mini-mansion is done being built in Beverly Hills."

Gary gives her a crazy look.

"You don't say," Mark says.

"No, you're right...I don't say," Gary says, rolling his eyes at Sheridan.

"How was it playing for the Dallas Enforcers?"

Gary's face lights up like a kid on Christmas day. "Wow, man...I was living the dream."

"Sheridan mentioned you were getting ready to sign with a new team," Mark says.

"She did...hmm...well, I have a little work to do before all that," he says, frowning at Sheridan and patting his wide girth. "Maybe I shouldn't have that beer after all."

"I'm sure one beer won't hurt," Mark says.

Shut up talking about alcohol!!!

"How do you stay in such good shape?" Gary asks.

"We have an exercise room here and at the church. If you ever decide you want to do something different, I could use a man with your talent and experience at New Hope. We have a competitive benefits package, and I'd be able to start you out with a good salary."

"That sounds kinda good. I'll keep that in mind," Gary says.

"Why don't we finish up the tour, so we can all freshen up and eat," Mark says.

We all nod and follow Mark and Faye to the next fabulous room in their fabulous house.

Chapter 12

Danielle

I power my iPad down and stretch, glad I was able to spend some time going over notes for my case. I'm representing a fifty-four year old attorney who was fired after she took a leave of absence to care for her elderly mother. I believe she was fired because of her age, gender, and family responsibilities. It's one of my many pro bono cases.

The Browns, Vicky, and I left Faye's mini-mansion a few hours ago. I believe Sheridan and Gary may still be hanging out. Lunch was delectable, but I ate very little so I'd be able to eat with Frankie. The sound of the toilet flushing in my hotel bathroom is my cue and I grab my purse. While I was away, Frankie scouted out what she thinks is the perfect restaurant. I hear her washing her hands and after a few moments she appears before me, all smiles.

"Are you done?" she asks.

"Yes, Danielle is done," I say.

"Are you ready to go?" she asks.

"Yes, Danielle is ready to go," I say.

She giggles and reaches for my hand. I take hers and we head out. Arms linked, we walk through the corridor and stop at the elevator bank. Frankie nudges me forward and points to the mirror that's on the wall above a long hallway table. We smile at our image.

"My, what a lovely couple," she says.

I nod and give her a peck on her soft full lips. "Thanks for waiting for me."

"Of course," she says, taking my hand.

The elevator door opens and I jerk my hand away from her at the sight of an elderly couple glowering at us with raised brows. Frankie snatches my hand back and pulls me into the elevator, giggling like an adolescent. The couple moves to the opposite end and faces forward.

"I can't wait to make love to you tonight," Frankie says.

I give her a murderous look and move away from her. We arrive at the lobby, the door opens, and the elderly couple shuffle out, mumbling and grumbling.

We get off and I ask Frankie, "What is wrong with you?"

"I'm just having fun."

"You know I don't like rubbing it in people's faces. Not everybody is on board, Frankie."

"Sometimes I wonder if you're on board."

"What does that mean?"

"Nothing," she says.

"Frankie, I don't want to fight. Between the funeral, the case, and you showing up unannounced, I feel really stressed. Let's just have a nice evening and take the first flight out in the morning."

"I thought—"

"I don't want to leave tonight. I'm exhausted."

"Okay, that's fine with me and I'll behave. I wanna hear some more about your day."

"Where's the restaurant?"

"We can walk there. Follow me," Frankie says.

The soft music resonating throughout the dimly lit Italian restaurant, coupled with the red wine I just drank, totally relaxes me. Frankie's beautiful candlelit face brings a smile to mine. "I like this place," I say, looking around at the other patrons.

"The concierge gave me the hook-up, but not before hitting on me," she says, flashing a coy grin.

"He has good taste," I say, twirling my spaghetti around my fork.

"Speaking of taste, how do you like the food?"

"It's great."

"So how much do you think Faye's place is worth?"

I chew, swallow, cast my eyes upward and say, "North of five million easily."

"Get out."

"It's almost ten thousand square feet."

"So her husband must be taking in millions."

"He writes a lot of books. She says that's where most of their money comes from. I think I've made some progress."

"That's awesome."

"Vicky and I had a conversation—a *real* conversation."

"About?" Frankie asks. She puts her fork down.

"We were both shocked when we saw Gary. I didn't

even recognize him."

"The football stud?"

"More like football dud. He's put on a lot of weight and he looks old. I mean he doesn't have a lot of wrinkles. He just looks hard, like he's had it rough. And he has a limp."

"It's amazing what time will do to some people. Right before we met, I had gone to my twentieth high school reunion and people had really changed, some not for the better."

"I just hope Sheridan's okay. She had a black eye."

"Is he abusive?"

"I don't know. She denied it. Oh...and Faye has been trying to have a baby for three years now."

Frankie takes a sip of her wine and shakes her head. "What's the problem?"

"She's thirty-eight and in spite of what Hollywood has led us to believe, eggs do not last forever. She says they've gone as far as In vitro but haven't had any success."

"When did she tell you all this?"

"Sheridan, Faye, Victoria, and I had a few moments to talk while the guys talked sports."

"So you did make progress."

"It was the first time in twenty-years that we were all in the same room together talking. I mean it wasn't like back in the day...there were some strained moments, some cold stares, and you can tell not everyone was being as open as they could have been. And if it wasn't for Mrs. Brown, I don't think we would have come together at all."

"That's understandable. What about Sheridan and Vicky?"

"They never spoke to each other, but Sheridan and Faye seemed to be hitting it off really well. Sheridan and Gary were there when I left."

"So do you think you ladies are going to be able to work it out?"

I take a gulp of my wine and press on my temples. "I

don't know. We really need to talk about what happened and that's the hard part. Bringing it all back — reliving it. I spent so much time trying to forget it." My eyes burn and I feel a cough coming on. Choking, I reach for my water.

"Drink up," Frankie says.

I do so and try to relax.

"I'm sorry for bringing it up."

"It's okay."

"So when do you think I might have an opportunity to meet the other members of The Fresh Five?"

"It's funny you ask because I was thinking about inviting Vicky to New York. I have more frequent flier miles than I know what to do with."

"Really?"

"Yeah, but she's a teacher and she's married with two kids. I don't know if she'll be able to get away. I feel like we really connected and that together we may be able to sort through things. I really think we should do group therapy."

"Really?"

"I don't know. Maybe not. Let's just focus on dinner. I'm tired of talking about it."

Frankie takes my hand, rubs it, and sprinkles it with soft kisses. She pauses, looks up, and juts her chin forward.

"What's wrong?" I ask.

"Danielle?"

I turn at the sound of a man's voice.

"Danielle, it's me, Walter."

I shift in my seat, wondering how long Walter has been standing behind me and if he saw Frankie kissing my hand. I try to read his doe shaped eyes but he averts them. "Hey, Walter," I say dryly. "How long have you been here...I mean what are you doing here?"

"I just came by to pick up my take out order and I noticed you from the back. Your hair cut is really distinctive. It caught my eye at the funeral," he says, holding up a brown paper bag with traces of juice at the bottom.

"Oh."

"I don't live too far from here. I come here all the time."

"I'm staying at the W up the street."

"That's a nice hotel," he says, his eyes shifting to Frankie.

There's a moment of uncomfortable silence and then Frankie stands with her hand outstretched. I get a kick in my gut and pray a silent prayer that she doesn't tell him we're married.

"Hi, I'm Frankie."

Relieved, I say, "I'm sorry. Forgive my poor manners. This is my friend Frankie. She's from New York and came out to give me some support. And Frankie, this is Walter, Sabrina's ex-husband."

"Nice to meet you," Walter says, shaking her hand.

"Nice to meet you, too," Frankie says, sitting.

"That's cool of you to have come all the way to L.A. to support Danielle. Were you at the funeral?"

"No," Frankie, says, motioning to Walter to sit.

I sit on my clammy hands and take a page out of Vicky's book and count to ten, silently.

"Did you know Sabrina?" Walter asks.

"No, she never had the opportunity to meet Sabrina," I say, wondering why Walter accepted Frankie's invitation to sit. He has a lot of nerve. I haven't spoken to or seen him in two years and he ran out on Sabrina.

"It was a beautiful service," Walter says.

"That's what I heard," Frankie says.

"How long have you known Danielle?"

Frankie and I exchange wary looks.

"We met a couple of years ago," Frankie says.

"That would have been around the time Sabrina was diagnosed with cancer," he says.

"That must have been hard for you," Frankie says.

Not able to take their banter anymore, I want to scream.

I really want to get up, but I'm afraid of what Frankie might tell Walter. I want to tell people about our relationship when I'm ready. And if Frankie tells Walter, he might go run and tell the Browns and the others.

"Are you okay?" Frankie asks.

"I'm fine. I just need to use the powder room. I'll be right back. And Walter, don't feel obligated to stay. Frankie will talk your ear off. But maybe she'll behave tonight," I say, giving her a "don't go there," look. She smiles knowingly and then resumes her conversation.

I walk away and look over my shoulder a couple of times. I nearly stumble when I see Walter remove his food from the bag. Great, that's all I need — dinner for three. Skipping the restroom, I step outside and breathe in the night air. The area is teeming with college students. Pacing in front of the restaurant, I wonder to myself when I'm going to get used to being in public with Frankie. I mean, not being in public, but being in public when she displays her love and affection for me. It really makes me uncomfortable. But when I think about it, Mitchell was very demonstrative, too and I was uncomfortable when he would act out in public.

I give my watch a gander, wondering how much longer I can stall. Flashing red lights and sirens give me pause. An intense wave of nausea surges through me. I wrap my arms around my waist. If only Sheridan would have kept her pregnancy to herself. If only we had cell phones that night. If only the paramedics would have gotten there on time. "If, if, if, if. Shoulda, woulda, coulda!"

"Danielle?"

"Walt. Hi."

"Are you okay?"

"Of course. I just needed a little fresh air. Are you leaving?" I ask, with my fingers crossed behind my back. While I wait for his answer, I search his face for any signs of disgust or disdain. I'm not sure what his stance is on homosexuality, but I do know Sabrina was open.

"I'm about to take off. I really enjoyed talking to your friend."

"Thanks. She's good people," I say.

"Take care, Danielle. And life is short. Don't be afraid to live in your truth," he says and walks away.

"'Don't be afraid to live in your truth.'" What did he mean by that? I stand there baffled. Did Frankie tell him we're married? He didn't seem like he knew. Gritting my teeth, I go into the restaurant ready for a fight, but Frankie is nowhere to be found. I cool my heels and have a seat. The door to the ladies' room opens and she appears. She walks toward me, passing by the bar.

"Where were you?" she asks, sitting.

"I needed some air."

"He's a nice guy," she says.

"That *nice guy* walked out on Sabrina a year after she was diagnosed with cancer."

"Shut up!"

"It's true."

"Wow, I wonder what I'd do if something terrible ever happened to you, Danny."

"I hope nothing terrible ever happens to either one of us. So what did you and Walt talk about?"

"His plumbing business and my column."

"That's all?" I ask.

"Why don't you just come out and ask, Danny?"

"Ask what?"

"If I told him we're married."

"Did you?"

"He noticed my ring and marriage came up. I told him I was married, but I didn't say to whom."

I breathe a huge sigh of relief and give Frankie an appreciative smile. "Thanks."

"No worries. Just let me know how much longer I'm going have to live your lie," she says, storming out of the restaurant.

I run after her but she flags down a cab and takes off before I can reach her.

"Good job, Danielle," I say, walking back to the hotel.

Chapter 13

Sheridan

Standing at the window in Faye's great room, I gaze at the boats in the bay, wishing I was Faye. She has it going on. She has really turnt it up! Lunch was the bomb and I could use a cigarette and a drink right about now. I can't believe we're still here. It's after eight. I tried to give Gary a clue that we might be overstaying our welcome, but when Mark took him into the theater room two hours ago, Faye and I haven't been able to get them out. Mark has some old football games on DVD, including some games from back in the day that feature Gary when he played with the Dallas Enforcers. I thought he was going to have a heart attack when he flashed on the screen in all his glory.

"Sheridan, I'm back."

"Hey, Faye," I say, moving away from the window. "This view is bananas!"

"Thanks, I really love this house. It's hard for me to leave it at times," she says, holding a large key.

"I feel you."

"I want to show you something," she says, motioning for me to follow her.

We leave the great room and I follow Faye down a long corridor. She stops at the end of the hallway and stands in front of an enormous wooden door. "What's in there?" I ask.

She unlocks the door and says, "Come in." She turns on the light and motions for me to enter.

I go in and my mouth drops. One wall is covered with a few of my paintings of The Fresh Five and another wall is covered with a bunch of photos of The Fresh Five from back in the day. The five us at Disneyland, Magic Mountain, church, school, the Downtown Mission feeding the homeless with Faye's father, our entire young lives in pictures. And the other two walls are lined with shelves that are filled with Faye's homemade dolls. "This is off the chain," I say.

"When we moved in five years ago, I had the room decorated, but I hadn't been in here since that day. After Mother Brown called and told us Sabrina had passed away, I ran to this room and cried and cried. I ended up sleeping in here for two days." She points to the wooden floor. "I slept right there. I wanted to be uncomfortable. I wanted to hurt — feel the pain that Sabrina had felt. Mark joined me the second day." She walks toward a photo of Vicky and me taken on the day we tried out for Bradshaw's cheerleading squad. "This is one of my favorites."

I study the picture and my scowl melts into a smile. I remember that day and I remember I hadn't started dating Gary yet. He was still up for grabs. We were both so happy with the thought of possibly making the squad together.

Vicky and I are all hugged up with bright eyes and wide grins. "Why is it your favorite picture?" I ask.

"Because it's one of the few times you and Vicky seemed happy with each other."

Faye gives me a guarded look while sitting on the small black leather sofa in the corner of the room. I join her and ask, "What's wrong?"

"I was just thinking about what happened in church today," she says.

"Yeah, what did happen? You ran out of there like the church was on fire," I say.

"I had a breakthrough."

"Really," I ask, scooting closer to her, not wanting to miss a word.

"I had to ask God to forgive me for some things I did back in the day."

I sit there wanting to laugh in her face, because everyone knows Faye was a square, a nerd, and scared to death to do anything her preacher father would frown upon.

"What kind of things? Cheat on an exam? We all did that."

"No...I can't get into it right now, but I did ask God to forgive me and I believe he has."

"Sure he has," I say.

"You know, Vicky was at the altar with me and I heard her say something that was strange."

"What? What did she say?"

"I probably shouldn't tell you...I mean what she said should stay at the altar."

"Faye, I'm going to my grave with a lot of secrets, one more ain't gonna hurt."

"Okay, but you have to promise me you won't say anything."

"I cross my heart and hope to die."

Faye shoots me a scolding look.

"I just cross my heart," I say.

"While Vicky was praying she said something about hurting her kids."

I get goose pimples and jump to my feet. "What the freak! She said the same thing to me. Something about them being molested."

Faye rises and asks, "Do you think she molested her own kids?"

"I don't know, but whatever she did, she was drinking up a storm because of it."

"When...when did you talk to her?" Faye asks.

"Last night at the Browns. After everybody left. I went to the cellar for a drink and she was down there holding a bottle of wine. We had a few drinks and that's when she mentioned about her kids being molested."

"Oh my God," Faye says, sitting. "I hope they're okay."

"According to Vicky, she's happily married and her and her husband and kids are fine," I say. "But then last night she did say something about them being molested."

"But is that the truth about everything being all good? She could have just said that to save face," Faye says.

"You mean she could be frontin'," I say.

"Yeah, people do that," Faye says.

Don't I know. "What do you think we should do?"

"We need to talk to her."

"We all need to talk," I say. "Maybe we can get some group therapy or something."

"You think we can talk Vicky and Danielle into it?"

"It's worth a shot," I say.

I flop down next to her and take her hand in mine. "Faye, I am so proud of you."

"Thanks...I'm...I'm proud of you, too."

"You don't have to say that. I know what my life is about. I'm old, I haven't accomplished anything and Gary is...let's just say...he's not the man he used to be."

"None of us is perfect, Sheridan."

"Stop calling me Sheridan! Call me Sherry like you used to."

"I will, if you call me Dimples like you used to."

"Okay, Dimples," I say, laughing.

"I've always loved your laugh, Sherry."

"And I've always hated that whiny voice of yours, Dimples."

She taps me on the arm and says, "You are not right — throwing shade like that."

"I'm sorry, but it's true."

"I know. Mark teases me about it, but he says it's cute."

"You are so lucky to have Mark in your life. I really hope you all get pregnant."

Faye rises abruptly and walks to my paintings. "You are a great artist. Why don't you try to sell your work?" she asks.

"I'm not that good," I say, joining her.

"Yes, you are. I want to give you a show."

"Stop messing with me, Dimples."

"I'm not. For real and a portion of the proceeds can go to the children's ministry at New Hope. We have a lot of ministries — programs for the homeless, work programs, you name it."

"You would do that for me?"

"I'd love to," she says.

"Why?"

"Because…because…I love you, Sherry. I never stopped loving you, Vicky, or Danielle. I just couldn't be around you after what happened."

"Why do you think we let it destroy our relationship?"

"I don't know, but we really should get help. We have to get past this. I don't want to see another one of us die before we fix this."

I unbuckle my seatbelt when Gary pulls into our driveway. We get out of the car and I notice some extra pep in his step. "Wait up for me. I'm not trying get smoked out here."

"You're too slow, woman," he says, stopping.

"Hold on a minute. I need to get the bag with the plates of food," I say, going back to the car. I grab the goodies and follow Gary into the house.

"Ma, we're home!" Gary yells.

"Why are you yelling?" I ask, going into the kitchen.

"I'm not yelling!" he yells.

I walk into the kitchen and sigh when I get a look at the stack of dishes in the sink. I did tell ma that I would wash them. My eyes shift to the dishwasher without a door. Gary yanked it off during one of his rampages. "Babe, when are you going to fix the dishwasher?"

"Not tonight, that's for sure," he says, grabbing a plate of food.

"Y'all finally made it back," Gary's mother says, entering.

"Sorry we were gone so long, ma," Gary says.

"Ma, did you eat?" I ask.

"I had some of the leftover repast food," she says.

"We brought some food from Faye's house. Her chef cooked it," Gary says.

"Chef!" ma says.

"Yep, she has a chef and a maid," I say.

"Are they rich?"

"Ma, you should see their house. It's a mansion — bigger than the place we had in Dallas. They even have a theater and Faye's husband had some old footage of me playing football back in the day."

"You don't say. No wonder you took so long getting back," she says, laughing. She sits at the table, looking at Gary with pride and admiration. I don't know who loves him more, me or her.

"Their house is almost ten-thousand square feet and the ceilings go on forever. It's something else," Gary says.

"He's not exaggerating, ma," I say.

"Speaking of exaggerating stuff. Sher, why did you tell Faye and Mark we're having a mini-mansion built in Beverly Hills?"

"Lord, have mercy," ma says.

"I just didn't want Vicky showing me up," I say.

"You and that girl still competing?" ma asks.

"Not really."

"I'm glad to hear that. Sabrina's leaving here should be a lesson for all of you. Life is short. You girls loved one another when you were in middle and high school. You were inseparable. You need to work it out."

"That's what I keep telling her, ma. Especially in light of everything Sabrina has done for us. And it was her dying wish, ma."

Gary and his mother shoot daggers at me. "I'm not in this alone. Faye and I talked today and we're going to try to get Vicky and Danielle to talk to us. We're going to try to get into some kind of group therapy." The kitchen fills with applause. I shake my head at Gary and his mother. "You two are too much," I say.

"I'm glad you and Faye are reconnecting and I'm digging Mark. He's restored my faith in preachers. I'm even thinking about joining New Hope."

"Are you for real?" I ask.

"Yeah, ma could join, too and get on the usher board. You'd make a good usher, ma."

"Will see," ma says.

"I'm glad you're feeling Mark and Faye, because Faye and I are gonna have a spa day tomorrow and lunch," I say.

"I'm not mad at you," Gary says. "Just don't be lettin' no thirsty —"

"Don't even go there," I say. "I don't know about you

and ma, but I'm tired. I'm going to bed," I say, leaving them in the kitchen.

"I'm eat a little more of this food and I'll be right there," Gary says.

I go into our bedroom, thinking about the time we spent at Faye's and my conversation with her. That was really sweet of her to offer to help me sell some of my paintings. It seems as if Faye has really changed. She seems genuine now.

I take off my dress and stand in the mirror checking myself out in my mismatched bra and panty set. Groaning, I think back to the day when I would go on shopping sprees at Victoria Secrets. Speaking of Victoria and secrets, I'm dying to know what happened to Victoria's kids. I turn around and look over my shoulder at my backside. I can't compete with Kim Kardashian, but my body doesn't look half bad for my age. I have a little cellulite, but who doesn't. I turn toward the door when I hear Gary whistling.

"That's what I'm talkin' bout," he says, approaching. He grabs me from the rear and wraps his arms around my waist. "You look good, baby."

"Thanks," I say. "Did you have fun with Mark?"

"Yeah, I'm digging him," he says, sitting on the bed. "But I'm digging *you* even more. Come and sit next to daddy." He presses down on the mattress.

"What's with you?" I ask, sitting next to him.

"Can't a black man admire his white wife?"

"You need to quit. You know, I feel sorry for Faye."

"Why would you feel sorry for her? She has it all."

"Yeah, but they want a baby and it's not happening."

Gary rises abruptly and walks to the dresser. He starts to undress.

"Shoot, Faye probably doesn't even know how to do it. That's probably why they can't get pregnant. You know she was a virgin all the way through high school and she probably was when she met Mark," I say.

Gary, now in his red boxers turns and glares at me. "Why are you all up in their business?"

"I'm not 'up in their business.' I just care about Faye."

"Sometimes you go too far, Sher."

"What do you mean?"

"Like when you had me take Faye from church that time. We both could have gotten in trouble. What if her father had found out?"

"I was worried about her and it worked. She made it through high school a virgin and childfree, unlike some people I know."

"Don't go blaming me. Sher, you told me you were on the pill."

"I didn't tell you that. You know I wasn't. You said you were gonna jump out. You should have used a rubber."

"Okay, that was twenty years ago. We have a kid now and we're married, so stop bitching."

"Maybe my life would have been different if I hadn't gotten pregnant. Maybe I could have gone to art school. I coulda been a famous painter."

"Oh really. Where is all this coming from, Sher? Oh, I get it. You see how large Faye is livin' and you're comparing yourself to her. You always do that. You're always tryin' be something you ain't. You need to be satisfied with what you have."

"Satisfied that I'm living in the ghetto in a section eight house with my husband's mother, driving a hooptie?"

"This is just like you. Kick a man when he's down. What about when you were living like a high society chick in Dallas when we had a mansion and we were driving luxury cars? Who do you think made that happen? I did and I busted my butt doing it. You saw that footage. I was the one out there running with the ball, getting banged up. Now I can barely walk. I sacrificed a lot for this family. I got a bum deal with the team. It ain't my fault.'"

"Yeah, but you wasted the money, Gary. Drinking and

drugging and God knows what else." He gets in my face, raises his hand and I rear back. "Don't you dare hit me!"

"I'm not gonna hit you. I'm out. I don't have to take this shit from you or nobody else! You need to grow up!" He goes to the closet, puts on a sweat suit, and storms out of the room.

"Good riddens!" I say, flopping down on the bed. I put the covers over my head and have a good cry.

Chapter 14

Faye

Sitting in front of my vanity mirror, I cup my hands around my face and moan. My weave is really showing out today. The devil is a liar. I'm going to get my hair to act right or else. I really do need to come out of this weave. I've been wearing a weave since high school. I'd love to wear my own hair, but I've never had much to work with. Seems like when God decided to give me dimples, he held back on the hair. I'd love to have a head full of frilly red hair like Sabrina had or long locks like Sheridan or even thick curls like Vicky. Even Danielle has a thick luxurious mane. That was before she decided to cut it all off. I, on the other hand, have been a chicken head from day one. Mark has asked me to come out of my weave, and I think before the year's out, I am. I need to get real on the inside and the outside.

Speaking of which, I really need to come clean with Sheridan. I felt like such a hypocrite yesterday spending time with her knowing I had slept with Gary and carried his child. But Mark says some things are better left unsaid, especially if they can hurt another person. But how can Sheridan and I really move forward with a relationship knowing what I did? It was such a long time ago. I don't see her *not* forgiving me...but then again, maybe I should keep it to myself. We're already dealing with what happened that night. Mark has forgiven me and he doesn't even want to know who I was pregnant by. Thank God for that because it seems like he and Gary really hit it off last night. "Lord, what is the right thing to do?"

"The right thing to do about what?" Mark asks, entering.

"Hi, babe."

"You okay?" he asks, standing behind me.

"I'm alright."

"What right thing are you trying to do?'

"Nothing...nothing...I'm just struggling with this dang weave."

"The right thing to do would be to wear your own hair."

"I am, sweetie. I plan to soon," I say, brushing my hair into a boring, but acceptable style.

"Where are you off to?" Mark asks.

"Sheridan and I are having a spa day."

"Nice. I really like Gary. Seems like a nice guy. So you all went to the same high school?"

"Yeah...that's right."

"Boy, he was something else on the field back in the day. Good-looking guy, strong."

"Right...uh...what are you doing today?"

"I have a meeting with New Hope's social media team. I want to start seeing how we can incorporate Facebook, Twitter, and Instagram into the worship service."

"Sounds good, sweetie. I better head out," I say, needing to clear my head.

"Okay, baby. Be good," he says, pulling me in close. "What time is your appointment? You sure you don't have time for a quickie?" he asks.

"Lord Jesus, man you are so nasty," I say, pulling myself out of his arms.

"No, I just happen to have a sexy wife and we *are* trying to get pregnant."

"You're right. I'll make sure I get back early," I say. "What time do you think you'll be home?"

"Around five or six. By the way, Montana's making lasagna for dinner. That's unless you want something else," he says.

"Lasagna's good." I kiss Mark and head out to my appointment.

I pull my black Lexus sedan up to Spalacious Experiences, Inc. located in Beverly Hills. A valet parker approaches and opens my door. "First Lady Davis, so good to see you."

"Thank you, Raymond," I say, getting out of the car. "I'm meeting a friend—"

Before I can complete my sentence, he points to the patio area where Sheridan's waiting, puffing on a cigarette. "She's right there," he says. "And I'll bring your gym bag inside."

"Thank you," I say. He hands me a ticket and I approach Sheridan. She looks up and pulls her shades off. Smiling, she passes her hands over her jeans. She takes her pack of cigarettes from her shirt pocket and thrusts them in a large red duffle bag that's on the ground next to her bare feet. My eyes search for her shoes. As if on cue, she removes a pair of yellow Flip Flops from her bag.

"Hey, lady," I say, approaching. She puts her cigarette out, slips into her shoes, and gives me a hug. The stench of smoke makes me cough.

"Are you okay?" Sheridan asks.

"It's the smoke," I say.

"I'm sorry. I really need to stop smoking."

"Yes, you do. When and why did you start?"

"I started right around the time Sabrina stop seeing or talking to me. So it's been about two years now. It calms me down."

I give her a look of disapproval. "It may calm you down, but it causes…"

"I know…I know. Gary, Kim, and my mother-in-law get on my case and they won't let me smoke in the house."

"Why don't you try yoga or just work out? That always helps me with stress."

Sheridan sighs, passes her hand over her red face and says, "Can we just do the spa thing and lunch and not talk about my cigarette smoking. I won't smoke while we're together today and I'm going to quit."

"Lord, have mercy. I'm sorry. I didn't mean to stress you out. Come on, let's go inside," I say, hugging her around the waist.

She pulls away, grabs her bag, and follows me into the facility. We go to the reception area and I approach the marble desk manned by a pretty twenty-something woman with locks. "First Lady, welcome back," she says, rising.

"Thank you, Lorraine. This is my friend Sheridan Hawkins."

"Yes, I have her right here," Lorraine says, staring at her computer. She extends her French manicured hand to Sheridan. "Welcome to Spalacious."

"Thank you," Sheridan says, shaking Lorraine's hand.

"This place is off the chain. I love the marble floors and the little chandeliers. I can't wait to see the rest of the place."

"If you ladies are ready, I'll call your chaperone."

"Chaperone!" Sheridan says, with raised brows.

"Monica, your guests are ready," Lorraine says into her phone. "She'll be right out."

We turn and a thirty-something Hispanic woman with a shaved head wearing a nose ring joins us at the desk. "First Lady, so good to have you back." She gives me an air kiss.

"It's good to be back. This is my good friend Sheridan Hawkins."

"Nice to meet you, Sheridan."

"Good to be here," Sheridan says.

"The Wilson twins will be giving you ladies your massages today."

"Perfect," I say.

"Who are the Wilson twins?" Sheridan asks.

"Some of the best masseuses in the country," Monica says.

"Wow… I can't wait," Sheridan says.

"Follow me," Monica says. We enter the spa area. "I have an idea. Why don't you ladies disrobe, take a dip in the hot tub, and then we'll take the tour, and by then it'll be time for your massages. And afterwards you can get your facials, mani's, and pedi's. What you do you think about that schedule?"

"Fine with me," I say.

"It's all good," Sheridan says.

"There's a name card on your lockers with your combinations. Inside, you'll find your robes, shower shoes, and brand new swimwear."

"Shut up!" Sheridan says.

"We aim to please at Spalacious," Monica says, ushering us into the locker area.

"See you later," I say.

Sheridan does a walk through, looking at herself in the

rows of lighted mirrors. "Dimples, this is awesome and they treat you like royalty. Do you come here all the time?"

"Every chance I get," I say, slipping out of my sun dress.

"Look at you, Miss Thang," Sheridan says, giving me the once over.

"What?"

"You are still tight. And how is it that you don't have any cellulite?"

"Girl, I work out at home and church. You see Mark, he's in perfect shape and trust me, I'm not the only one at New Hope with eyes for my husband. I have to keep it together."

Sheridan and I share a laugh.

"Mark's lucky to have you," Sheridan says, slipping out of her jeans and top.

"Look at you, Sherry. You look good, too."

"Not bad for an old white broad," she says.

"Girl, we're all the same age."

"I know, but I have to admit, I haven't taken care of myself as well as I should have."

"You can start by dumping those Kools and getting yourself a jar of Spalacious night cream."

"You got a point. Hold up." She goes to her bag, grabs the cigarettes, and dumps them in the wastebasket. "I'm done!"

I stand there with my mouth open. "Are you sure? I mean you're not going to have nicotine fit are you?"

"I hope not," she says, opening her locker.

I open my locker and we both change into our two piece bathing suits. Mine is white and Sheridan's is red. We secure our purses and clothes and head to the hot tub area. Sheridan's blue eyes widen when we enter the candle lit room filled with a half dozen hot tubs. She moves her head to the new age music that resonates throughout and points to a bar area stocked with a variety of water, juices, and fresh fruit. A trio of women on the opposite end wave at us. We wave back, hang our robes on the wall hooks, and then sink into the hot steamy water.

Sheridan points to a button on the floor. "What's that?"

"It's for privacy. Push it."

She does so and a wall of plexiglass slowly rises, sealing us off from the other women. "Damn! I mean, dang."

I laugh and say, "It's okay, I've heard worse."

"That's another bad habit I need to break," she says, leaning back, looking up at the ceiling. "Dimples, you are truly living the life."

"The other day I was thinking that maybe God has blessed me so much because I lost my mother at such a young age…you know making up for that loss. Giving me a loving forgiving husband in Mark and letting our ministry take off in such a big way."

"I never thought of it like that. You may have a point. But my situation growing up was worse than yours. At least you had a father. By the way, where is your father?"

"He remarried and is living in Las Vegas."

"Oh…well, I didn't have any parents and I was in the system. Why didn't God try to make it up to me?"

"But He did. You finally ended up with a good set of foster parents, you married the boy that every girl in high school wanted, you guys had a great life in Dallas. Now you're having a mansion built in Beverly Hills, not to mention Gary's about to sign another NFL contract. So from what I can see, God *has* blessed you." Sheridan kicks her feet underwater and sucks on her teeth. "What's wrong?" I ask.

"I have a confession to make."

"What?" I ask, sitting at attention.

"I lied, Dimples."

"What do you mean you lied? Lied about what?"

"Gary and I are broke and are living with his mama. The only income we have is his retirement money and that's not much. Gary took a partial lump sum and squandered most of it."

I wrap my arms around my knees while I listen to Sheridan's confession. Her eyes fill with tears and she wipes them away.

"And I don't have a Lexus in the shop. The Honda is the only car we own and it's on its last leg and if it wasn't for Sabrina, Kim would have had to go to community college. She got a partial scholarship, not a full one like I said. So you see, Vicky wasn't the only one frontin'."

I sit there thinking about the day I found out I was pregnant with Gary's baby and how much I wanted him to tell me I didn't have to get an abortion and that he would marry me. But it didn't happen like that. We always want what we want, not realizing God knows what we need and He can see into the future. If Gary had fulfilled my teenaged fantasy, I would be the one sitting in the hot tub shedding tears. Now I see why Gary was giving Sheridan all those crazy looks last night. I can't judge her. I know how it feels to want people to think the best of you. She looks so pitiful. I know to her, outside of losing my mother, I've led a charmed life, but it hasn't been that way at all.

"Did you hear me, Dimples? I'm a liar."

"Join the club I say."

"What do you mean?"

"Remember in church when I ran out?"

"Yeah."

"I ran out because Mark overhead my prayer."

"What do you mean he 'overheard' your prayer?"

"Victoria wasn't the only one telling dark secrets at the altar."

Sheridan rolls her eyes and laughs. "Dimples, you are such a drama queen. You've been a nerd all your life."

"Have I?"

"What are you talking about?"

"Mark heard me asking God to forgive me for aborting my baby."

The blood drains from Sheridan's face and she has a coughing fit. She flails her hands and kicks up her legs. The women in the other hot tub give us looks of alarm. I press the button and the plexiglass wall goes down. I hop over it, run to the bar, and grab a bottle of water. I remove the cap, give it to Sheridan and she guzzles. I get back in the tub and put the glass back up. Sheridan composes herself and stares at me.

"You're lying. Abortion? How could you have had an abortion when you were a virgin?"

"I wasn't a virgin. I mean I was, but not all through high school."

"You have got to be kidding me. When did you have sex? You were always with us or at chur...oh my God."

"What?"

"The bet. Did you get with one of the football players after Gary talked to you? We told you, Dimples. Please tell me you didn't fall for the okie doke."

My stomach flips and my armpits fill with perspiration. "No, I mean...yes...I mean...no. I mean."

"What's wrong with you? Who's your baby's daddy? Who popped your cherry?"

I cringe. "Don't say it like that."

"Okay, I don't believe any of it. Dimples, you were just a green country bumpkin in high school. How would you even know where to get an abortion? If you're making all this up to make me feel better, you can stop. Don't feel guilty about living a charmed life, Dimples. It's okay. You don't have to create drama. You don't need street cred. I love you unconditionally."

"Do you?"

"Of course."

"So whatever I tell you about what happened, you'll be cool with it."

"Yes!"

"Okay…remember when you had Gary come and get me from church to teach me a lesson and to tell me about the bet."

"Right. Of course I remember. We talked right after."

"Well, something happened that night—something I didn't tell you."

Sheridan's eyes widen. "What happened?"

"Gary…Gary and…Gary and I…"

"You and Gary what?"

"We…we…we made love and I ended up getting pregnant with his baby. When he found out, he took me to get an abortion."

Sheridan is motionless. She looks at me and then asks. "When did you get the abortion?"

Her stoic response sends chills though me. "It was about two months later. Remember when we were all going to go to Sabrina's after school to study for that big English exam and I said I couldn't go because I had to do something at church. That was the day."

"Yeah….I remember that…and I remember you being unavailable a lot around that time," she says, looking off into space.

"Sherry, I'm so, so, sorry. I really am. Please for—"

Before I can ask her forgiveness, she hauls off and slaps me so hard I hit my head on the plexiglass. "That's for being a lying fake tramp bitch," she says. She presses the button, the glass goes down, and she storms out. The women in the other hot tub point and talk among themselves. I slide down into the water and contemplate drowning myself.

Chapter 15

Victoria

Sitting in the back of the classroom, I go over the spelling papers for Mrs. Hamilton. She says I'm the best teacher's assistant she's ever had. How could I not be with a Master's degree in education and fourteen years of teaching my own class? I didn't have the courage to tell the others I had been demoted to a T.A. position, because if I had, then I would have had to tell them that when the district got wind of my home situation, they didn't feel comfortable with me teaching at Bradshaw or anywhere for that matter. The best they could offer me was a T.A. position at Washington Elementary. It's all supposed to be temporary, but it seems like this nightmare is never going to end.

Mrs. Hamilton presses down on her bushy brown hair and goes to the chalkboard where she scribbles a few math problems. She reminds me of myself when I made my foray into education — eager, bright-eyed, and determined to produce the next Einstein. She smiles at the twenty-five boys and girls with her perfect white teeth. They look up at her with adoration — so innocent, so expectant. I can't help but think about Matt and Tangie. I've spoken to them on the phone, but I haven't seen them in a week. I can't wait for the bell to sound in the next fifteen minutes so I can see my babies. They're living with Curtis and his parents right now. I told Curtis I would leave our house, but he insisted that the kids be taken to his parents' home.

"Who wants to take a stab at this algebra problem?" Mrs. Hamilton asks.

All hands go up and she grins even wider. I can't believe they're studying Algebra. We didn't until high school. I glance at the clock on the wall that's surrounded by artwork and story assignments bearing smiling faces and stars. This is an advanced fifth grade class and the children are not only brilliant, but well-behaved. My children are brilliant and well-behaved. It's their mother that's a dunce and a screw-up.

Five minutes to go and now my heart is racing and my palms are sweaty. I always get this way when it comes time to see my babies. The last time I saw them they ran to me with open arms and wouldn't let me go. I'm grateful Curtis isn't turning them against me.

I finish grading the last paper and stack them all in a neat pile. The bell rings and the children jump up from their seats. Mrs. Hamilton cautions them to slow down and not to run. They grab their backpacks and bolt.

"How'd they do?" she asks.

"Not bad for a pop quiz," I say, handing her the graded exams. "I have a word for next week."

"What is that, Vicky?"

"Archrival."

"Hmmm. That's a good one. What made you think of that?"

"It came to me while I was at the repast for my best friend Saturday."

Her brown eyes widen and she says, "That's right. My condolences again. How was the service?"

"It was beautiful. There were over a thousand people there—her family, friends, and patients. She was really loved."

She presses her stubby hands together and tilts her head. "How wonderful. You know you could have taken some more time off if you needed to."

"Now that you mention it, a good friend of mine, who was also at the funeral, was hoping I could spend some time with her. Sabrina's death has taken a toll on all of us. She lives in New York and it would only be for a few days."

"That wouldn't be a problem at all, Vicky. You're a great asset to the class, and I plan to give the district a stellar report about your performance."

Now *I grin* like a Cheshire cat. "I'd really appreciate that and I'll let you know as soon as I have my travel dates. I need to head out now."

"Okay, Vicky. Take care."

"Bye," I say, leaving.

I slowly drive up Curtis parents' block in Leimert Park, a small neighborhood in Los Angeles, being extra careful not to hit any of the neighborhood children who are returning home from school. I take a deep breath and hope I get a second wind sooner than later. I am really exhausted after this past weekend. The funeral, repast, church, and the visit to Faye's mansion really took a lot out of me, and after I see my babies, I have a meeting with my sponsor. She wants to talk to me about Step 5: Admitted to God, to ourselves, and to another human being the exact nature of our wrongs. Two out of three isn't bad. Sunday I finally admitted to God and myself, and now I need to admit to my sponsor. We've done all the steps, including five, but I never told her about what happened with Tangie and Matt, and she thinks that's why I drank again. Thank God I've managed not to drink since Saturday. I'm on my second day of sobriety. Whoopie! Right. I don't know what's going to happen when Curtis finds out I went back out. Per our court agreement, if I'm able to hold down a job and remain sober for eighteen months, I can see our kids unsupervised and Curtis says he will definitely think about us reconciling. Now I've totally screwed that up. I really need to go see my parents today, but that's going to have to wait. After I'm done with my sponsor, I'm going to be drained.

I park my BMW behind a gold Lexus SUV, and Faye pops in my head. Her and Sheridan seemed to have really hit it off yesterday. Maybe there's some hope for us. I couldn't believe it when Danielle called me last night and invited me to come and visit her in New York. I've never been and it would be good for me to get out of town—not so I can run from my problems, but to just be in a different environment. My sponsor calls running to another location to escape your problems a "geographic." Seems like she has sayings for everything.

While I'm getting out of the car, I catch Tangie and Matt in the picture window waving at me. My eyes sting and tear up. They still love me. I grab tissue out of my purse and dab at my eyes. I don't want them to see me cry. My eight-year-old daughter Tangie has my green eyes and my nine-year-old son Matt has my curly hair. I lock the car and go to the front door of the little white house trimmed in brown wood. The door opens and Tangie and Matt cling to me like Super Glue.

"Mom, what took you so long?" Matt asks.

"We miss you," Tangie says, pulling me into the house.

"Where's dad?" I ask, choking up.

"I'm right here," Curtis says, approaching. I pull my eyes away from my children and take in their father. He's as handsome as he was the day I first laid eyes on him. Medium brown complexion, clean shaven, with close cropped hair—he's a sight to behold. My eyes scan his well-built, six-two inch frame, and I get weak in the knees. Gary Hawkins who? Curtis is my dream man—my knight in shining armor. An investment banker with a prosperous firm in Century City, he's done quite well. The kids are in private school and we have a three-thousand square foot home in Los Feliz. Our house doesn't compare to Faye's, but it's fabulous just the same.

"How's it going, Vick?"

Why did he call me that? He knows that gets me all wet between the legs. Especially when he says it all deep and sexy-like.

"Fine. How's everybody here?"

"The kids are great now that you're here and mom and dad are out playing cards with the Smiths."

"Mom, come and see our report cards," Matt says, dragging me to the family room. I look over my shoulder at Curtis who's flashing his pearly whites and shaking his head.

"Take it easy on your mother, you two."

"It's okay, I love being wanted," I say.

Tangie and Matt run to a table in front of the green sectional sofa and grab their report cards. Before I go over them, I take a good hard look at my children and pull them onto my bosom. I smell them, hug them, and whisper "I love you's" in their small ears.

"We love you, too, mom."

I pick up their cards and feign shock when I get a gander at their straight A's. I fall back and faint and they laugh their heads off.

"Mom, you're so funny," Tangie says.

"And you two are the smartest kids in the whole world."

"Smarter than your students?" Matt asks.

"Of course," I say.

"Mom, when are we going to be able to come home? We miss you and our friends."

"I need to make sure I'm well first so I can be there to protect you. Not let anyone hurt you."

"It wasn't your fault, mom," Tangie and Matt say.

"It *was* my fault. It's important that when you do something wrong to own it. Remember what your father and I taught you?"

They nod. "We forgive you!"

"I know you do," I say, wondering how I ended up with such fabulous kids.

"Matt, Tangie, it's time for you to do your homework and when you're done, you can have dinner with mom and me."

"Okay, dad," they say.

"We'll be right back, mom. Don't go anywhere," Matt says.

"I'll be waiting," I say, hugging them again.

They pull out of my embrace and run to the living room. I watch them wistfully, thanking God that no permanent damage was done. Curtis, wearing a pair of shorts and a sweatshirt, sits on the love seat across from me, passing his large hands over his toned thighs. My vajayjay twitches and I clamp my legs shut. It's been a year since I've been with Curtis…well actually six months ago we had a little rendezvous, but it feels like forever.

"You look good," I say.

"Thanks, I'm on vacation right now."

"Curtis David Williams is on vacation? I don't believe it."

"Yeah, it's true. I wanted to spend some time with the kids. I've been volunteering at their school."

"That's wonderful, Curtis. So are you thinking about giving up banking for teaching?"

He laughs huskily. "No…not at all. I'll leave teaching to you. How's that going?"

"Mrs. Hamilton says she's going to give me a stellar recommendation. The board report is coming up."

"That's great. So in six months you should be all set."

I cast my eyes downward and interlace my fingers. *1, 2, 3, 4, 5, 6, 7, 8, 9, 10.*

"What's wrong, Vicky?"

"I…I may need a little longer than six months."

He rises and thrusts his hands into his pockets. "Please, don't tell me you drank again."

I rise and go to him. "Curtis, I wish I could tell you I didn't, but I did, and please don't beat me up about it. I've already skinned myself alive. I had a whole year!"

"Keep your voice down," he says, looking toward the living room. "What happened?" He sits and I join him.

"The funeral, seeing Sheridan, Faye, and Danielle. All those memories coming back, the guilt about the kids. It was all too much."

"I thought AA was supposed to help you. Have you spoken to your sponsor?"

"I did. I'm going to meet with her when I leave here. I never told her what happened with Matt and Tangie. I was too ashamed. She says that's why I drank again. She says I'm as sick as my darkest secret."

"You're going to have to get it together. Our kids may seem happy on the outside, but they cry in their sleep. They're missing you and so am I."

My heart sinks and I burst into tears. Curtis pulls me

onto his chest and passes his hand over my hair. "I'm so sorry for everything. For what happened twenty years ago and for what happened with the kids. Please forgive me, Curtis."

"I do, but you're going to have to forgive yourself, Vick. Do you understand me?" I nod and he kisses my tears away. "Baby, I miss you so much. I could make love to you right here and now. I want my wife back. I want my family back, but I can't take a chance with our kids. Please promise me you'll listen to your sponsor and that you'll stay sober. I'm even willing to go back to court and ask them to amend the time to six months."

"Would you do that for me, Curt?"

"Woman, I'd give my life for you. Now get it together."

Sitting in my sponsor Darlene's home office, I feel like a little girl waiting to be punished. She says emotionally I'm not even a girl—I'm a baby—a two-day old baby. She's been sober for thirty-years and eats, drinks, and sleeps AA. I look up when she enters carrying two cups of coffee on a silver tray. She makes a path with her foot. The office has been taken over by self-help books.

"Here you go," she says, leaning a little forward.

"Thank you," I say, taking the brown mug off of the silver tray. I put the glass up to my mouth and blow. "This smells great."

"Thanks," she says, sitting. She picks her mug up and takes a sip. "Careful, it's hot," she warns.

"I'll let it cool down." I place the mug on a coaster on her desk.

"How was your visit with the kids?" she asks

"Awesome. They got straight A's on their report

cards."

"Smart like their mother," she says.

I drop my gaze to the books on the floor, not feeling very smart after going back out. "Right."

"Stop that!" she says.

"What?"

"Beating yourself up. So you drank. That's what alkies do best. You're going to have to get to the point where you have no reservations, Vicky."

"What do you mean by that?"

"Meaning, you don't drink no matter what!"

"How will I be able to do that?"

"You're going to have to first start by cleaning house. Now you told me you left something out of your inventory—the reason Matt and Tangie are no longer at home."

I wring my hands, grab the coffee, and take a long sip. "Right...uh...the reason."

Darlene leans back with her hands folded over her drooping breasts and waits for me to speak. I stare at her brown mole-covered face trying to muster courage. "As you know, I started drinking three years ago. Prior to that I had sworn off drinking of any kind. In high school I used to drink a lot of Wine Coolers and other things, but after that night with Sheridan, Faye, and Danielle, I vowed to never drink again. But three years ago, I started having flashbacks about that night. I really don't know what triggered them. Maybe it was because Curtis and I were at the peak of our lives. Life was so good. We were both doing so well and the kids were, too. I think I felt guilty. Yeah, I felt, because of what I had done, I didn't deserve to have the life I had. My drinking started slow. I was just drinking socially. Like when Curtis would have to attend a dinner for the bank. He was surprised when I started drinking because he thought I didn't drink. It just got progressively worse, like the Big Book says. By the beginning of the second year, I started having blackouts. I remember not showing up for a lunch appointment with Sabrina. Then she dropped out of my life and I started drinking more."

"Get to what happened with the kids."

"Right. Curtis was on an IPO Roadshow."

"What's an IPO Roadshow?"

"He along with some other bankers from his company were taking a private company public and they were going across the country offering up shares. Something like that. I really needed him and I was losing it. So I went out that night to a local club. But I called the kids' babysitter first and she came right over. Valerie is her name. She's wonderful, loves the kids, and they love her."

"Keep going," Darlene says.

"I was having a good time. I wasn't thinking about twenty years ago or having any guilty feelings. There was a man there that kept looking at me. I wasn't trying to cheat on Curtis or anything. I wasn't there to catch anyone. Just drink and have a good time. The man came over, bought me a few drinks, and we started talking. He told me how pretty I was and asked for my number. I told him I was married. He took one look at my three carat diamond ring and got the picture. Around ten, I started to head out. What I didn't realize is that the man had followed me home."

Darlene's eyes widen and she grabs her coffee and takes a swig as if she were drinking a beer. "And…keep going."

"I thanked God for letting me get home safely because I was plastered. I don't even know how I made it home without…without…anyway, Valerie ran to the door when I stumbled in. She was shocked that I was drunk. She told me she would stay the night, but I told her I would be okay. She got me some coffee and helped me to bed. She checked on the kids and left. After she left, I managed to fall asleep, but I woke up when I heard the doorbell. I thought it was her and

I wondered why she was ringing the doorbell when she had a key to the house.

I made it to the door and I looked out the window and it was the man from the bar. He was standing there holding my purse. I couldn't believe I had left my purse behind. He was pointing to it and beckoning for me to let him in. I was so grateful he had brought my purse to me, that I cast all caution to the wind. I didn't take into consideration that he was a perfect stranger. I let him in and he asked me if he could use the restroom. He did and then we ended up talking. Before I knew it, he pulled out a bottle of whiskey from his coat jacket and we started drinking. Unbeknownst to me he had spiked my drink and I was going under. He put me back in bed and I started babbling. He kept trying to get away from me. Unfortunately at the bar I had mentioned to him that I had two kids and that Curtis was out of town.

The next thing I knew I was coming to with Valerie and the police standing over me. They told me that after I passed out, this man slithered his way into Matt's and Tangie's rooms. Being the smart kids they are, they had gotten up and saw what was happening and called Valerie. She told them to lock themselves in the bathroom and that she and the police were on the way. After not finding them in their rooms, the man figured out they were in the bathroom. Matt said that he told them I was sick and going to die and that they needed to come out. The man didn't know that Valerie and the police were on their way to the house. The kids, worried about me, opened the door, and he grabbed them and took them to Matt's room. God is a good God. Just before he got his slimy hands on them, Valerie and the police arrived and got his no good child molesting ass before he could hurt my babies. The next morning Curtis cut his trip short and came home. He took the kids and left me without a word. The judge sent me to AA and you know the rest.

Darlene hands me tissue and I wipe the tears and snot

off of my face. "That's it. That's the whole sordid story."

"Do you see your part in this?" she asks.

"Of course!" I say.

"You need to forgive yourself and that asshole who tried to molest your babies."

"What the fu…"

"Yes, you have to forgive him, just like you had to forgive the boy in second grade that pulled your hair. And you're going to have to forgive yourself just like you had to forgive yourself for what happened twenty years ago. Just like you had to forgive Sheridan, Faye, and Danielle for what happened twenty years ago."

"I…I…I"

"What?" she asks.

"I forgave the boy who pulled my hair, but I didn't do the other forgiving."

"I want you to now. Repeat after me."

I look at her and let go and let God as Faye says.

"I Victoria Williams forgive the following people."

"I Victoria Williams forgive the following people."

"Myself, Sheridan, Faye, Danielle, and the asshole who tried to molest my children."

"Myself, Sheridan, Faye, Danielle, and the asshole who tried to molest my children."

"Feel better?" she asks.

"I guess, but I feel like I was just saying words."

"Just keep repeating it. Fake it 'til you make it. Eventually you'll believe it. Just keep saying it over and over."

"Okay, Darlene. Okay. I Victoria Williams forgive the following people. Myself, Sheridan, Faye, Danielle, and the asshole who tried to molest my children."

"That a girl."

Darlene hugs me and sends me on my way. I leave there and go home singing my song of forgiveness, hoping that it will eventually leave my lips and sink into the depths of my heart and soul.

Chapter 16

Danielle

Dear Danny,

Jerome and I deeply appreciate you coming to the funeral all the way from New York. I'm sure Sabrina (in spirit) is overjoyed to know you and the other Fresh Five girls were there to see her make her transition. Please know that we love you dearly and are still praying that you girls reconcile. Please give our love to your hubby Frankie. I am looking forward to meeting him, and I'm looking forward to the day when all my girls, their husbands, and children can have a big barbeque at our house. Take care and stay in touch.

Love, Mother Brown

P.S. I love the photo!

I lean back in my office chair, staring at the thank you note I received from Mother Brown today. I can't believe it's been a week since Sabrina's funeral and I can't believe Frankie hasn't spoken to me in a week. In fact, she's been sleeping in the guestroom. It's like we're roommates now — no, more like strangers. She says she won't speak to me until I'm ready to introduce her to at least one of my friends. Looks like I'll have the opportunity to next weekend when Vicky gets here.

My ringing iPhone takes me out of my head. Tossing the card, I pick it up and scrunch my face when I see the 562 area code. Hmm. "Hel...lo?" I say, tentatively.

"Danielle, this is Faye."

"Faye?" I ask.

"Dimples."

"I know...I mean...I'm just surprised to hear from you. What's going on? Are the Brown's okay?"

"Yes, they're fine. I'm calling you because...I don't know...I just need to talk to someone and it seems like out of the four of us, you seem to have it all together."

I snigger at the irony. "Okay, what's going on?"

"It's a long story."

"Is there any way you can tell me the short version? I have a lunch meeting with a client."

"Can I talk to you when you have more time?"

"That would be a good idea. I'll be home around eight tonight. Can you call me then?"

"Yes, I can."

"By the way, how did you get my number?"

"Mother Brown gave it to me."

"Of course."

"Thank you so much, Danielle. I'll call you right at eight."

Before she hangs up, I stop her. "Faye, by the way, what is this concerning?"

"It's about me and Sheridan. I did something really terrible to her and I need some advice on how to fix things."

"Oh, okay. I'll talk to you later. And Faye, I'll call you. Is this your number on my phone?"

"Yes it is and I appreciate you calling me, Danielle."

She hangs up and I set my phone on my desk that's covered in accordion files. What in the world did she do to Sheridan? During the visit to her house, she and Sheridan were all over each other. And why is she calling me? She has a husband and friends at church. I glance at Mother Brown's note and I think about how much she wants us to get back together. Maybe this could be a segue.

"Danny."

I look toward the door at my assistant Pamela. "What is it?"

"Did you see the email from Jacqueline?" she asks, tossing her micro braids over her shoulder.

"No, I was just on the phone," I say.

"She copied me on it," she says.

"What's it about?" I ask, clicking on my mouse. "Never mind, I see it now."

"Okay, let me know if you need me to get her on the phone."

"Will do," I say, noticing an email from **Shawkins@heresnail.net**. Shawkins? Is Sheridan emailing me? What the...I click it open and sure enough it's an email from Sheridan. Okay, a phone call from Faye about Sheridan and now an email from Sheridan apparently about Faye. The subject line says *Call me about Faye*. Why do I suddenly feel like I'm back in high school? This is just how it used to go down. If Sheridan was mad at Faye, she would try to get me to be on her side and if Faye was mad at Sheridan, she would try to get me to be on her side. They didn't dare go to

Sabrina with their petty fights because Sabrina would shut it down in a hot minute and Sheridan would die before she went to Vicky, and Faye knew Vicky didn't have the patience to deal with her. So that left moi. I stare at the email, wishing that Mother Brown hadn't given Sheridan my work email. She had to be the one to have given it to her, because she's the only one in the group outside of Sabrina who has it.

Sorry to bother you at work, Danielle, but I need to talk to you about something ratchet Faye did to me. It's really messed up because we seemed to be getting close and ready to deal with what happened that night. And then I find out this whack crap she did behind my back and I'm not sure where to go with it. Please call me as soon as you can. My cell is 310-555-4986.

Wow, okay. Maybe I'll do a conference call. Talk to them both at once. There are three sides to every story: Faye's, Sheridan's, and the truth. I click on the email my assistant mentioned and focus.

From: Jacqueline Burton
To: Danielle C. Wiley
Subject: My case
Danielle,
I've been thinking about my lawsuit and I think I might want to settle outside of court.

What the! No she didn't just say that. After all my work!
Please don't be upset with me.

I push away from the computer and get out of my chair, wondering why Jacqueline is backing down. We have an airtight case and I know I can get her high six figures if not seven. Pacing, I contemplate how I'm going to get her back on track. I start to call her, but I decide to cancel my appointment and try to meet with her instead.

I buzz Pamela.

"What is it, Danny?"

"Can you reschedule my lunch appointment with Mr. Kaplan? And get Jacqueline on the phone and have her meet me at Sparks Steak House."

"Will do."

"Thanks. And by the way, have I missed any calls from Frankie?"

"No. No calls."

"Did the roses go out?"

"About an hour ago."

"Thanks, Pam."

I stand in the lobby of the Chrysler Building where my firm is located, with iPad in tow, thinking about the phone call I received from Faye and the email I received from Sheridan, wondering what could have happened. I focus and press the doors open and step onto Lexington Avenue. I look up at the building squinting. The Chrysler Building is the fourth tallest building in New York and thought to be a leading example of Art Deco architecture. The building was declared a National Historic Landmark in 1976. Hmm, in 1976 I was a year old. If only I could go back in time and change everything. Richard would—

My ringing iPhone interrupts my thoughts and I take the call. My stomach flips when I see "Frankie" on the screen. "Hey, what's up?" I say, trying to sound nonchalant.

"You're what's up—you and these beautiful freaking roses!"

Standing at the stoplight, I catch my breath, excited to hear her voice and glad she appreciates the roses.

"Are you there?"

"I'm here. It's just weird hearing your voice. You haven't spoken to me in a week." The light turns green and I, along with countless other New Yorkers, continue walking. Sparks Steak House is just a couple blocks from the office, so I feel comfortable taking a moment to chat with Frankie.

"I know and I'm sorry. But I was hurt."

"I know you were and I'm going to fix things. Vicky is flying in next weekend and we're all going to get together...oh, I have a conference call with Faye and Sheridan tonight. I'll introduce you to them, too."

"A conference call? What's that about?"

"Apparently Faye did something to Sheridan. I'm at Sparks. I have a meeting with Jacqueline."

"I thought you were meeting with Kaplan."

"I was, but Jacqueline dropped a bomb and told me she wants to settle," I say, walking into the restaurant.

"What the freak!"

"No worries. Danielle will tell you all about it tonight. Talk to you later."

"Hello, Mrs. Wiley," the hostess says.

"Hi, Nellie."

"Do you want your table?"

"Yes, please," I say, heading to the rear of the restaurant.

Before I have a chance to sit, I notice Jacqueline entering. She scans the restaurant with her big blue eyes and passes her hand over her blonde bob. At 5'10", with never ending legs, if she were thirty years younger, she'd be mistaken for a runway model rather than a corporate tax attorney. I wave and she looks my way. She gives me a smile that fails to reach her eyes. I beckon for her to join me.

"Thanks for meeting me with so little notice," she says, sitting. She crosses her bare legs that are covered with spider veins and places her hands on the table. I give her pink silk blouse and black skirt a gander, wondering where she buys her clothes and if I paid too much for the navy blue Dolce Gabbana pant suit I'm wearing today.

"It's okay."

"I know my email probably freaked you out."

"You think?" I say, forcing a smile.

The waiter approaches. "Have you ladies had a chance to look at the menu?"

"Taylor, I'll have my usual," I say.

"Nothing for me...I mean can you bring me some water?" Jacqueline says.

"Definitely, I'll bring you both water and your salad will be here shortly, Mrs. Wiley."

"Thanks," I say.

The waiter leaves and Jacqueline leans forward.

"Please don't be upset with me, Danny."

"I'm not. It's just that I asked you early on if you wanted to settle and you were adamant that you wanted to fight this thing on principle. I've had a team of folk working on this case with me. A lot of time has gone into this, Jackie. What your firm did was unconscionable and they need to be held accountable."

We remain quiet when the waiter returns with water. He sets two glasses down and then leaves.

Red in the face, she wrings her hands. I notice for the first time numerous brown spots—age spots. I glance at my hands, wondering how many more years I have before I get my own. "I want them to be held accountable, too, but I just don't want to fight them anymore. I can't endure a court battle. I just can't," she says, tearing up.

"What's wrong, Jackie?" She sobs and shivers. I take the napkin off of the table and hand it to her. "Please tell me what's wrong."

"My...my...mother died last night," she says. She takes the napkin and dabs at her tears.

Nearly choking, I grab my water and take a big gulp. "I'm...I'm sorry. My God, I didn't know."

"It's okay. As you know, she had been ill, but it's still hard...you know...it hurts."

"I'm sure it does." I place my hand on hers in a weak attempt to show sympathy.

"Danny, I have a lot to do and I don't have time to fight this, and if I did have the time, I still wouldn't want to fight. Life is so short. I don't want to spend it in somebody's courtroom. Let's just take what they're offering and call it a day. No grudges. I just want to be free."

Sitting there watching tears stream down Jacqueline's face, I want to hold her in my arms and make it all better. But we're in public and I have to be professional. Look at me—always afraid to show affection in public. What the freak is wrong with me? I rise and walk to the other side of the table. I stoop down and put my arms around her. "It's going to be okay. We can settle. Don't worry and I'm here for you. Please let me know how I can help."

"Thanks so much for understanding."

"Of course," I say, returning to my seat. "Are you going to be okay?"

"I'll be fine. I'm going to head out. I have a meeting with my mom's attorney. I'll be in touch," she says, rising.

I rise and hug her again. She leaves and I flop down in my seat, a little dazed. This is the second person I know who's died within the past week. I hate death. It's so final. The waiter arrives with my salad and I'm hit with a wave of nausea.

"Are you okay, Mrs. Wiley?"

"Yes, I'll take it to go."

"Sure thing," he says.

While I wait for him to return, Jacqueline's words resonate in my head. *"Danny, I have a lot to do and I don't have time to fight this, and if I did have the time, I still wouldn't want to fight. Life is so short. I don't want to spend it in somebody's courtroom. Let's just take what they're offering and call it a day. No grudges. I just want to be free."*

She's right. Life is too short. Sheridan, Faye, Vicky, and I have wasted so much time. I wonder what our lives would be like today if we had stayed friends. The waiter returns with a takeout bag. I grab and it and head back to the office.

"That feels so good," I say, while Frankie massages my shoulders. I turn over in our king sized bed and give her a warm smile. "It's good to be talking again," I say.

"I agree," she says, sitting on the bed. She kisses me on my lips gently and a bolt of electricity shoots up my leg. "Hmm, careful I say."

"I want you," she says, opening my robe, staring at my naked body. "You're so beautiful, Danny."

"You are, too," I say, tying my robe and leaving her on the bed, wanting.

"Where are you going?"

"I have to make that call I told you about."

"Can't it wait?"

"I'm only going to be a few minutes. Come with me. I want to introduce you to Faye and Sheridan. I'm going to Skype."

"Cool," she says, running behind me.

Chapter 17

Sheridan

"Mother Brown!"

"What's wrong, Sherry?"

"I did a test with this Sky thing and I don't see anything. Can you help me? I don't wanna miss Danielle's call."

"Just hold on a minute. I'll fix it," she says.

I look around Sabrina's office while Mrs. Brown fidgets with the little portable camera on top of Sabrina's computer. I moved in a few days ago. When I confronted Gary about Faye's story he refused to talk to me about it. Fed up, I moved out and the only way I'm going back is if he convinces me it didn't happen. But deep down I know it did. Why would Faye make up something like that? And to make matters even worse, I remember spying on Gary around that time because he was acting strange and the very day Faye says she got the abortion is the same week I saw Gary coming out of the clinic. I didn't think anything of it, because we had discussed possibly aborting the baby we had and he said he was going to check around to see if we could get it done at a good price. But then we both had a change of heart and decided to keep our baby.

"There you are. You're all set," Mother Brown says.

"How did you get so good at this?"

"Sabrina, trying to get Jerome and me out of her hair — well, out of what little hair she had left — convinced us to take a class last summer. We learned about the Internet, Facebook, Twitter, texting, email, Instagram, all of that stuff. And it's called Skype, not Sky."

"My bad. I'm impressed and thank you again for letting me stay here. You know my foster parents still take care of kids, so there's no room at the house on Avalon."

"No problem, we love having you here. I just hope you and Gary can work things out."

A beeping noise brings our conversation to a halt.

"Looks like your call is coming in. Tell Danny I said hello. I'll give you some privacy."

"Thanks, Mother Brown."

I peer at the screen and a smile spreads across my face when I see Danny wearing a white terry cloth robe looking back at me. Her face is a little distorted. I wonder what I look like. Oh...okay...there I am. Yuck, I look a hot mess. "Hi, Danielle."

"First of all, stop calling me Danielle and call me Danny like you did back in the day."

"I will if you call me Sherry, like you used to back in the

day!"

We laugh.

"Okay, Sherry, are you ready for me to get Faye on the line?"

"Not yet."

"What happened?" she asks.

"Remember when we had that big English exam our senior year. The one that would determine whether we would graduate?"

"Unfortunately I do. What about it?"

"Remember we were going to meet at Sabrina's house to study."

"Right."

"And remember Faye couldn't go because she had something to do at church."

"Danielle remembers and…what about it?"

"The reason Faye couldn't go is because she was at the clinic getting an abortion."

Danielle's mouth falls opens and her eyes bulge. "Stop messing with me, Sherry."

"If I'm lying I'm dying."

"Abortion? How could she have had an abortion? She was a virgin."

"So we thought. She was pregnant."

"I can't believe it."

"Believe it. Now guess who the baby's daddy is?"

"Who?"

My armpits perspire and I get a kick in my gut just thinking about it. I force out, "Gary!"

"Gary who?" Danielle asks.

"Gary Hawkins. My Gary!"

Danielle jumps up and her robe flies open, revealing her coochie hair that's shaved like a landing strip.

"Girl, you just flashed me!"

"I'm sorry," she says, closing her robe. "OMG. Did you confront Gary?"

"I tried to but he won't talk. I left three days ago and I've been staying at the Browns. That's where I am now — in Sabrina's office." I scoot the chair away from the video camera so Danielle can get a look at the room.

"Forget the office, I'm still trying to wrap my head around Faye having sex. She was so green, I didn't even think she knew where her private parts were."

"Well, my asshole husband showed her."

"So what did you say to her?"

"I called her a fake tramp bitch and slapped the taste out of her mouth."

"Wow, Sherry."

"I know…but I just lost it."

"We're not in high school anymore. She could press charges and you of all people should not be putting your hands on anybody."

"What do you mean by that?"

"The black eye?"

"Please let that go. Gary did not hit me. I really did run into a door."

"Okay, if you say so. Faye and Gary getting together was so long ago and Faye didn't know what she was doing and you know Gary was a horn dog."

"But all this time, she's been grinning and skinning in my face, knowing she had my man and was carrying his baby."

"All what time? You haven't seen each other in twenty years."

"That's true," I say.

"You need to let that go. You and Gary have been together for two decades… please. And you've been blessed. You're getting ready to move into a mansion in Beverly Hills for goodness sake. You have a daughter going to USC tuition free. Girl please, you need to count your blessings."

"Danny."

"What?"

"I hear what you're saying...but...I need to set the record straight. Gary and I are broke and living with his mama. And Kim got a partial scholarship and Sabrina set up a fund for her to go to school. And Gary is too old and injured to ever play ball again." I wait to see and hear Danielle's response. She just looks at me, silent. "Aren't you gonna say anything?"

"Are you alive? Are you above ground, Sherry? Are you and Gary breathing?"

"Yeah...but..."

"Then the possibilities are endless," she says. "Like I said, let it go. Faye is married now. Let bygone's be bygones. Did she apologize?"

"Yeah, she did."

"Then you need to accept it. Life is too short and we've wasted so much time. I really think we need to do group therapy. We have to get past what happened. And we all need to grow up! Damn, we're still acting like we're in high school and I'm sick of it."

I sit there knowing that Danielle's right. It's funny how we hide from the truth. I had a funny suspicion Gary had gotten somebody else at Brad pregnant, but never in a million years did I think it was Faye. She's also right about us needing to grow up. Gary said the same thing.

"Are you ready for me to put Faye on the line?"

"Go ahead."

"And Sherry, please keep your cool."

"I will," I say.

I squirm in my seat and after a few minutes there's a beeping sound. I cringe when I hear Faye's whiny voice. "Danielle, it's me."

"I know , Faye and please call me, Danny."

"Okay, Danny."

"Sheridan is on."

"I know. I can see her," Faye says.

I pass my hand over my hair while I stare at Faye's dimpled face. Curious, I wonder where she's making her call from—home, church. Who knows?

"I thought it would be a good idea to get you both on the phone. Sherry told me what happened."

Faye casts her eyes down. "I told her I was sorry. Sherry, I really am. It just happened."

"Don't say it just happened. It didn't just happen," I say, putting my face in the camera.

"I didn't know you were going to have Gary come to church and take me to that abandoned house."

Danielle furs her brows. "What abandoned house?"

"Sherry and Gary were trying to teach me a lesson. They told me some of the guys on the football team were going to try to have sex with me. There was a bet and Gary didn't want me to fall for it. So he brought me to this empty house and then he went off on me for going with him."

"How did you guys end up having sex?" Danielle asks.

I listen hard, praying to God Gary didn't rape her.

"After Gary filled me in on what was going on, I felt like a fool. You guys were always putting me down. Treating me like I was this church girl who didn't know anything and it pissed me off. So I went crazy. I attacked Gary."

"What the freak," I say.

"Yeah, Sherry, it wasn't his fault. I forced him."

"I'll be damned," I say, trying to stifle a laugh. The image of Faye attacking Gary with her weave going every which way, but the right way, is just too much for me and I burst out laughing. The next thing I know Danielle is laughing and then Faye joins in. We're laughing so hard, we start crying.

A knock on the door snaps me out of my laughing fit. "Sherry, are you okay?"

"I'm fine, Mother Brown."

"Okay."

I turn my attention back to Danielle and Faye who are both trying to compose themselves. "I'm sorry, Faye, but it's still hard for me to imagine...but anyway, what happened was a long time ago and I'm sorry for slapping you."

"I deserved it. Will you please forgive me?"

"Yes, I forgive you."

"I'm glad that's over with," Danielle says. "While I have you on the phone, I want to know if you all would be open to participating in a little group therapy. We need to bring closure to that night."

"I am," Faye and I say.

"When?" Faye asks.

"Vicky's coming to visit me next weekend. I'm going to settle the case I was working on, so I'll have some free time. I think I'm going to fly back to L.A. with her."

"Do you know of a good therapist?" I ask.

"Mother Brown says Sabrina's therapist is really good," Danielle says.

"I can get the information from Mother Brown," I say.

"That'll be good," Danielle says.

"Thanks, Danny for setting this call up," Faye says.

"Yeah, thanks, Danny," I say.

"Before we end the call, I have someone I want you all to meet," Danielle says.

"Who?" Faye and I ask.

"Frankie," I say.

"Great, I've been dying to meet him," Faye says.

"Me, too," I say.

"Frankie, come in," Danielle says.

I sit there wondering if Danielle's husband will look like I imagined him—tall, dark, with a short afro. Buff, with a baritone voice. Somebody with a little gangsta, but some class. Danielle has a hard streak that only a strong brotha could tame.

A thin white woman with grey eyes, long brownish

hair, and a pretty smile fills the screen. "Hi, everybody!"

I shake the camera, thinking it switched channels or that there's some kind of party line. "Danny, something's wrong with my reception. There's a white woman on the screen."

"That's my wife—Frankie."

I fall out of the chair onto my butt, looking up at the screen, wondering if I had heard Danielle correctly. I get up, brush myself off, and my eyes shift to Faye whose mouth is wide open. "Did you say wife?" I ask.

"Yep," Danielle says.

My head is spinning and I feel like I'm in the Twilight Zone. I have so many questions. First of all when did Danielle turn gay? Was she gay back in high school like Gary claims? Why didn't she tell us she was married to a woman? Wow, this is a trip.

I watch Faye, wondering what she's going to say. The Bible clearly says homosexuality is a sin and an abomination. Faye closes her mouth and says, "Uh…nice to meet you, Frankie."

"It's nice to meet you, too. I've heard so much about The Fresh Five and I can't wait to meet you all in person."

"Me, too," Faye says.

"Right," I say, still in shock. "Danielle, uh…we need to talk" I say.

"Sure, but not tonight. I'll touch base with you tomorrow."

"Okay," I say.

"I'm glad you and Faye are working things out. Frankie and I have to go. I'll talk to you tomorrow."

Before I can say another word, Danielle and her wife are gone.

Faye and I exchange looks of surprise. "Did you see that?" I ask.

"Yeah, I can't believe it," Faye says.

"Wow, there's just one surprise after another," I say.

"Did you know Danielle was gay?" Faye asks.

"No, she dated guys at Brad."

"I can't wait to find out how she ended up with a woman," Faye says.

"Me, too. Doesn't the Bible teach against homosexuality?" I ask.

"It does, but we have a lot of gay people in our church."

"Really?" I say.

"God doesn't discriminate, Sherry."

"Hmm, I need to call Gary."

"And I need to get home."

"Where are you? I didn't think you'd want Mark to know you were pregnant with Gary's baby."

"I'm at my office at the church. Mark doesn't want to know any details."

"Girl, you are so lucky to have Mark."

"And you're lucky to have Gary. He loves you. He told me you were pregnant, and I asked him if he was going to have you get rid of it. Girl, if looks could kill. Don't blame him. It was my fault."

"It was all of our faults. I'm glad Danielle is open to group therapy. I'm going to get the info from Mother Brown and then we need to set an appointment that will work for all of us."

"Just keep me in the loop."

"Will do….oh…and, Faye."

"What?"

"Do you think we can finish our spa day?"

"Of course."

"And guess what, Faye?"

"What?"

"I haven't smoked a cigarette since that day I threw them out at the spa."

"Wonderful, just wonderful, girl. I love you."

"I love you too, Dimples."

Chapter 18

Faye

I sit in my office at church, shaking my head, thinking about what just happened. Happy Sheridan and I are back on track, I stop shaking my head and sit back in my chair with a smile on my face. And I'm thrilled the others are open to getting closure on that night. It seems like we might just be able to fulfill Sabrina's death bed wish after all. Now Danielle, that's a whole nother story. "Lord, have mercy. She's married to a woman." Who knew? I never would have imagined. Wow, she didn't just get married to a woman, she's married to a *white* woman. Not that her race matters, but a relationship with a *man* of the *same race* can be challenging. I wonder how they manage to get along. She is pretty and seems nice. Hmm, nowadays, you have to be careful what you say about gay people or do to gay people. Say or do the wrong thing, you can lose everything you've ever worked for. It's getting late and I have to make a stop before I go home.

I grab my purse and make my way to the sanctuary. I can hear the security guards in the back cracking jokes and laughing. When I come to the entrance of the sanctuary, I notice someone sitting in the rear. I squint, but can't make out the person. I start to turn and go the other way, but something propels me forward. If this person was up to no good, he never would have been allowed to come in after hours. When I step forward, the person calls out to me.

"Faye, it's me. Gary."

"Gary?" It feels like déjà vu. I flash back to that night when Gary was sitting in the back of my father's church. And now here it is twenty years later and he's sitting in the back of my husband's church. But this time, I won't be going anywhere with him. This time we won't have sex. I continue to walk toward him, wondering what he wants. He rises and limping, comes toward me. I stop and let him approach. The transformation is still jarring. Gone is all his thick curly hair, six pack, and youthful glow.

We stand a few feet from each other, both silent. "What do you want?" I ask.

"Why...why did you tell Sherry what had happened? We both swore to take that shi...I mean stuff to the grave," he says, looking up at the stained glass picture of the black Jesus hanging over the pulpit. "Now she's gone. She left me. She's all I had left. In case you haven't noticed, my looks are gone. I'm too old and broke down to get another NFL contract, and I don't have a pot to crap in or a window to throw it out of. All that stuff Sherry said was a lie. We're not you and Mark. We don't have a lot, but we had each other. I know Vicky and a lot of the girls at Bradshaw were pissed I got with Sherry, but it wasn't because she was white. Truth be told, I've always had a thing for chocolate skin like yours. I fell for Sherry because of her spirit. I had found out about her moms dumping her off at a fire station and how she grew up in the foster care system. I couldn't believe that somebody who had gone through all that could cheer like she did. She used to cheer like her life depended on it. I believed that a white chick that could hold her own with some tough sistahs like y'all had to be special. That's what I was attracted to, Faye. I don't wanna lose her. Do you understand me? You have to talk to her."

"Gary, first of all, what happened shouldn't have. I've had to live with what I did for twenty years. It wasn't easy. I killed my own baby and now I want to have a baby and I can't. Do you know how that feels? I've asked God to forgive me and he has and I've forgiven myself. I want to start fresh—new. I love Sherry and I just didn't feel right being in a relationship with her with a secret like that."

"Why didn't you at least talk to me first? Give me a heads-up or something. How do you think I felt when she jammed me up about that stuff? You ain't right, Faye."

"No, *we* weren't right, Gary."

"Does Mark know what went down?"

I swallow hard and say, "Yes, he knows."

"Damn…I mean dang. So I guess I'm a have to deal with him next. Now he probably has beef with me."

"I didn't tell him it was you."

"What?"

"No, I didn't and he doesn't want to know."

"What the—what kind of man is he?"

"A good one," I say.

"You got that right. You did good, Dimples. I'm proud of you. But you got to talk to my wife."

"I already did."

"When?"

"Just before you got here. I told her I was the one who came onto you."

"What did she say?"

"She laughed."

"Laughed?"

"Yep. She's at Sabrina's house. Go see her. I'm sure it's gonna work out."

"Yeah, maybe you're right."

"Is everything okay in here?" a loud voice rings out.

"Yes, Lamont. I'm fine."

"Just checking," he says, and leaves.

"Dang, you're like a celebrity, Dimples. You've come a long way."

"We all have. Now, go get that wife of yours."

"Will do," he says. He leans in and kisses me on the cheek. "Stay sweet."

"You, too. And Gary…you're not broke down. You're older and wiser and you still have a beautiful soul."

"What…why…why you say that?" he asks, choking up with tears in his eyes.

"Because you do. I saw it that night in that abandoned house and I see it now. Don't base your worth on material things, Gary. I've been living the good life for years now, but I was miserable because I had so many dark secrets and lies and now for the first time I'm happy and almost free."

"I feel you, Dimples. I feel you," he says, leaving.

The sheet of paper Mrs. Brown gave me with Vicky's address on it gives me pause. I reach over and take it off the passenger seat of my car. Hopefully, she's home. I don't want to call because I don't think she'll see me if she knows I'm coming. I can't shake what she said at the altar, and I feel I need to reach out to her. Sitting behind the wheel of my car, I bow my head and close my eyes. "Dear, Lord please guide and direct me in dealing with Vicky. Give me the right words to say. Help me say the right things, Lord and help me to help her. In Jesus name I pray, Amen."

A knock on my window makes me jump. "First Lady, are you okay?" Lamont asks.

I roll my window down and ask, "Is Mark still in his meeting?"

"Yes, he told me to tell you not to wait up for him."

"Okay, Lamont, I'm fine. Tell him I'm going to stop by my friend Vicky's house before I go home. I'll text him the address."

"Will do and stay safe," Lamont says.

"Thanks and I will and by the way, you do a wonderful job. Mark and I should tell you that more often."

"I love it here. All of us do. Because of y'all, we're not in the streets doing what we used to do back in the day."

"I'm glad to hear it." I start my car and pull out of the parking lot and head to Vicky's house in Los Feliz.

What a beautiful neighborhood, I think to myself when I pull up to Vicky's large yellow house surrounded by a white picket fence. I smile thinking about meeting her husband and kids. She's so lucky to have kids. I park my car, lock it, and make my way to the fence. It opens easily and I take a deep breath and walk to the white door with yellow trim. The yard is filled with colorful plants and trees. I'm not surprised. Vicky loved all things green. She used to tell me she really wanted to go into horticultural but took up cheerleading instead to please her mother. Don't I know about people-pleasing. It's unfortunate we go through life never being ourselves, who we really are, who God meant for us to be.

I ring the doorbell and peer into the window. I see a light on and I can hear music playing. It sounds like Jagged Edge's "Walked Outta Heaven." I put my ear to the door. The song continues..."asking God to please forgive me..."Maybe I should have called. She might be having an at home date night with her husband. I start to turn, but a shrill scream stops me in my tracks. I run to the door and ring the bell, and then I knock. There's another scream and something tells me to turn the knob. I do so and the door opens. I slowly enter. "Vicky! Vicky! Are you okay?" My heart is racing and I know I'm putting myself in harm's way, but that little voice inside me I call the voice of God tells me to keep moving. "Vicky where are you?"

"In here," she says, sobbing.

"Where?" I ask.

"The living room. Follow the light."

"As I near the living room, the music gets louder."

I stop at the entry way and gasp. The room is filled with buckets and there are empty wine, whisky, and beer bottles strewn across the floor. Vicky, butt naked, sits on a large tan leather sofa with her arms wrapped around her knees. Her hair and face are wet. I look for any signs of injury, but I don't see any. The room is dark. I go the wall switch, but she stops me.

"No, don't turn on the light."

"What's going on? Why are you in here like this?" I walk to the CD player and turn it off.

"Don't ask," she says. "What did you do to the music?"

I ignore her question and look in the buckets. They're full and based on the smell wafting up my nose, they're filled with alcohol.

"Where's the restroom?"

"Over there," she points.

I go to the restroom for a towel to put around her because she's shivering. When I get there, I notice the tub and sink filled with brown liquid that I surmise is also alcohol. My Lord, what is going on? I grab a bath towel and a robe that's hanging on the back of the door and rush back to the living room. I attempt to dry her hair but she shakes her head.

"Be still, Vicky, you're going to get pneumonia."

"This reminds me of that time we went to that church picnic with your father and it started raining and we were all trying to get out of the rain before it messed up our hair. Then when we got inside, we were fighting over the one dry towel we had. Remember?"

"I remember," I say. "Here put this on. My Lord, you smell like a brewery. Is that alcohol in your hair?"

She nods.

"Why did you put it in your hair?"'

"Because I didn't want to put it in my mouth."

"What are you talking about, Vicky?"

She doesn't answer me. She puts the robe on and asks, "Why are you here. Who sent you?"

"God. God sent me, Vicky. And I'm glad I listened to Him."

"God is good. He forgave me, Faye. Listen to this; I Victoria Williams forgive the following people. Myself, Sheridan, Faye, Danielle, and the asshole that tried to molest my children."

"What do you mean? Who tried to molest your children?" I ask, looking around. "Where are your children and where is your husband?"

"Curtis took Tangie and Matt away. He took them away a year ago. We're separated. You see, I was a bad mother. I let a strange man I met at a bar come into my house and he almost molested my babies. But the babysitter and the cops stopped him. Not me, I was too drunk. I'm an alcoholic, Faye. After that night twenty years ago, I stopped drinking, but three years ago, I started up again, and I haven't been able to stop. I stopped for a year, but the day of the funeral, I drank again. I woke up Sunday morning with puke all over me in Sabrina's cellar. Yep, I dragged myself to church in spite of it. I was a bad mother, but God forgave me. Do you think he really forgave me, Faye? Did he? Did your God forgive me or am I fooling myself?" She grabs me around the collar and starts to shake me. "Did he?"

I pull away from her. "Yes, yes he did, Vicky. He did. He forgave you. You have to believe it."

"Did he forgive me for that night, Faye? What about that night? I want to drink because of that night, but I want my kids more. I went to the store today and I bought all this liquor and I was going to drink it, but I did what my sponsor told me, she said to say 'God help me!' and I said it and God did for me what I couldn't do for myself. But I can't get over that night. It keeps haunting me, Faye. Does it haunt you?"

My eyes sting and I begin to cry. "Yes, yes, it does. We have to get past it. Danny, Sherry, and I talked tonight. We're going to meet with Sabrina's therapist and we're going to get help. We're going to do group therapy. I want you to go with us."

"That's a good idea."

"And Vicky, you're not the only one with demons and secrets. I got pregnant with Gary's baby when I was in high school and had an abortion. Sheridan is dirt poor and living with Gary's mama, and Danielle is married to a white woman."

Vicky looks at me wide-eyed and her face starts to twitch and she starts to howl. She laughs so hard she falls over. "You have got to be kidding," she says.

"No, it's true."

"I don't know what part of what you told me is harder to believe — you being pregnant or Danny being gay."

"Believe it all. We're all works in progress and it's time we grow up. It's time we start acting like women. We're no longer in high school."

"You're right, Faye."

"Why don't we start by dumping all these buckets and getting rid of all this alcohol," I suggest.

"Good idea," she says, getting off of the sofa.

She gives me a crazy look.

"What?"

"I can't believe you had sex with Gary…uh…how was it?"

I shake my head and roll my eyes.

"Come on, I always wondered what it would be like to have sex with him."

"Girl, it was horrible. Not because of anything he did. I was a virgin, so it hurt like hell and I didn't feel anything. You know it takes a while to get used to sex."

"Dang…I hope you enjoy sex now."

"I am not going to discuss my sex life, with my preacher husband, with you."

"My bad. Let's get this place cleaned up."

"Like I said, we really need to grow up, Vicky."

"You're right, Faye."

I roll my sleeves up and get busy.

Chapter 19

Victoria

It's been two weeks since the funeral and a week since Faye found me at home fighting a fierce desire to drink. If she hadn't shown up, I wouldn't have fourteen days of sobriety and I wouldn't be on my way to The Big Apple. So when she asked me to get my cheerleading outfit out of storage and meet her at Bradshaw High School today, I agreed — reluctantly, but I said, "Okay." She thinks it would be cool to have a photo of me wearing my uniform today juxtaposed with a photo of me in my uniform twenty years ago. In addition to doll making, Faye dabbles in photography. She's actually not half bad. It's a miracle I can still fit it, but I've worked hard to maintain my figure over the years. Okay, I did have to take it to the tailor so the hip area on the skirt and bust area on the top could be adjusted.

Standing in front of the mirror in my bedroom, I twist, turn, and kick my legs up. "You better watch out, you better get back, the Bradshaw Bears are on the attack. We're gonna knock you out and win the game, because we're the best and you're so lame." Winded, I stumble back a bit, thinking about how *lame* the cheer is. I need to get back in the gym.

"Look at you!"

"Curtis, you frightened me. I didn't hear you come in."

"I'm sorry. What's going on?"

"This is Faye's crazy idea. She wants to do a photo shoot and then she's gonna put the picture she takes of me today in a frame next to the photo she took of me in my uniform twenty years ago."

"You probably won't be able to tell them apart," Curtis says, walking toward me. He wraps his arms around my waist and plants a kiss on my lips.

"Don't start something you can't finish," I say.

"What time is your photo shoot?"

"In an hour and then I have to come back here and pack."

"Do you need a ride to the airport in the morning?"

"Faye's taking me."

"You two seem to be getting along quite nicely."

"I guess we are. It seems like old times, but better."

"What do you mean?"

"I don't know…just more honest, more open and when I get back, we're going to try to get into a group therapy session."

"That's wonderful, Vick. I'm so proud of you."

"Just keep praying for me. I have six months…well, five months and two weeks."

"No, you only have today. You only have to get through today, Vick. One day at a time."

"You're right, sweetie. Are the kids here?"

"They're in the backyard. Why don't you come out back? They'll get a kick out of you in your cheerleading outfit."

I laugh at the thought. "Shoot, I wish I had some pompoms."

"Come on," Curtis says, grabbing my hand.

We sprint to the yard, like we're in our teens and not late thirties. Curtis motions for me to wait and then he goes to the yard. I get full watching Matt and Tangie playing on the swing set Curtis bought them for Christmas last year.

"Matt and Tangie, I have a surprise for you."

"What surprise?" they ask.

"Introducing your mother the cheerleader."

I run outside, kicking my legs up and spinning around. Matt and Tangie stare at me with wide eyes and open mouths.

"Mom, you look hot," Matt says.

Curtis and I exchange curious looks. "'Hot'? What do you know about hot?" I ask.

"He means you look nice, mom," Tangie says.

"Do a cheer, baby," Curtis says.

"Yeah, do a cheer," Matt and Tangie say.

I stand there, wanting to do something special for them, and then say, "Two, four, six, eight, Matt and Tangie are so great. Five, six, seven, eight, I love them so much it truly aches."

"Yeah!" they scream. They barrel toward me and knock me to the ground. I lie there while they smother me in kisses, thanking God for the moment and asking him to never let it end.

Still buoyant about the time I spent with Curtis and the kids, I sing along to an early copy of Beyoncé's "Drunk in Love" playing on my CD player in the car, while I pull up to Bradshaw. I must be getting stronger to be able to listen to this song and not want a drink. Curtis and I had a quickie before I left the house and I told him I wanted to do it to this song. When he heard the lyrics he started to shut it down, but I went down on him before he had a chance to. I get hot just thinking about our tryst. Thank goodness the kids were preoccupied in the backyard. While I was pleasuring Curtis he was able to keep an eye on the kids from the bedroom window, the entire time and vice versa. I wonder if my parents ever did anything kinky like that when we were kids.

I pull into the faculty parking lot. It's Saturday, and the school is deserted. I look around for Faye's black Lexus, wondering where she is. When I look in my rearview mirror I spot a silver Honda. While squinting, the door opens and Sheridan emerges wearing a cheerleader outfit. "What the hell?" I peer at her with my jaw in my lap while she slowly approaches my car. She stops halfway and stands with her hands on her wide hips. I take this as my cue to get out of the car. I do so tentatively.

"Funny meeting you here," Sheridan says. "You can close your mouth now."

"Right," I say. I step back when she walks toward me.

"I don't bite," she says, with a chuckle.

"What are you doing here?" I ask.

"Faye told me to meet her here. She's going to take a photo of me—"

"In your cheerleading outfit and then put it in a frame next to—"

"The picture she took of me twenty years ago," Sheridan concludes. "How did you know?"

"Because she told me the same thing."

"Looks like we've been set up," Sheridan says.

"Yep," I say.

There's a moment of uncomfortable silence and then we both ask, "Were you able to fit it or did you have to have it altered?"

We laugh and then both say, "I had to have it altered."

More laughter and then again we say, "I never did like the brown and gold school colors."

We share incredulous looks and curl over roaring.

"What is this…wow…what are you a ventriloquist?" Sheridan asks.

"You know we used to talk at the same time back in day," I say.

"I know," she says.

I look around, thinking about all the good times and the bad times we had at Bradshaw. Sheridan points to a bench near a fence. I nod and we walk to it and have a seat. She passes her long slender hands over her long legs and we both sigh loudly.

"What's wrong?" I ask.

"I wish I had a cigarette," Sheridan says. "What's wrong with you?" she asks.

"I wish I had a drink," I say.

Sheridan rises and walks to the fence. She leans back and says, "Speaking of drinks, what was going on with you at Sabrina's house? You know down in the wine cellar. We never talked about it. You were really on one. I'm sorry for leaving you, but you kinda freaked me out."

"I'm sorry, Sheridan."

"You don't have to call me Sheridan. Call me what you all called me back in the day."

"Okay, Sherry. Well, uh…Sherry, I'm an alcoholic."

"What the fu…freak. Shut up."

"Yeah, I am."

"That explains a lot. I mean…I was wondering why you

acted the way you did at the repast. You know…after what happened twenty years ago, I was surprised to see that you still drink."

I get up from the bench and join her at the fence. "I did stop drinking after that night. I didn't start up until three years ago. And on the day of the funeral I had a whole year of sobriety."

"Why did you drink again?"

"Guilt. You know it can eat you alive."

"Tell me about it," Sheridan says. "Are your kids okay? You said they had been molested."

"They're fine. All credit goes to God. He had mercy on me. The police and the kids' babysitter stopped the asshole who was trying to hurt my babies."

"What asshole?"

"A piece of scumbag that followed me home from this club."

"Damn!"

"I forgave him…and you, Faye, and Danielle."

Sheridan gives me a crazy look.

"That's what my sponsor told me I would have to do if I don't ever want to drink again."

"How long have you been sober now?"

"Two weeks."

"I haven't smoked a cigarette in three weeks, and I'm going crazy."

"I'm glad you stopped. Every time you get the urge to smoke just say, 'God help me.'"

"Is that what you say when you get an urge to drink?"

"Yep," I say.

"Does it work?"

"So far it has and the urges are getting less frequent," I say.

We both fall silent and then say, "God help me."

We laugh again.

"Victoria, you're not—"

"Vicky…call me Vicky like you used to."

"Right. Vicky, you're not the only one with secrets."

"Faye already told me. You and Gary are broke, Faye had sex with Gary, got pregnant, got an abortion, and Danielle's married to a white woman."

"Are we a hot mess or what?" Sheridan asks, shaking her head.

"The thing that surprises me most is that Faye got to Gary when I couldn't. I mean, it's no secret that I wanted him…I mean… he was actually interested in me first," I say.

"Wait a minute, Vicky, you have it a little twisted. I saw and spoke to Gary before you even knew he existed."

"What?"

"Remember our first week at Brad in the cafeteria when I fell down."

"Yeah, I remember," I say.

"Gary was the boy who helped me get up off of the floor. He told me his name and that he had just made the football team. We were really making a connection. You were standing behind him and then when he asked me my name, you blurted out your name and he turned around and started talking to you. After that, I went back to our table and sat with the others."

I stand there trying to remember everything that happened that day in the cafeteria and it starts coming back to me. Sabrina had seen a group of boys sitting at a table next to ours and I got all excited and started flirting with them. Then I decided to walk to the vending machine so they could see my green eyes and one boy did notice. The next thing I heard was a bunch of laughter and when I turned around Sheridan was on the floor and this tall guy was reaching down to her. I couldn't see his face, but when I took a look at all the girls in the cafeteria with their eyes bulging and their jaws on the floor, I knew he had to be cute. So I ran up and stood behind him, waiting for the right moment. He asked Sheridan what her name was and that's when I told him my name. Once Sheridan left, I tried to keep his interest by talking about everything I had learned from my father and two brothers about football. I wanted him to ask me for my number but he never did. From that point on I tried to talk to Gary to no avail. Then when we were juniors, I found out Sheridan was dating him. I thought that was the worst news ever, but the night she told us she was pregnant with Gary's baby was the end of the world for me, literally and figuratively.

"Vicky!"

"I'm sorry, you're right. He did talk to you first. That's in the past and I'm married now."

"How's that going?"

"We're separated, but I'm working on getting back together with him and my kids."

"Curtis...right?"

"Right."

"I'd love to meet him and your kids," Sheridan says.

"I'd love for you to meet them, too. How's Kim?"

"Beautiful and doing well in school. You know Sabrina set up a trust fund for her. That's how she was able to go to SC and live on campus."

"Sabrina...hmm...I miss her so much," I say.

"I do, too."

"Did Faye mention doing group therapy?" I ask.

"Yeah, I'm game."

"I am, too. I'm going to New York in the morning to spend a few days with Danielle."

"Wow, I'd love to go to New York. Too bad we didn't make it a group trip," Sheridan says.

"I know. Maybe once we get through therapy, we'll be able to do a group trip."

We turn at the sound of a car approaching.

"Look who decided to show up?" I say.

Sheridan and I walk to Faye's car. She grins and waves. She gets out with her digital camera on her arm. "Sorry, I'm late."

"You set us up!" we scream.

"My bad," she says, through laughter. "I just wanted to give you guys a little time to get reacquainted."

"Faye, you're just full of surprises. We're gonna have to keep an eye on you," I say.

"Let's get these shots," Faye says, surveying the area. "Over there is good," she says, pointing to a tree. Sheridan and I follow her. We stop at the tree and she says, "I need you ladies to loosen up. Give me a cheer."

"Faye!" we say.

"Come on. By the way, you look great. Both of you!"

"You'd be proud of me, Faye. I haven't had a cigarette in three weeks."

"And I haven't had a drink in two weeks," I say.

Faye applauds "Wonderful! Now that cheer."

Sheridan and I share a smile. "You ready?" she asks.

I nod and we lift our hands and shake our hips. "You better watch out, you better get back, the Bradshaw Bears are on the attack. We're gonna knock you out and win the game, because we're the best and you're so lame."

"That's it. Right there. Good, ladies. I'm gonna take a few more shots of you together and then we'll do individual shots," Faye says.

Sheridan and I nod and I notice tears in her eyes. Then my eyes sting and tear up. Without words, we walk to each other and hug and then Faye joins us and I thank God for this moment, too, and I say a silent prayer asking him to give us the strength to make it through therapy.

Chapter 20

Danielle

Standing at the bottom of the escalator in the American Airlines terminal at JFK, I move out of the way of the drivers carrying signs covered in names like, Desjardin, Hurst, Schmidt, wondering to myself, who the people are and if they live in New York or are just visiting. Vicky should be coming down anytime now. Her flight landed ten minutes ago. Perspiration drips from my hairline onto my face when I think about Frankie and Vicky meeting for the first time. She told me Faye already told her about my situation, but hearing about it and seeing it are two different things.

Vicky's never been the judgmental type, but compared to her normal life, might lifestyle may be a bit off putting. She seems to have it together—a nice husband, two kids, and an admirable profession. She's really done well for herself. It seems as if she really learned a big lesson since that night that changed our lives for—"

"Danny!" Vicky says, waving wildly.

I smile and wave back. She reaches the bottom of the escalator and I meet her with open arms. We hug and she whispers in my ear. "So good to be here."

"It's good to have you here," I say, pulling out of our embrace and giving her the once over. "You look good."

"You look good, too, but you're sweating up a storm," she says, pointing to my face. She reaches into her bag and hands me a piece of tissue. "It's clean. Don't tell me you're already in menopause. Girl, we're too young for that," she adds.

"No, maybe perimenopause, but not menopause," I say, looking around, hoping no one is ear hustling, as Sheridan would say. "To be honest with you, I'm a little nervous about you meeting Frankie." I dab at the sweat on my brow and toss the tissue into a nearby wastebasket.

"Don't be and where is Frankie?" she asks.

"At home finishing up her column. She's had writer's block for the past week and she's running behind. She can't wait to meet you," I say.

"Let's get my bags," she says.

"Right."

Headed to my Upper Westside condominium, I listen to Vicky go on and on about a photo shoot she and Sheridan had with Faye. It sounds like Sheridan and Vicky have come to terms with their rivalry. I have to give it to Faye; she has played a significant role in bringing us all together.

"Do you remember that crazy cheer?" Vicky asks.

"Not really...I mean, I think it said something about lame and game. That's all I can remember," I say, stopping at a red light.

"Girl, this place is crowded," she says, looking out the window. "Where do all these people come from?" she asks.

"All over the world. There are over eight million people living in New York and over a million of those live in Manhattan. New York isn't spread out like L.A. is, that's why we're all on top of one another."

"Geez," she says. "Do you think you'll ever move back to L.A.?"

"Danielle doesn't know. Maybe she will." The light turns green and I continue on. "That's Central Park right there," I say, pointing.

"Wow, I've seen it in hundreds of movies. Can we go there? And I want to visit the Statue of Liberty, The Empire State Building, Apollo Theater, the museums, the Chrysler Building—"

"Whoa, slow down, girl," I say, laughing. "You're only here for three days."

"I know, but I'm excited."

"I know you are. By the way, my law office is in the Chrysler building."

"Perfect, we can go there and I can see where you work."

"We can go there, but I'm not going into the office. This is my time off, to spend with you."

"I appreciate it."

I slow down and point to a building on the corner. "It costs a fortune to live there. Denzel Washington has a place there."

"Where?" she asks, stretching her thick neck.

"Fifteen Central Park West. A lot of famous people live

there. A duplex in the building is on sale for sixty million plus."

"Shut up!"

"Yep."

"How can you afford it?"

"Danielle can't. Danielle lives over there. It's costly, but with my income and Frankie's, we manage," I say, parking my Mercedes. We get out of the car, grab her two bags out of the trunk, and walk into my building. "The elevator's right over here," I say. "We're on the twelfth floor."

"How long have you all lived here?" she asks, when we get on the elevator.

"Five years. Where do you live?"

"Los Feliz."

"That's a nice area," I say.

The elevator stops and we get out. Before we reach the door to my condo, it opens and Frankie appears, red in the face, all smiles and giggles. "Danny, I finished. I finished my column and it's brilliant!"

I stand there wondering how she knew we were here, but knowing Frankie, she probably saw us from the window. "Great," I say.

"And you must be Victoria," she says, grabbing the suitcase out of Vicky's hand.

"You can call me Vicky."

"Cool," Frankie says.

I move past them and go into the house. The smell of spicy spaghetti sauce wafts up my nose.

"Something smells good," Vicky says, entering.

"I'm making my secret pasta dish," Frankie says, closing the door.

"We're going out to dinner, Vicky. Frankie can't cook and wants to use you as a guinea pig."

"That's not fair, Danny," Frankie whines.

"It may not be fair, but it's true."

"See how she does me?" Frankie says. "I'm excited

about you being here and please make yourself at home."

"Vicky, come with me. I'll show you to your room," I say.

"How many bedrooms does this place have? It's huge."

"We have three bedrooms—the master, a guest bedroom, and an extra room."

I motion for Vicky to follow me and we come to the room at the end of the hall. I usher her in and she stands back taking in the décor. "I love the purple walls and gold comforter set," she says.

"It was Frankie's idea. She's really into loud colors," I say.

"Nice," she says, sitting on the bed.

"I'll be right back. Let me get your other bag. The dressers are empty. You can put your clothes in there."

"Thanks."

I give her a welcoming smile and head back to the living room. Frankie sits on the sofa reading what appears to be her column. She looks up and asks, "Is everything okay?"

"It's fine," I say, getting Vicky's other bag.

"I can't wait to read this to you," Frankie says.

"Okay, sure. Just give me a minute. I want to help Vicky get settled."

"Of course," she says, without looking up. "By the way, her green eyes and curly hair are to die for. You didn't tell me she was a looker. You might have competition, sweetie."

"Don't start," I say, frowning. "She's married, remember?" I leave her there and go back to the room. I love Frankie, but sometimes she plays too much. She's just so in your face with our lifestyle. I guess I can't blame her for being proud and free. "Here's your other bag, Vicky."

"Thanks. Sit down for a minute," she says, patting the bed.

"What's up?"

"I just want you to know I'm okay with you and

Frankie."

"Danielle knows this," I say.

"I'm not so sure you do…I mean…you don't seem like your usual confident, cocky self," she says.

"I'm not cocky," I say, laughing.

She rises and shuts the door. "I know you, Danny. You've always followed the status quo, with your dad being a judge and all. After Sabrina, you were the smartest one out of all of us. Look at you—you're a big time attorney now. I'm so proud of you."

"I'm good. It does take some time to get used to it. I mean, don't get me wrong, I'm crazy about Frankie, but I've still yet to determine whether I'm gay or not. Maybe I'm not…I don't know."

"Just take it easy on yourself, Danny."

"I'm proud of you, too. You seem to be the only one out of all of us living the American dream."

"What do you mean?" she asks.

"Sheridan, as you know, is struggling with finances, Faye is struggling with fertility issues, and I don't have you know…the normal type of relationship. You on the other hand, have a great husband, two kids, and a wonderful teaching career." I peer at her, waiting for a smile or a "thank you" or something, but she just gives me a blank stare. "Are you okay?"

"There is something—"

Before she can finish her sentence there's a knock at the door.

"Who is it?" I ask, with a knowing chuckle.

"Me, silly."

"Come in, Frankie," I say.

The door opens and Frankie says, "Sorry to interrupt, but I have a great idea. Why don't we take Vicky to the Bronx?"

"The Bronx," I say, wondering what's gotten into Frankie.

"Not just the Bronx, but to the Botanical Garden there. You said she likes plants and stuff."

"Yeah, I do," Vicky says.

"It has more than forty different gardens and plant collections. There's so much to see and it's such a beautiful day outside. Then after we could go to dinner."

"I like the sound of that," Vicky says.

"Danny, what do you think?"

"It's up to Vicky?"

"I'm only here for three days and I wanna make the best of it. I'd love to see the Gardens."

Danny claps and we all laugh. "It doesn't take much to get her going," I say.

"Forgive me, Vicky, I can get a little giddy at times. I guess I'm excited about doing something wholesome. Most of my friends are into boozing and rock 'n roll. I'm mean, you're a teacher for goodness sake and into gardening and stuff. I feel like I'm hosting Donna Reed or somebody. I know she's way before all of our time, but I used to be addicted to 'Nick at Nite' when I was in high school."

"My kids are addicted to Nickelodeon," Vicky says.

"Okay, let me know when you're ready to go. I'll be in the living room."

"Will do," Vicky and I say.

"Wow, she's really full of energy," Vicky says.

"That's putting it mildly," I say. "Oh, you were going to tell me something."

"It's okay. It can wait. Why don't we go? I'm getting hungry. Maybe we can eat before we tour the gardens," she says.

"No problem," I say.

Standing underneath the breathtaking trees at the Bronx Botanical Garden, I watch Vicky's eyes widen at the sight of the fall foliage. A sea of orange, crimson, and gold hovers above. "This is incredible," she says.

"That's one of the many things I love about New York," I say.

"What?" Vicky asks.

"The seasons! In L.A. there are only two."

"What are those?" Frankie asks.

"Sunshine and rain," I say.

We all laugh and Vicky continues to marvel at the sights.

"Do you like Azaleas?"

"Frankie, I love Azaleas," Vicky says.

"Let's check out the Azalea Garden and then I promise we'll eat."

"No problem," Vicky says.

Danny walks ahead of us taking notes. She decided she would turn our little adventure into a story for her next column. I sidle up next to Vicky and notice her mood has somewhat changed. "You okay?" I ask.

"Yeah, I'm having a good time."

"Be honest."

"No, I am. I do miss Tangie and Matt a little and Curtis."

"That's understandable."

"And I was also thinking about the therapy session idea that's being bounced around."

"Are you okay with it?"

"One part of me is and another part of me is a little afraid. I mean, look, we all seem to be getting to know one another again...you know...we're getting along now. Sherry and Faye. Me, Sherry, and Faye. You, Sherry, and Faye. Why dig up what happened? Why not just forget about it?"

"Because it's still there—lurking beneath the surface. I still have nightmares. It's been twenty years, and I still have nightmares, Vicky."

"I do, too."

"I can't believe I didn't do something sooner. I should have listened to Sabrina. She tried to get me to get past it. To talk to you all, but I wouldn't...especially the first few months after it happened. I was so full of rage. I wanted to kill—" I stop and get hold of myself. My fists are balled and red.

"Calm down, Danny. I'm sorry I brought it up."

"Don't be sorry. We have to deal with it. Get closure," I say.

"How are your parents?"

"They retired and moved to Florida six months after the funeral. They didn't want to be in L.A. anymore—too many memories."

"Is that why you ended up going to Cornell? To get away? You know...do a geographic?" Vicky asks.

"What's a geographic?"

"It's when you make a physical move to get away from emotional baggage."

"I don't think so. I mean, I was accepted to UCLA, but I was always curious about the East Coast."

"I wish I would have listened to Sabrina, too. I think I could have saved myself a lot of heartache. And I missed you guys. Look at all the years we threw away. I would have loved to have been there for you and Frankie's wedding. I missed Faye's wedding and I wouldn't even recognize Kimberly."

"You see, all the more reason, we have to go through with it."

"You're right, Danny."

"Hey, you two, come on!"

We laugh and run to catch up with, Frankie.

Chapter 21

Sheridan

The sound of the bed squeaking fills the room. I grip the side of the mattress while Gary thrusts himself in and out of me from the rear.

"Hmm...you feel so good, Sher—nice and juicy like I like it." He grabs my titties and squeezes. "I don't know what feels the best, your kitty cat or your tits. You're driving me crazy, woman. Hmm...damn, this is goooooooood. Is it good for you?"

It could be good for me if I could get images of Gary and Faye screwing like rabbits out of my head. This is the first time we've gotten together since I jammed Gary up and he came to me on his hands and knees with my real wedding ring, begging for me to forgive him and take him back. I open my eyes and glance at our wedding photo on the nightstand, trying to get into it. I was three months pregnant in that picture. You couldn't tell though. My stomach was flat as a pancake. Right when I'm starting to feel good, Gary groans and shivers.

"Don't...don't...move, Sher. Please don't. Hmm...damn!" he says, falling off of me onto the bed. "That was great!!! I feel like Tony the Tiger."

I roll my eyes and sit up in bed.

"What's with you?" he asks. "All that work I was doing and you didn't enjoy it?"

"I could have, but I kept thinking about you and Faye knockin' boots."

"Sher, you told me you weren't going to bring it up."

"I know, but it's hard not to think about it."

"You need to let it go. It was twenty years ago and trust me it wasn't all that."

"Tell me anything," I say.

"Don't you have bigger and better things to do than think about some whack stuff like that? When are you meeting with Faye?"

"Tomorrow. We're going to take a look at the artwork I have in storage."

"Okay then. Focus on that." I shake my head while he kneads his balls. "I still can't believe Danny is gay. I don't know why I'm surprised though. See, if she had gotten with a real man back in the day, she would be straight."

"Oh, really...what real man...you?"

"Hell no, I'm just talking."

"You need to stop talkin' because you don't know what you're talkin' about. Having good sex isn't gonna keep a person from being gay. Some people are born that way."

"The Bible says it's wrong. Ask Faye, she'll tell you."

"The Bible says a lot of things are wrong—like

fornication, lying…sound familiar."

"Okay, you are really messing up my mood, Sher. I'm gonna get up, take a shower, and go by New Hope."

"New Hope?"

"Gary invited me to come down so he could talk to me about New Hope's Rites of Passage Program for boys. I told him no at first because I wanted to spend the day with you, but you seem set on arguing all day, and that's not how I want to spend my Monday."

I watch him get up and head to the shower. I get a tingle in my choochie while staring at his ass. He may not be what he once was, but he still has a nice butt. My ringing phone on the nightstand snaps me out of my sensual stupor. I grab the phone and smile when I see Vicky's name appear. I can't believe she's calling me all the way from New York.

"Vicky!"

"Hey, Sher, what's up?"

"What's up with you? How's The Big Apple?"

"Good. It's day two and I'm having a blast. Yesterday we went to the Botanical Gardens in the Bronx."

"That sounds awesome. How's Danny and Frankie?"

"Good."

"Is it weird? I mean…you know, hanging out with them," I ask.

"No, they're really cool. The reason I called is to see if you still think group therapy's a good idea. I know I told Faye it was, but I'm having second thoughts. I'm having such a great time with Danielle, and I had a great time with you at Brad that day and with Faye. We're all getting along now. I just think it might not be a good time to drag everything up."

I sit there listening to Vicky's logic, but not quite agreeing with her. Vicky played the biggest role in what went down that night and it would be to her advantage not to revisit things, but we need to. "No, Vicky, we need to get closure and Mrs. Brown gave me the name of Sabrina's therapist. I've already set up an appointment for when you and Danielle get back to LA." I wait for her response, but there's silence. "Vicky?"

"I'm here. I guess you're right."

"Of course I am. Now go and enjoy the rest of your trip, and I'll see you when you get back."

"Okay, Sher, talk to you later."

I hang up the phone and breathe a deep sigh of relief, wanting to get this therapy thing over with so we can move forward with our lives. The thought of my upcoming art show puts a smile on my face and hope in my heart. I imagine it being successful and making a lot of money. Wouldn't that be ironic if I got rich and famous and was able to move us out of this hell hole?

"Who was on the phone?" Gary asks, coming out of the bathroom, dripping wet. He grabs a towel out of the basket of newly washed laundry next to the dresser and dries himself.

"Vicky."

"I thought she was in New York."

"She is."

"Why is she calling?"

"She's trying to get out of doing group therapy."

"Wow, ain't that nothin'. Y'all gonna still do it?"

"Of course."

"Good."

I pull up to Faye's mini-mansion with a gut full of butterflies. Gripping the steering wheel with my sweaty hands, I try to pull it together. I could really use a cigarette right now, but I'm glad I don't have any. "God help me!" Okay, that's better. I pull the visor down and look at myself in the mirror. I can already see the difference since I've stopped smoking. A lot of the fine lines under my eyes are going away. When Faye and I go to the Spa again, I'm going to get a bottle of that Spalacious night cream. Shoot, I'm gonna have it going on in a minute. I don't know why I'm so nervous about seeing my old paintings. I guess because it's been so long since I've seen them and Faye may not think they're good enough. My phone rings and I pick it up off of the passenger seat. It's Faye. "I'm right outside, " I say.

"You can come in for a minute or we can head out. I'm going to drive us," Faye says.

"I'll come in for a minute. I have to use the restroom."

"Okay."

I hang up the phone and walk to the front of her house. I stand back, still in awe of her crib and the tall arch glass door. I reach for the bell and the door opens.

"Hello, Sheridan, so glad to see you again."

"Hi, Melba, it's good to see you, too. Where's Faye? She just called me."

"She's in the kitchen. She said you had to use the restroom. Go to the one right down the hall. I just finished cleaning it and it smells like roses!"

"Thank you, but I can't promise you it's going to still smell like roses when I'm done."

Melba turns red and we both laugh. "You are so funny, Sheridan."

"Sherry," Faye says, entering.

"I'm just going to the restroom. I'll be right out."

"Okay," she says.

I make my way to the restroom and the smell of roses gives me pause. I chuckle, thinking about what I told Melba. It's so clean in here, I could eat off of the floor. I close the door and do my business. Tapping my feet on the rust colored marble tile, I wonder how much a bathroom like this would cost. The matching green marble tub and sink with gold plated faucets is off the chain. If my art show is a hit...wow. I finish up, wash my hands, and take another look at my face. I look five years younger. I turn to leave, but then a thought crosses my mind to peek into Faye's medicine cabinet. I know it's wrong, but the curiosity is killing me. I quickly open it before I lose the nerve and give it a once over. There's aspirin, a couple of toothbrushes still in the original packaging, some toothpaste, a few prescription bottles, and a box of home pregnancy tests. Two in the box...hmm.

"Sherry, are you okay?"

I shut the cabinet door and say, "Yes. I'll be right out." That was close. I spray the air freshener and exit.

"I love your restroom," I say, joining Faye in the foyer.

"Thanks, you look nice. There's something different about you."

I point to my face. "It's because I don't smoke anymore. I can already see a difference."

"I can, too. You look great."

"I feel better, too. I think I'm going to start working out."

"That's fabulous, Sherry. I'm so happy for you."

"You look good, too."

"Thanks," she says. "But I haven't been feeling well lately."

"What's wrong?"

"It's just a lot going on up at the church. I think I'm stressed. Oh, guess who called me today?"

"Who?" I ask.

"Vicky."

"You're kidding," I say.

"No, I'm not. She called me all the way from New York."

"She called me, yesterday," I say. "Let me guess, she wanted to know if you still wanted to do group therapy."

"Exactly. I told her yes. Girl, I'm so ready to close that

chapter to my life," Faye says.

"You and me both," I say.

Faye turns toward the dining room and calls Melba. She enters the foyer, with a rag draped over her arm. "What is it First Lady?"

"Melba, please, you know you don't have to call me First Lady."

"I know…I just slip sometimes. What can I do for you?"

"Can you tell Montana I changed my mind. I'd like Cornish Hens tonight. Tell her to save the fish for Friday."

"Will do."

"We'll see you later," Faye says.

"Bye, Melba," I say, wishing I had a Melba and Montana of my own.

Faye pulls into the storage company parking lot. She parks and then passes her hand over her stomach and shuts her eyes.

"Are you going to be okay?" I ask.

"Yeah, I'm fine. I ate too fast this morning."

"Don't front. If you're not feeling well, we can do this on another day."

"No you don't," she says, wagging her finger at me.

"What?"

"You're not getting out of this. You have a show next month and it'll be here before you know it. November is perfect because it's right before Christmas and you'll get a lot of sales."

"Are you sure Mark is okay with us having it at the church? You know I keep thinking about that message your father preached when we were in high school about Jesus chasing those money changers out of the temple."

"Girl, he is more than okay with it, especially with a

portion of the proceeds going to the children's ministry. Come on, let's go check your work out."

I follow Faye to the office like she's the one who's going to conduct business. She motions for me to hurry. We enter and an obese man wearing bifocals grins, revealing tobacco-stained teeth. I'm so glad I don't smoke anymore.

"How can I help?" he asks, putting his cigarette out in the full ashtray on the counter.

I set my paperwork next to the ashtray. "I'd like to access my storage."

He takes the paper, reads it over, and nods. "No problem. You're a very luck lady."

"What do you mean?"

"You're way past due on your bill and your unit is up for auction tomorrow."

"Are you serious?"

"Dead serious," he says, pointing to a bulletin board on the wall.

"I need my stuff. Please don't sell it."

"Pay up and you can get it all today."

"How much do I owe?"

Faye and I exchange glances while the man pulls out a file. He takes out what looks like an invoice and slams it on the desk. I skim the paper and groan. "Hell, this is almost more than my mortgage was on my house in Dallas."

"Let me see it," Faye says, taking the paper.

"I can't believe this!" I say.

"Calm down. I got this."

"Faye, I don't want you paying my storage bill."

She ignores me and turns toward the man. "If I give you cash would it be possible to cut the bill in half?"

The man grins and chortles. "I'd be open to that." Faye reaches in her purse and takes out a wad of money. What the hell. She's ballin'. She counts out what I owe and the man snatches it. "Nice doing busy with you." He stamps paid on the invoice and then says, "I have a key that will get you in." He reaches in a drawer and hands me a key. "Take the elevator out back. It'll take you right to your unit."

Faye and I leave and head to my space. "Girl, I'm gonna pay you back. I can't believe you did that."

"You don't have to pay me back. We'll make it all back with the sale," she says.

I shake my head in disbelief and accept the blessing. When we get to my unit, I unlock the door and turn the light on. Faye gasps when she sees the stacks and stacks of paintings, some propped up and some lying down. My stomach drops at her reaction.

"You hate it?"

"No, I love it. Girl, this is fabulous."

"I did a lot of it after Gary got drafted. It kept me busy…that and taking care of Kim."

"We're gonna need a truck to haul this out of here."

I give Faye a questioning look.

"Don't worry, New Hope has several trucks."

"Why don't we go through it and pick out the best pieces," I suggest.

"That's a good idea," Faye says.

She goes straight to a panting of Gary in uniform on the football field. "I'm loving this one," she says.

I clear my throat and she averts her eyes. "Not because…not…it's just a good painting, Sher."

"I know, don't mind me. I'm tripping. Don't laugh at me, but Gary and I were doin' it and all I could see was the two of you getting it on."

Faye stumbles backward and bats her eyes. "TMI! That is way too much information. Please, please, keep me out of your bedroom. Trust me, there was nothing romantic or sexy about what Gary and I did. It hurt like crazy."

"I know. I try not to think about it."

"Please, Sherry, please don't. Can we just put it to bed, no pun intended, right here and now?"

"I promise," I say.
"Thank you!" she says.

Chapter 22

Faye

Brushing the dust off of my jeans, I watch Sheridan put my second favorite painting with the others that we've set aside for her art show. It's a painting of the Cathedral Santuario de Gaudalupe in Dallas, Texas. The church was built in the 1800's and it has the second largest Catholic church membership in the United States. I have a thing for old churches of all denominations. Sheridan painted it while she was living in Dallas. She really captured the mystic feel of the building. We've been going through her artwork for a couple of hours now and I'm beat. She has some great pieces, and I think she's going to do well. I just wish she would move forward and let go of what happened with Gary and me. I guess I have to be patient with her. It was a shock and I don't know how I'd react if some sister at New Hope came to me and told me she had had sex with Mark twenty years ago, got pregnant, and had an abortion. I'd probably banish her from the church.

"So you think we have enough?" Sheridan asks.

"More than enough. With everything we want set aside, it'll be easy for the guys to load it all."

"Thank you so much, Faye."

"Don't thank me, thank God. All perfect gifts come from Him. Are you ready to go? I'm starving," I say.

"Yeah, let's go and get something to eat. Food tastes so much better now since I've stopped smoking."

"I told you it would," I say.

Sheridan turns the light off and locks up. We turn to each other and high five and make our way to my car. A few feet away, I'm hit with a wave of nausea and curl over.

"Okay, hold up, Faye, you're not well and you're going home right now!"

"No, I'm fine," I say, standing upright.

"You're not." Sheridan takes my keys, puts me in the passenger seat, and gets behind the wheel.

"What are you doing?" I ask.

"Taking you home. You're in no condition to drive."

"You are really overreacting, Sherry."

"I don't know what's wrong with you, Faye, but I'm not going to let anything happen to you on my watch. No lady," she says, starting up my car.

"But—"

"But nothing," she says.

We put our seatbelts on and I put my seat back and let her drive. I think about the pregnancy tests I have hidden away in the guest bathroom medicine cabinet. It's taken everything in me not to use them. My period's a week late, but I'm afraid to take a test. I don't think I could endure a negative test result. It would be devastating. I'd have a better chance at winning the lottery than getting pregnant. Sheridan continues to sneak peeks at me while she drives.

"Does Mark know you haven't been feeling well?"

"No, I didn't want to worry him unnecessarily. He has a lot on his plate."

"If you don't tell him, I will."

"Wow, Sherry, it's probably nothing—probably just a little virus."

"I've lost one good friend and I don't intend on losing another one—at least not for a very long time!"

I watch Sherry wipe away the tears falling from her eyes and get choked up. She's still reeling over Sabrina's death. We all are. It still hurts every time I think about losing her and not being able to have been there. "I miss Sabrina, too, Sherry."

"I just hate I wasn't allowed to be there," Sherry hisses.

"Me, too. That's the hardest part," I say. "Sometimes, I think about what I would have said to her."

"I do, too," Sheridan says. "'Sabrina, if I could trade places with you, I would. I love you and I'll always love you. You're one of the most special people I've ever known.'"

"That's beautiful, Sherry. I'm sure she would have loved that," I say.

"What would you have told her in the end?" Sherry asks.

I think about Sheridan's question, wondering what I would have told Sabrina. I probably would have been so devastated I wouldn't have been able to talk. "I don't know…maybe I would have said, 'Sabrina, I'll always remember how you took charge in math class when we all first met. I was so scared that day, but you were an inspiration. And now you have ovarian cancer and you're handling it like a champ. One more time, you inspire me…'

I'd say something like that. Yuck, that sounds silly," I say.

"No it doesn't and Sabrina is probably looking down at us right now, thrilled because we're fulfilling her dying wish. Look at us, we're the Fresh Fi...Four. The Fresh Four now."

"You're right, Sherry. Take the next exit."

"Thanks. I can't believe I remembered how to get to your house."

"I appreciate you having my back, Sherry."

"Of course."

Standing in the guest bathroom, I open the medicine cabinet and stare at the box containing the little stick that will tell me if I'm going to be a mommie again. I've been standing here for ten minutes now. Sherry left right after she dropped me off about two hours ago. She made me promise I would call Mark and let him know I'm not feeling well. I have yet to make the call, but I plan to. I'm hoping I'll be able to tell him I'm pregnant when I do make the call. I take a deep breath and reach for the box. I can't believe I have so much riding on this box and what's inside it. Then I think back to the last time I took a home pregnancy test and how painful it was when it came back negative. With that thought in mind, I slam the medicine cabinet shut and leave the restroom. I just don't have the courage to do it and maybe I actually do have a virus and am not pregnant.

I head to the kitchen where Montana is busy cooking dinner. The sun is setting and I peer out the window at the golden, hazy sky. "Smells good, Montana."

"Thanks."

"Are you okay?" Montana asks.

"Yes, why?"

"You haven't seemed like yourself lately," she says.

"I guess I just have a lot on my mind."

"Let me know if I can fix you anything special to cheer you up," she says.

"That's sweet of you."

"Lucy, I'm home!"

We turn at the sound of Mark's voice.

"My crazy husband is home, Montana."

"I see," she says with a glint in her eye.

I leave the kitchen and meet Mark in the foyer. He drops his briefcase and gives me a hug and a kiss. "How's everything?" he asks.

"Good. Sherry left a couple of hours ago."

"Did you get to see her paintings?"

"Yep and we got a gold mine—about a hundred pieces."

"Wow!"

"She's really talented, Mark."

"I'm impressed. I guess it runs in the family."

"What do you mean?" I ask.

"You know I met with Gary about the Rites of Passage Program. He has some really good ideas."

"That's great," I say.

"I think he'll be a good asset."

"Did he say anything about joining New Hope?"

"No, but I think there's a good chance he will. What about, Sherry?" Mark asks.

"No, but I think she will, too. Wouldn't that be wonderful if Vicky joined, too."

"Yeah...isn't she in New York?"

"She is. She comes back Wednesday. Her and Danny. We're scheduled to do group therapy this weekend."

"That's great. I'll be praying for you ladies. What's for dinner?"

"Cornish Hens."

"Let's eat."

"Okay, baby," I say, following Mark to the kitchen.

Sweat sprouts from my forehead while I stare at the open medicine cabinet. I wring my wet hands and force my feet to move forward. Taking a deep breath, I pass my hands over my nightgown and shut and open my eyes. I make it to the edge of the sink and press forward, slowly lifting my arm. I snatch the box containing the home pregnancy test and move away from the sink. My heart is racing and I feel faint. "Dear God, give me the strength to take this test and to accept the outcome." I sit on the toilet and slowly open the box, repelling the images from my last encounter with a home pregnancy test. The stick covered in white paper stares at me, mocking me. The devil is a liar! I pull the stick out and remove the paper covering. There's a round window and horizontal window. A plus sign in the window means I'm pregnant. "Lord, please let me get a plus sign." I rise, lift my gown, and sit on the toilet, with the stick between my legs. I relax my muscles and let my urine flow. After five or so seconds I stand and with a trembling hand, set the stick on the sink. I fall back on the bathroom door a nervous wreck, afraid to see the results. "Give me the strength, Lord." I inch my way over and look down at the stick. NEGATIVE! I fall to the floor, shaking and sobbing. The sound of laughter gives me pause. I look up and a baby is sitting on the edge of the sink. He's laughing and pointing at me. His eyes are blood shot and bulging. His mouth is wide. He stops laughing and sticks his serpent tongue at me, hissing, and wheezing. "NEGATIVE, BITCH! YOU AIN'T PREGNANT AND YOU'RE NEVER GONNA GET PREGANT, BECAUSE YOU KILLED ME, BITCH. YOU MURDERED ME!"

I jump to my feet and grab the demon baby around its neck. I choke it so hard, the veins in its forehead protrude. "The devil is a liar. You're a liar. You're a liar! I am going to get pregnant. I deserve to be pregnant. You're a liar! A liar! A liar!"

"Faye, Faye, wake up! Wake up, baby."

I open my eyes and Mark is trying to get the pillow out of my grip. "Oh my God, Mark. My God. I had a demonic dream. Satan himself was trying to curse me." I release the pillow and fall onto Mark's chest. He holds me and passes his hand over my arm.

"It's okay, baby. Satan can't hurt you. You're a child of God."

"I know he can't. He has no power over me and we're going to get pregnant. I know that now, because if we weren't, I wouldn't have had that dream. Satan is on the attack. He knows that we love God and that any child we have is going to love God, too. He doesn't want that."

"You're right, baby."

"I haven't been feeling well. I think I might be pregnant, Mark?"

Mark sits up straight and stares at me. "Are you serious?"

"Yes, I am."

"What kind of symptoms have you had?"

"I feel nauseous in the mornings and a little faint at times."

"Do you want to take a pregnancy test?"

"I will. Not now, in the morning."

"Sure, we'll do it together. Do you want me there with you?"

"Yeah, that would be nice."

"Okay, I'm excited," Mark says.

"I am, too, baby. Let's get some sleep."

"Okay, Dimples."

"Dear Lord, we thank You for giving us sleep grace and for waking us up this morning. Father God, we're asking You for a miracle. We're asking You to let Faye be pregnant this morning, Lord. We know You're a merciful and loving God and that You promised to give us the desires of our heart if we follow and obey You. Well, Lord, we're asking You to keep Your promise this morning. These prayers we pray, in the mighty name of Jesus, Amen."

"Amen," I say, looking up at Mark. "Thank you, baby."

"No, thank you, for being my wife and for being my friend."

We let go of each other's hands and I go into the bathroom boldly.

"You sure you don't want me to come in?"

"I'll be fine, baby. No matter what the outcome," I say.

I close the door and get the test from the medicine cabinet. I stop and notice that my hands are no longer shaking. I remove the test stick from the box and its protective covering, lift my gown, and sit on the toilet. I pee on the stick as directed and when done, I set it on the edge of the sink.

"Is everything okay?" Mark asks, on the other side of the door.

"I'm fine, baby. I just finished." I wait a couple more minutes and then I go to the stick. I pick it up and I stare at the window. My heart starts racing and I'm suddenly short of breath. I can't breathe. I put the stick down and gasp for air.

"What's going on, Faye? Faye? Faye!"

I try to answer Mark, but I'm too busy trying to get some air. The next thing I know he bursts through the door. "My God, Faye." I motion to him that I can't breathe. He cups my face in his hands. "Listen to me, baby, you're having a panic attack. I want you to breathe. Look at me and breathe along with me." I began to breathe with him and I find air. After a couple of moments I calm down. My eyes fill with tears and I fall onto his chest, trembling. "Don't worry about it. It's not God's will yet. I still love you—baby or no baby."

"But—"

"Sshh, it's okay," he says.

I pull out of his embrace and grab the stick. "Mark, I got a plus sign! I got a plus sign! We're pregnant! We're pregnant! That's what I was trying to tell you. I was so shocked, I panicked."

He snatches the stick from me and looks at it and shouts, "Glory be to God! Glory be to God! Thank you, Jesus. We're pregnant!"

Melba appears in the bathroom doorway, red in face. "What's wrong?" she asks.

"We're pregnant, Melba!" Mark screams.

"That's wonderful, Mr. Mark. So wonderful. I'm so happy for you, both." She hugs us and runs down the hallway. "They're pregnant, Montana, they're pregnant!"

Mark and I laugh and bask in our good news.

Chapter 23

Victoria

Sitting in Sparks Steak House, Frankie and I exchange smiles while Danielle wraps up her call with Faye. Ten minutes ago Danielle received a call from Faye telling us she's pregnant. She said she found out this morning and that the doctor confirmed it this afternoon. I'm ecstatic for Faye and Mark, but I can't help but think about the last time we got news about someone being pregnant in the group and that someone was Sheridan. Up until the moment she told us, I still thought I had a chance with Gary. In fact, I had spoken to him the day before without Sheridan knowing. We had planned to meet. I told him I had something very important to tell him and that we needed to be alone. I had planned to seduce him and get pregnant myself. I had concocted the seduction for months and I timed it so I'd be ovulating. He and Sheridan had been having some problems and she suspected he was cheating on her. She was even spying on him and following him. I felt my timing couldn't have been more perfect. But I never got a chance to execute my plan, because Sheridan beat me to the punch.

"Isn't that wonderful?"

"What?" I ask.

"Isn't it wonderful that Faye is pregnant?" Danielle asks.

"Yes, I'm thrilled for her and Mark. It couldn't have happened to a nicer couple," I say, shifting in my seat.

"She must be on cloud nine," Frankie says.

"She is," Danielle says.

We all exchange curious glances and turn our attention to the waiter when he approaches.

"Can I get you ladies anything else?"

"Actually, you can," Danielle says. "Bring us a bottle of champagne. We have something to celebrate."

"I will do just that and if you don't mind me asking, what's the special occasion?"

"A good friend of ours just found out she's going to have a baby."

"Excellent, I'll be back right away," he says, turning on his heel.

I swallow hard and wring my hands underneath the table. I haven't had the opportunity to tell Danielle about my situation and I really don't want to. She and Frankie have me on a pedestal so high, I can't seem to climb down. After feeling like the scum of the earth for so long, I'm relishing my new reputation—even though it's not merited. I know I'm going to have to tell her the truth about me sooner than later. I can't believe Faye didn't mention it. I just don't want to bring everybody down with my drama. But then they're going to wonder why I won't drink with them. Maybe one drink won't hurt. Crap, what am I saying? If only I could control it. But I can't.

"Vicky, are you okay?" Danielle asks.

"I'm fine."

"You don't look fine. You look ill."

"I hope you didn't get food poisoning," Frankie says.

"No, I'm sure I didn't," I say, looking at the small piece of steak left on my plate. "The steak was good. I'm just a little sad the trip is ending so soon."

"We can pick up where we left off once we get back to L.A. I plan to stay for at least a week," Danielle says.

"Right."

"What was your favorite tourist attraction?" Frankie asks.

"The Gardens."

"I told you it would be great."

"The Empire State building was good, too. All of it was nice and you and Danny have been wonderful hostesses. Don't mind me."

"Ladies, here's your champagne."

My stomach flips when the waiter sets three glasses down and pops the cork. Danielle and Frankie giggle and clap. I sit there and try not to panic. My mouth waters while I watch the waiter pour the bubbly into the glasses. I reach my trembling hand out to stop him when he comes to my glass. He raises his brow.

"None for me," I say.

He looks at Danielle and says, "Okay, as you wish." He sets the bottle down, nods, and leaves.

"You're not having any?"

"No, I think I'll pass, Danny."

"Aww, come on and have a celebratory drink with us," Frankie urges.

"Thanks, but I'll pass," I say.

"You're hurting my feelings," Frankie says. She picks up the bottle and attempts to pour champagne into my glass.

"I said, I'll pass, dammit!" I knock the bottle away and it falls onto the table. Champagne spills on the table and onto Frankie's lap. She jumps up, grabs the napkin from the table, and dabs at her wet jeans. She looks at me, rolls her grey eyes, and pulls the scrunchie out of her hair. Her locks fall onto her shoulders. Before she has a chance to part her full lips, I say, "I'm sorry. I'm sorry," and bolt to the ladies room.

I press the door open and pray the restroom is vacant. I hear a toilet flushing and a young woman comes out. She ignores me, washes her hands, and exits. I stand at the sink looking at myself, wondering when I'm ever going to be able to be around alcohol without it stressing me out. The door to the ladies' room opens and Danielle enters with a face coated in concern.

"Are you okay?" she asks, standing next to me.

I shake my head.

"What's wrong?"

"I didn't want anything to drink."

"Yeah, I can see that."

"Please tell Frankie, I'm sorry. I didn't mean to knock the bottle out of her hand."

"You can tell her yourself. You don't have to drink. It's okay."

"It's more to it than that."

"What do you mean?"

"I *can't* drink."

"*Can't* drink?"

"I'm an al—"

Two teenaged girls flounce in yapping and talking too loud for indoors.

"Can we go somewhere and talk, Danielle?"

"Sure, follow me," she says.

I follow her out of the restroom into a small private

dining area.

"We can talk here."

I look around, wondering if it's really okay to be in the small room with one long table and about a dozen chairs.

"It's okay, Vicky, I'm a regular here. We sit down and she cups her chin with her hand, seemingly waiting for me to talk. "What's going on? Why did you react like that?"

"I'm an alcoholic."

"What?"

"Yes, I *can't* drink. I stopped drinking right after…you know…and I didn't start drinking again until three years ago. I notice Danielle's jaw tense and I pause.

"Why three years ago?"

"Curtis and I were really doing well at that time. He had been promoted to a managing director at the bank and I was getting all kind of teaching awards, the kids were excelling in school…life was great."

Vicky rubs her eyes. "I'm confused. If life was so great, why would you drink?"

"Because I didn't feel like I deserved my life after…after…what happened."

Tears well up in Danielle's eyes and her face reddens. "Right."

"Sabrina didn't even know I was drinking. Then when she dropped out of my life, my drinking intensified."

"When did you stop?"

"A week before Sabrina's funeral I had a whole year of sobriety."

"What do you mean '*had* a whole year of sobriety.'"

"I had gone a year without drinking and that night at the repast I ended up in the cellar drinking again."

Danielle rolls her eyes and shakes her head.

"I felt guilty about what had happened with us and about what had happened to my kids."

"What happened to your kids?"

"They were almost molested by this man I met at a bar. I was drunk and he followed me home. He brought my purse to me and I let him in. If it weren't for the police and my babysitter, he would have hurt my babies." I wipe at the tears falling down my face and wait for Danielle to give me some words of encouragement. She just stares at me—through me.

"So let me get this straight…after everything that happened with us, you decided to drink again three years ago and you got so drunk you put your kids in harm's way, not to mention other innocent drivers and pedestrians. And then you got sober and got drunk again?"

I nod.

"You are freaking pitiful! You haven't changed, Vicky. You're still a self-centered, conniving, lying bitch. It's always been about you. Always! You tried to destroy Gary and Sheridan's relationship. You're just a destructive asshole."

I sit there mortified while Danielle goes off on me, wondering where the sweet Danielle who met me at JFK is. "But, Danny—"

"But nothing! You always have an excuse. If it wasn't for you, Richard would be alive today. You killed my brother, bitch! You did. It's all because of you! I hate you! I hate you!"

"Danny, calm down," I say, reaching out to her.

"Don't tell me to fucking calm down, and don't touch me! You ruined my life, my parents' life, get out of my face. I can't stand to be in the same room with you!"

"What's going on?" Frankie, accompanied by a man who looks like security, approaches.

"I want her out of our house. Now! Get her out now!"

"Calm, down, Danny," Frankie says.

"She killed my brother and let some pervert almost molest her kids."

"Stop, Danny. Get hold of yourself," Frankie says.

"Ma'am, do you need me to call a cab?" the man asks.

"No, we drove."

"Can you call me a cab?" I ask. "Frankie, I'll call you about my things."

"Where are you going?"

"I'll find a place to stay the night. My flight is in the morning. And I guess, it's safe to assume you won't be going back with me and you won't be participating in the group therapy session," I say to Danielle.

"Bitch, I wouldn't go around the corner with you and screw therapy. You're a hopeless case, *Victoria!*"

"On that note, bye," I say.

I leave the restaurant with my tail between my shaky legs. The man who intervened with Frankie ushers me to the exit where a cab is standing by. I look over my shoulder wistfully, hoping Danielle has had a change of heart, but I don't see her or Frankie. I get in the cab and the driver asks, "Where to?"

"I need a hotel near JFK."

"How about the Hilton?"

"That's fine," I say.

The driver takes off and I sit there going over what just happened. I feel like I had an out of body experience. Danielle couldn't have said those things to me. She couldn't have meant what she said. I reach for my phone and start to call Faye, but I don't want to spoil things for her. She sounded so happy on the phone about being pregnant. Scanning my contacts on my phone, Sheridan's name comes up. I hit the call button and Teena Marie's " I Need Your Lovin'" fills my ear. "I can use some lovin' myself right about now." I wait for Sheridan to answer, thinking about the day Teena Marie died. It was the day after Christmas in 2010. I was so tempted to call Sheridan, but I never made the call. Even if I had had the courage, I didn't have her number.

"Vicky...what's up?"

"Sherry...hi."

"Hi, girl, what's going on? Aren't you still in The Big Apple?"

"Yeah and I've made a *big* mess of things."

"What else is new?" she asks, laughing.

"It's not a funny matter."

"My bad. What's going on?"

"I told Danny I was an alcoholic and she went off of me." I look up and meet the driver's eyes in the rearview mirror. He quickly looks away.

"Really?"

"She called me a bitch and said I killed Richard. It was horrible."

"Dang. When and where did all of this happen?"

"At a restaurant less than twenty minutes ago."

"What did her wife do?"

The driver clears his throat and shakes his head.

"Frankie was trying to calm her down, but couldn't. She told me to get out of her house. Girl, I'm on my way to the Hilton, and I'll be on the first flight back to L.A. tomorrow."

"What the— "

"And get this…she's not coming to L.A. and she's not going to participate in our group therapy session."

"Now, that's jacked up," Sheridan says. "Are you sure you can't make up with her?"

"Sheridan, she acted like she wanted to kill me. I've never seen her that pissed before."

""She's hurting, Vicky. Her rage is just pain inverted."

"Wow, you sound like you know what you're talking about."

"Don't give me too much credit. I read that on Dr. Hayes's website."

"Is that the therapist?"

"Yeah, Phyllis Hayes. So what are you going to do now?"

"Try to get some rest and come home in the morning."

233

"Whatever you do, don't drink," Sheridan says.

"OMG!" I say.

"What?"

"Sherry, during this whole time, I never once thought about having a drink. It's a miracle!"

"Yeah it is. That and Faye being pregnant. Now let's just see if God will give us another one with Danielle. We need her at that therapy session."

"You're right. Okay, I'll see you when I get back."

"Vicky, I'll call Faye and see if she's available for lunch. The three of us can put our heads together about this Danny situation."

"Okay, that sounds like a good idea. Bye."

"Love you, Vicky."

"I love you, too, Sherry."

Chapter 24

Danielle

Pressing on my head, I follow Frankie to the elevator of our building. I need an aspirin, no, I need a lobotomy to stop this searing pain in my head. Frankie looks over her shoulder at me, her eyes filled with worry. She's never seen me get as upset as I did at the restaurant. She's probably glad it was *Victoria* I went off on and not her. I have to make a mental note not to ever say that woman's name again. All she ever did was cause problems. I remember the first day we met in math class when we were in middle school. The teacher put us in a group and Sabrina wanted to give us a name. Sheridan wanted to call us the Fabulous Five, but Vicky didn't like it. She was the only person who didn't like the name, so I suggested we be called The Fresh Five to keep the peace.

The elevator door opens and Frankie and I get on, silent, sharing knowing glances. Thank God I don't have to go to the office tomorrow. I need to call the others to let them know I'm not coming to L.A. The elevator stops on the twelfth floor and we get off and make our way to the condo. Frankie unlocks the door and we enter. She goes to the kitchen and I toss my purse onto the coffee table and sit on the sofa, wondering where my cell phone is. I don't remember putting it in my purse, but then again I could have.

"Looking for this?" Frankie asks, handing me my phone.

"Thanks."

"Are you going to be okay? You know you could have had a stroke back there."

"I'm fine, Frankie, and I wasn't going to have a stroke."

"You don't know that. Women our age have to be careful."

"Frankie, I know you mean well, but can you give me some space please? I need to make a few calls."

"Why don't you talk to me? Why do you have to call L.A. when I'm right here?"

"I know you're here, but you weren't there."

"Where?"

"You weren't there when my brother was killed."

"Danny, you won't even talk to me about it. That's not my fault."

I rise and with my hand on my head say, "If you want to do me a favor, please get me a glass of water and some aspirin."

"No problem," she says, heading toward the restroom.

I sit down and go through my contacts. I would call Faye, but I don't want to put a damper on her baby bliss right now. I get to Sheridan and I hit call. I listen to Teena

Marie sing her heart out while I wait for Sheridan to pick up. Fifty-four…Teena died at fifty-four. Why do the good die so young? Richard was only twenty. He wasn't even old enough to legally drink. How ironic.

"Danny!"

"Hey, Sheridan."

"What's going on?" she asks.

"Not a whole lot," I say. "What are you doing?"

"Going over my RSVPs for my art show. A lot of people have responded."

"Oh…okay…you know what, don't worry. I'll talk to you later."

"No…talk now."

"I don't want to bore you with—"

"Vicky already called, Danny. She told me you're not coming to L.A. and you're not going to do group therapy."

"Please don't mention that woman's name to me. Hold on a minute, Sherry." I look up at Frankie and take the glass of water and aspirin from her and down it all. "Thanks, babe," I say to Frankie.

"Let me know when you're ready to talk," she says, walking away.

"Will do," I say, handing her the glass.

"Danny…you there?"

"I'm sorry. I'm here. I have this huge headache and I just took some aspirin. As you know, that woman and I had a blow up."

"She told me you went off on her when she told you she was an alcoholic."

"She told me more than that, Sheridan. She almost got her kids molested with her drunk ass. Not to mention she's the reason Richard isn't with us today."

"She's not the only one responsible for Richard's death, Danny."

I swallow hard and drop my head.

"Danny?"

"I'm here."

"Please do me a favor and sleep on this thing. Don't quit five minutes before the miracle."

"I'm going to let you go. I need to talk to my wife."

"Think about what I said, Danny. We're too close to turn back now. I don't want Sabrina's death to have been in vain."

"Okay, Sherry, we'll talk," I say, hanging up.

I toss my phone onto the coffee table and drag myself to the master bedroom. Frankie, in her bra and panties, sits on the bed reading her column. "Are you done with your calls?"

"Yes, Danielle is done," I say, sitting on the bed. "Is that your column?"

"Yep."

"Why don't you read it to me?"

"You sure you wanna hear it?"

I give her a blank stare.

"Okay, it's called, 'Gender Blind Love.'"

"I like the title."

"Thanks."

"Okay, here it goes. Whoever said love…"

I lie back on the bed while Frankie reads her column to me. I hear her and I don't hear her, because her words are being drowned out by Sheridan's. *Think about what I said, Danny. We're too close to turn back now. I don't want Sabrina's death to have been in vain.* Sheridan's words reverberate in my head that's actually starting to feel better. I close my eyes and say a prayer for God to lead me in the right direction.

Standing at the American Airlines carousel in baggage claim at LAX, I crane my neck looking for Mother Brown. I told her I would meet her out front, but she insisted on meeting me inside the terminal. I turn my attention back to the bags being spit out and spot mine. I grab them and stop in my tracks when I hear Walter's voice. What the? My bags hit the ground with a thud.

"Danny!"

Wow…no Mother Brown didn't. What is he doing here? He sprints to me and gives me a bear hug. I stand there with my arms dangling at my side. "Where's Mother Brown?" I ask, pulling away from him.

"Mr. Brown had to run an errand and hadn't made it home yet. Mother Brown didn't want you to have to wait, so she asked me to come and get you. I was at Sabrina's mowing the lawn and doing some handyman work and a little plumbing. The guest bathroom toilet was stopped up."

This is way too much information. "Thanks," I say, trying not to sound too ungrateful. The last thing I want to do is ride anywhere with Walter.

He forces a smile and gives me a wary look. I motion to the bags and he grabs them. "I'm parked right across the way," he says. "By the way, how's your friend?"

"Frankie?"

"Right," he says.

"She's not just my friend, she's my *wife*." I wait for Walter to trip and fall and hit his head on the terminal floor, but he doesn't flinch. He presses the door leading outside open with his foot, and I help him get through with the bags. "Did you hear me?"

"I heard you, Danny. It's no big deal. I guessed as much when I saw her kissing your hand."

"You saw that?" I ask, while we cross the street.

"Yep."

"Boy, you sure played it cool."

"What was I supposed to do, burn you both at the stake?"

"So you're pro-gay marriage?"

"No, I'm pro-minding my own business and letting people be who they are."

"Okay."

"Here's my ride," he says, stopping at a blue pickup truck. He dumps my bags in the bed of the truck. I get in and he gets behind the wheel, and takes off. I sit there contemplating his stance on gay-marriage and life and smile. There's more to Walter than meets the eye. He's pretty progressive for a blue collar guy. But then again, I shouldn't be surprised. Sabrina was in love with him, so that speaks volumes to what Walter has to offer. Albeit, he was a coward and left her when she needed him most, but nobody's perfect. Trust me, I should definitely know.

He drives onto Century Boulevard with his eyes glued to the road. I wonder what he's thinking and if he knows about all the drama going on with the Fresh Four. "So have you uh…talked to anybody else lately?"

"You mean, Sheridan, Faye, or Vicky?"

"Yeah," I say.

"No, but Mother Brown did tell me Faye's expecting. I'm really happy for her."

"I am, too."

"Sabrina and I were talking about having kids right before she found out she had cancer."

My stomach quivers and I find myself putting my hand on Walter's that's resting on his knee. "I'm sorry."

"It's okay. In a way, it's good we didn't have kids. That would have made things even worse. I know Sabrina would have been even more devastated if she knew she wouldn't be able to see her kids grow up."

"I agree," I say, removing my hand. "Walter, is what Mother Brown said true? Did Sabrina not tell us she was sick because she was upset that we weren't talking to each other?"

"It's true," he says, turning onto La Cienega Boulevard.

"The Browns and I both tried to get her to get in contact with you all, but she wouldn't let us and we didn't want to go against her will…you know…with everything going on. She was hoping her death would shock you all into getting back together." He gives me a questioning look and asks, "Has it?"

"Time will tell," I say. "Can you do me a favor?"

"Sure."

"Don't tell any of the others that I'm here. I was supposed to come back with Vicky on Wednesday. But I'm a day late."

"Better late than never," he says, turning onto Sabrina's street.

"Right," I say.

Walter pulls into the driveway behind the Brown's car. Just as I'm about to get out, my phone rings. I put it on speaker and say, "I made it, Frankie."

"Tell her I said hello."

"Walter says hello."

"I heard him. Hello, Walter."

"We just got here. I'll call you later."

"Okay, sweetie. Love you."

"Love you, too."

"And I'm proud of you, Danny."

"For what?"

"For going?"

"It's still early. Let's just see if I can make it until Saturday."

"You will," she says.

"Bye."

Walter gets my bags. "What's going on Saturday?" he asks.

I scrunch my face, wishing I hadn't been on speaker.

"I'm sorry. It's none of my business."

"No worries." I follow him into the house and before we reach the door, Mrs. Brown flings it open and greets me with open arms.

"Danny, I'm sorry I didn't pick you up. Jerome took off with the car and was late getting back, and I don't feel comfortable driving Sabrina's car."

"No problem," I say, entering.

"You can have the master bedroom or the guest bedroom."

"I'll take the guest bedroom."

"Is that, Danny?" Mr. Brown asks, joining us in the foyer.

"It's me."

Mr. Brown hugs me and looks at my head. "I see you're letting your hair grow out. I like that better than that boy cut."

"Jerome, please," Mrs. Brown says. "Now tell me why you didn't bring your husband on this trip. When are we going to meet Frankie?"

Walter and I exchange conspiratorial looks. "I'll put your luggage in the guest bedroom," he says, leaving me to fend for myself.

"Mother Brown and Mr. Brown, my husband is actually my wife."

The Browns look at me like I had just told them the rapture had already taken place and that they had been left behind. "What do you mean your husband is your wife?" they ask.

"Frankie is Francine. He is a she."

Mr. Brown rubs his bald head and says, "Frankie is a woman."

"Right."

"You're married to a woman?" Mrs. Brown asks.

"Yes."

"So that means you're a lesbian."

"Not exactly, Mother Brown."

"Danielle, you are confusing the hell out of us," Mrs.

Brown says. "Forgive my language but…"

"It's a long story and I was hoping I could get some of your good cooking before I tell it to you."

"Of course. Come in the kitchen. I'm cooking up a storm."

"I'm going to wash up a bit and I'll be right in," I say, leaving them there with puzzled looks on their faces.

I run into Walter on my way to the guest bedroom. "So how did they take it?"

"I'm not sure," I say.

"They'll be cool. They're just happy to have you here. I hope you all work it out. It would make the Browns so happy and me, too."

"You, too?"

"Sabrina used to always tell me about you guys and all the stuff you did in middle and high school. So I felt like I knew the group…not just each of you separately and I used to fantasize about you all showing up to the house one day…surprising her. Let me be quiet. I'm talking way too much."

"It's okay, Walter. I miss Sabrina, too."

Walter hugs me and this time I hug him back—hard.

Chapter 25

Sheridan

Sitting on the patio at the Breeze restaurant in Century City, I lean back in my chair, looking up at the clear blue sky, feeling better than I have in a long time. Thanksgiving is right around the corner and so is my art show. I have a lot to be thankful for. The waitress approaches and before I have a chance to order another diet coke, Vicky and Faye call out to me.

"Do you want me to come back?" the waitress asks.

"Can you? I want my friends to have a chance to get seated."

"No problem."

I rise and meet Vicky and Faye half way. We group hug

and then stand back giving each other the once over. "Faye, you're glowing!" I say.

"You think so? I'm only a few weeks pregnant," she says.

"You *are* glowing," Vicky says. "And I love your little maternity outfit."

Faye passes her hand over her stomach. "I don't look ridiculous? I'm just so excited about being pregnant I couldn't resist buying some maternity clothes." She does a three-hundred and sixty degree turn, showing off her pink knit pants and matching top.

"Girl, knock yourself out," I say. "Why don't we have a seat and go over the menu. I'm starving."

"I am, too," Faye says. "You know I'm eating—"

"For two," Vicky and I say though laughter.

"You, two or not right," Faye says. "Lord, have mercy, it's a beautiful day," she continues, looking up at the sky.

"I was just thinking the same thing," I say.

We all pick up our menus and fall silent. I feel eyes on me and look up. "What's wrong, Vicky? You're staring at me."

"Did you have some work done?"

"What kind of work?" I ask.

"Botox, plastic surgery?"

"Heck no. Why?"

"Girl, you look ten years younger."

"I quit smoking and I'm using Spalacious Night Cream."

"It's working."

"She looks fabulous," Faye says. "In fact, we all do."

"We should change our name to the Fabulous Four," Vicky says.

"That's what I wanted to call us back in the day," I say.

"What do you guys think? Wanna change it?" Vicky asks.

We exchange tentative looks. "We probably should see

if Danielle would be open to changing the name," I say.

"I don't think she would mind," Vicky says.

"Has anyone talked to her?" I ask.

"I haven't," Faye says.

"Me neither," Vicky says.

"You think we should call her?" I ask.

"We probably should give her some time to cool off," Vicky says.

"But our therapy session is Saturday—two days away. We really need her to participate," I say.

"Let's pray on it," Faye suggests.

"You ladies decide yet?" the waitress asks, approaching.

"Can you bring us all water and I'd like another diet coke," I say.

"I'll take a diet coke, too," Vicky says.

"Cranberry juice for me," Faye says.

"Coming right up." The waitress leaves and we study our menus.

"I think I'm gonna have a cheeseburger with fries," I say. "I've been cutting back lately, but I feel like treating myself today."

"The salmon looks good," Vicky says.

"I think I'll have the Cobb Salad," Faye says. "Speaking of food, I want to have Thanksgiving over my house. Montana and Mother Brown are going to cook."

"That sounds good," I say.

"Are you excited about your art show?" Vicky asks.

"Yeah, I can't believe November 30th is right around the corner, and over two-hundred people have RSVP'd."

"Get out!" Vicky says.

"A lot of them are church members. But we got a lot of calls from Gary's old teammates and the coach and they're coming with their families. Gary's more excited than I am."

"We're going to raise a lot of money," Faye says.

The waitress returns with our drinks and we place our orders. After she leaves, we sit in silence that's quickly broken by Vicky. "I don't know about you all, but I'm nervous about Saturday."

"I am, too," Faye says.

"Me, too," I confess.

"What if we end up hating one another all over again? We've come so far," Vicky says.

"We have to promise one another that no matter what happens or what's said or discovered, that we won't let it come between us," Faye says. She reaches a hand out to each of us and we hold hands. "Come on you guys. Who are we?"

"THE FABULOUS FOUR!" We pick up our glasses, clink them, and drink up.

I think about Danielle, wondering how she's doing in New York and if we'll ever see her again. It would be a shame if she misses the therapy session and we move forward without her. I guess three is better than none. We'll be called The Fabulous Three or maybe we should be called The Together Three. That sucks. I don't know what we should be called. I just want the best for all of us.

When I pull into my driveway, I'm taken aback at the open garage. I squint looking for all the boxes and junk that was stacked from floor to ceiling. In its place are a treadmill, an elliptical machine, and a punching bag. In the center of the garage is Gary, jumping rope. He stumbles a bit, but isn't doing too badly. I get out of the car, wondering when he cleaned the garage out and where he got the gym equipment. I know he didn't get it on credit, because our FICA score is so low, it's in the single-digits.

"Hey, baby, how was lunch with the girls?"

"It was great. Where did all this stuff come from?"

"Mark gave it to me. He upgraded his home gym and he let me have all this equipment, and as you can see, I've started a workout program."

"That's great," I say, punching the oblong bag that's hanging from the ceiling.

"Careful, you don't want to mess up your hands. You're gonna need them to paint more pictures after your art show sells out."

"Baby, you think I'm gonna sell out?"

"Of course. You know the guys on my old team are going to buy you out. And with Christmas around the corner, you're gonna clean up."

"You know part of the money is going to the children's ministry at church."

"I know and that's a good thing."

"I'm glad you think so. Where's ma?"

"Next door at Mrs. Jenson's house. Speaking of mothers, babe, I was wondering, have you ever thought about finding your moms?"

I get a kick in my gut and my eyes sting and tear up. "No, what made you bring that up?"

"Since I've been working with the Rites of Passage Program at New Hope, I've come in contact with a lot of foster kids. It just made me think about your situation."

"There was a time I wondered about her, but not to the point of wanting to find her."

"If you ever decide you want to, let me know and I'll help you."

"I appreciate that, Gary. I really do. But right now I have my hands full with our lives. Shoot, who knows what my mother is even in to or if she's even alive. We're about to get on our feet and I don't want anything to mess that up."

"I feel you, babe" Gary says.

"I'm a get dinner on."

"Oh, Sher, by the way, I'm a need the car Saturday. I

have another meeting at church."

"What? I need the car Saturday. I like that you're hanging out with Mark, but you're starting to spend a lot of time at New Hope. There are a lot of things around here that need taken care of like—"

"The dishwasher?"

"Yes, the dishwasher."

"I fixed it."

"When?"

"This afternoon, right after you left."

"Oh…well thanks. But I need the car to go to my group therapy session."

"You can't have it!"

"Gary, what is your problem? You know I've had this meeting scheduled for two weeks, and I really don't want to bother Faye or Vicky for a ride."

"You don't have to bother them."

"So how am I gonna get there, on the bus?"

"No, in that," he says, pointing across the street.

I walk out of the garage and scan the cars parked across from our house, wondering what he's talking about. There's an old broke down, Toyota, a Honda like ours, but only black, and a gold Lexus, not a new one. It looks to be about five years old, but whoever owns it, is taking good care of it. Gary comes behind me and takes my hand. He puts a key in it. I stare at the Lexus logo on the key and then my eyes shift to the car and then to Gary, who's grinning from ear to ear.

"What's going on?" I ask.

"You don't have to go to your meeting on the bus, because you're going to go in your Lexus."

"My Lexus?"

He grabs my hand and pulls me across the street. He takes the key from me and I hear two chirps and the doors unlock. I get behind the wheel and he gets in the passenger seat. "Gary Devon Hawkins, what is going on? Where did you get this car?"

"I bought it today."

"How?"

"I bought it at a dealership."

"With what money and what credit?"

"With my own money."

"What money?"

"Money I've been saving, Sher."

"You've been holding out on me?"

"After Sabrina cut you off, I started putting a little money here and a little money there for a rainy day and it just added up."

"You paid cash for this?"

"Woman, calm down. I put a down payment on it and with my new job they gave me a deal."

"What new job?"

"I'm working at the church now. I'm the Director of the Boys Rites of Passage Program, and I'm also going to be coaching the boy members who are interested in playing football."

I sit in my new car feeling like the luckiest woman in the world. Faye's right, when you appreciate the little things in your life, God will bless you with even more. "That's wonderful, baby. I'm so happy for you."

"Why don't we take your new car for a spin?"

"Okay, and you know what?"

"What?"

"I'm so glad I don't smoke anymore. I wouldn't want to have my Lexus smelling like smoke."

"I feel you, Sher. Can I feel you, Sher?" he asks, putting his hands up my skirt.

"Man, you better stop."

"You know we need to christen your new baby?"

He grabs my boob and I slap his hand away. "If you don't stop, I'm gonna kick you out of my car."

He laughs. "Okay, I'll back off, but you better give it up

tonight."

"We'll see," I say.

Gary kisses me on the nape of my neck while spooning me. "That was so good, Sher. Did you enjoy it?"

For the first time in a long while I can honestly say I did. "It was off the chain."

"Just wait until I get in shape. I'm gonna really turn you out," he says, with a chuckle.

I turn over and peer up at the ceiling. "How long do you think it's gonna be before we move out of here?"

"Not long, baby. I'm working now. Mark's not paying me a mint, but thirty grand a year ain't nothin' to sneeze at. That combined with what's left of my pension…and then who knows what's going to happen with your artwork. I see us moving out of here by next summer. That's only seven months away. You think you can hold on 'til then?"

I nod and sigh. "I hope so. I really want to get a bigger and better place. You know…so Kim can bring her friends from school home. She called today. I'm so proud of her."

"I am, too. You did a good job raising her while I was playing ball, Sher. I appreciate that."

"She's always been a good kid," I say. "Sometimes I feel guilty…you know she's the same age Richard was when he died."

"Stop talking like that. I can't wait for you to go see that doctor so you can let go of the past."

"Saturday you'll get your wish. You know it's not just a one-time thing. Dr. Hayes says we may need several months of counseling."

"Who's paying for this?"

"Sabrina."

"Sabrina?" Gary asks.

"According to Dr. Hayes, Sabrina put money aside for us to get counseling."

"Dang, she thought of everything. She really wanted to see you guys get together."

"Now that may never happen because of Danielle."

"Have you tried calling her?"

"Yeah, but I just get her answering machine. Vicky and Faye tried, too. She's really pissed at Vicky."

"Don't get yourself all worked up. You, Faye, and Vicky do the right thing—do it for Sabrina, with or without Danielle."

"You're right," I say.

Chapter 26

Faye

Sitting at my vanity table, I read over Sabrina's obituary. I can't believe it's going on two months since we buried her. I put the obituary in the drawer closest to me and finish putting on my makeup. I decide not to wear any eyeliner or mascara because I have a feeling I'm going to do a lot of crying today. In two hours, our first therapy session starts and no one has yet to hear from Danielle. I prayed and asked God to move her heart, but I guess it just wasn't His will. There was a rumor going around that she was in L.A. at one point, but has since gone back to New York. I'm not sure who started the rumor. Sheridan said Gary ran into Walter on the Westside and Walter told him he had picked Danielle up from LAX a couple of days ago. Now we all know Walter is the last person Danielle would be seen with or take a ride from. Nonetheless, I plan to do everything I can to fulfill Sabrina's dying wish.

I put my lipstick on and run my fingers through my hair. Yes, *my* hair. I got my weave taken out after lunch with the girls Thursday. They're going to be so surprised. It feels good to wear my own hair. It has some length, but it's see-through thin. Nonetheless, I'm proud of it and Mark loves it. My obstetrician says that the prenatal vitamins I'm on should help thicken and grow it. Oh well, it is what it is.

I turn toward the door at the sound of whistling. "There she is...Mrs. America."

"Mark, you need to stop. You know I look a hot mess with my chicken-headed self."

"Woman, you better stop talking about my baby's mama!"

We laugh and hug each other. Mark drops to his knees and puts his ear to my belly. "Do you hear anything?"

"I sure do. Sshh."

"What's she saying?"

"You mean what's *he* saying?"

"Mark, I don't care if it's a boy or a girl, I just want our baby to be born healthy."

"He's saying, 'I have the prettiest mommie in the whole world and I can't wait to be born, so I can meet her. And I have the smartest father in the whole world and I can't wait to meet him, too.'"

I push Gary away and fall onto the bed, laughing and cackling. "Man, you are too much for me."

He sits next to me. "Are you sure you don't want me to drive you to your appointment?"

"No, I'll be fine."

"Have you heard from Danielle?"

"No, none of us have, but you know what, three is

better than none. That's what Sheridan said after lunch the other day."

"Hey, Father, Son, and Holy Ghost," Mark says.

"You're right," I say. "Is Montana done with breakfast?"

"Yeah."

"I better go ahead and eat so I can be there on time."

"I love you, First Lady."

"I love you too, Preacher Man."

I pull into the parking lot of the medical building on Wilshire Boulevard looking for any signs of Sheridan and Vicky. A thought sends chills through me. What if they don't show? Perspiration beads on my upper lip and I get short of breath. Lord, please don't let me have a panic attack. "Jesus, Jesus, Jesus." Suddenly a feeling of calm comes over me that puts me completely at ease. My peaceful feeling is interrupted by the sound of a horn. Squinting, I look in my rearview mirror at a gold Lexus coming my way. "Thank you, Jesus. It's Danny. Danny showed. It has to be her in a rental." I get out of my car and run to her. When I look in the passenger window of the car, Sheridan waves at me. My heart sinks.

Sheridan gets out of the car with a frown on her face. "What's wrong? Did I do something wrong?"

"No, I thought you were Danny in a rental car."

"Sorry to disappoint you," Sheridan says.

"No apologies necessary. It's me. I need to let it go. Give me a hug, girl."

Sheridan walks to me and holds me in a tight embrace. I look over her shoulder and take another look at the car. "Is that your car?" I ask, pulling out of our hug.

"Yep, Gary bought it for me."

"It's nice!" I say.

"It's not new...I mean...it's new for me, but not a new car like your Lexus."

"Girl, it's better to buy a car used than new because it depreciates as soon as you drive it off of the lot. Gary did good."

"Thanks, Dimples...OMG!!! OMG!!!"

"What's wrong with you, Sherry?"

"Your hair. You're wearing your own hair. When did this happen?"

"I had my weave taken out after lunch Thursday."

"I love it. Can I touch it?"

"Sherry, I guess you *are* a white girl after all...asking to touch my hair like it's some foreign object or something."

We laugh and she gently passes her hand over my little locks. "It's so soft. I bet Mark loves it."

"He does."

We get focused again and then Sheridan says, "I wonder where Vicky is."

"I think we better go in. We're running a little late," I say.

"You're right," Sheridan says.

We hold hands and briskly walk to the building. Sheridan opens the glass door and I enter first. She follows me and we go to the elevator bank.

"Dr. Hayes's office is on the 9th floor," Sheridan says.

We wait a few minutes and then the elevator door opens.

"Vicky!" Sheridan and I scream.

"Hey you guys," she says, nonchalantly.

"How long have you been here?" Sheridan asks.

"For about twenty minutes. I gave myself a little extra time because I didn't know how traffic was going to be."

"Where's your car? We didn't see your car."

"I drove Curtis's car today. It's the bronze Mercedes.

He took my car in for service. You guys better come on in. The elevator door is trying to close." We get on and she says, "I was coming to see if you guys were here yet. Did either of you happen to hear from Danielle?"

We shake our heads. "Let's just put Danielle behind us and do this," I say.

The elevator stops on the 9th floor. We get off and I swing my arm forward with my palm down. "Who are we Ladies?"

"The Triumphant Three," they say, placing their hands on top of mine.

We breakout in a gust of giggles that ends when Vicky yelps. "Faye! Wow! I just noticed. You're weave is gone. When did you take it out?" Vicky asks.

"After lunch Thursday."

"I love it," Vicky says. "The shorter hair makes you look even younger."

"Lord, if I knew I was going to get this kind of reaction, I would have gotten it taken out a long time ago. Thanks."

"We better get to our appointment," Sheridan says, leading the way.

We come to a closed door with a placard on it that says *Phyllis Hayes, Ph.D.* We enter and are greeted by a twenty-something receptionist with luxurious brown hair. She gives us a camera-ready smile. "How can I help you ladies?"

"We have an eleven o'clock appointment with Dr. Hayes," Sheridan says.

"That's right. You're Sabrina's friends," she says.

We all exchange looks of surprise.

"Sabrina talked about you all the time. Give me just a minute."

We share curious glances and wait for the receptionist to return. She comes back carrying a photo. She thrusts it forward and I take it from her. It's a picture of us in the seventh grade the day after we had won a math contest. Our teacher, Mrs. Crowley, had given us all ribbons and she pinned them to our clothes and took the photo and eventually gave us all a copy. I wonder why Sabrina gave the photo to the receptionist and why this photo. The receptionist must read my mind, because she says, "Sabrina gave me that photo because she said it represents the beginning—when you all were innocent and full of hope. She used to tell me she believed if she focused on that photo that it would help to bring you all back together. Something like coming full circle. She would bring it with her to her sessions with Dr. Hayes. Right before she passed away she gave it to me and told me to keep it and to give it to you all if you ever showed up. So, it's yours to keep."

The receptionist reaches for a box of tissue and hands it to us. We dab at the tears pouring from our eyes. Dr. Hayes comes out of her office. "Hey, no tears, ladies. I'm Dr. Hayes."

All watery eyes go to the tall woman with an afro bigger than Angela Davis's. She shakes our hands and asks, "Did you all meet Monica?"

"We did, but not formally," I say, putting the photo in my purse.

"Hello," Monica we say.

"Hello, everyone. Wait a minute, someone's missing," she says.

"Danielle," I say.

"Where is she?" Dr. Hayes asks.

"It's a long story," Vicky says.

"Why don't we get started," Dr. Hayes says. "Do any of you need to use the restroom?"

We shake our heads.

"Would you like some water?"

"I would," I say.

"Me, too," Sheridan and Vicky say.

"Monica, can you bring in some bottled water."

"Sure."

We follow Dr. Hayes into her office. I perk up when the smell of fresh potpourri wafts up my nose. "It smells good in here," I say.

"Thank you. Please have a seat," she says, motioning to several chairs surrounding a small round table.

Sheridan, Victoria, and I sit. I notice several degrees on the wall and a collage of photos. A large plant sits in the corner. Vicky's eyes are glued to it. I want to ask Vicky what kind of plant it is, but I try to stay focused. Monica enters with the water. She hands us each a bottle and we thank her. She quickly leaves and Dr. Hayes joins us at the table. She crosses her long legs and smiles. She lights up the room with her smile and her personality. I get a warm comforting feeling being in her presence. It all makes sense. I wonder what kind of conversations she and Sabrina had. We'll never know, because any and all things discussed in this office are confidential.

"Welcome, ladies!"

We giggle like school girls and sit at attention.

"It's been a long time getting you all here. Sshh...listen...can you hear that?"

"What?" we ask.

"Sabrina dancing and laughing because you all made it here. This is all she ever talked about. The Fresh Five! Who came up with that name?"

"Danielle," we say.

"We've recently changed our name to the Triumphant Three," I say.

"No more five?"

"Sabrina's no longer with us and we don't think Danielle is coming back to the group. She doesn't even live in L.A. anymore. She lives in—"

"New York," Dr. Hayes says. "Sabrina kept me abreast. I want you ladies to relax and stop thinking about Danielle. We're going to start with meditation. And that's going to consist of focusing on your breathing. Do you ladies mind getting on the floor?"

"No," we say.

"Perfect." Dr. Hayes removes the chairs and table and goes to a closet in the corner. She brings out four cushions. I wonder to myself why four. Like her assistant, she reads my mind.

"The fourth cushion represents Danielle."

"Okay," we say, sitting.

"Uh…Dr. Hayes, I recently found out I'm with child. I just want to make sure nothing we do today will hurt my baby," I say.

"No, not at all. What we do today is going to help you, and as a result your baby will benefit as well."

I smile and get comfortable.

"I want you ladies to sit up straight with your legs extended straight out in front of you."

"I thought we were going to do a lotus position," Sheridan says.

"No, I want you to be comfortable," Dr. Hayes says.

We all do as instructed.

"Okay, ladies, take a deep breath in."

The room fills with the sound of air being taken in.

"Now release it slowly."

We do so.

"How did that feel?"

"Good," we say.

"Repeat it."

We breathe in and out again—deeply and slowly.

"Now close your eyes and see your breath coming in and going out. Put a color to it. Whatever color you're comfortable with. You don't have to tell anyone."

I close my eyes and breathe in deeply and out slowly. I imagine my breath is yellow. I think I choose yellow because I'm afraid.

"Now think about why you chose the color you did,"

she says.

Wow, I'm way ahead of her.

"Now this time when you breathe in and out, I want you to think about how you want to feel and what color that feeling would be."

I want my breath to be like the rainbow…colorful…happy.

"Keep breathing in deeply and out slowly. Now that you have your color, I want you to focus on your breath, and I'm going to count down to ten, and as I count down, I want you to lie back on your cushions with your eyes closed, your legs stretched out, and your arms by your side, and I want you to imagine that you're floating in the ocean in warm, clear blue water. 10, 9, 8, 7, 6, 5, 4, 3, 2, 1."

I continue to breathe as she instructed. A wave of heat spreads through my body, and I feel as calm as I did earlier when I called on the name of Jesus. I feel myself floating. I'm no longer in Dr. Hayes's office. I'm in an ocean of bliss. I wonder if Vicky and Sheridan feel as good as I do.

"Don't focus on anyone but yourself."

What is she, a mind reader? I forget about Vicky and Sheridan and float and watch my rainbow breath.

"Now I want you to go back to the day that everything fell apart. I want you to go back to that morning. Go back to the moment you woke up that morning. How were you feeling? What was going on? What were your plans? I want you to imagine yourself in high school…a high school senior…soon to graduate. Imagine yourself and the other members of The Fresh Five. I want you to go back in time and relive those moments leading up to what happened. You're in a safe place to do this. You're in your ocean…your safe cocoon. Let go and experience what happened…the truth of what happened. You don't have to run from it anymore. You don't have to suppress it or hide from it. Today you're going to face it and release it."

Chapter 27

Victoria

Turning over in bed, a crafty smile creeps over my face. I had a dream about my phone conversation with Gary. He sounded so good. I can't believe he agreed to meet me tomorrow. I've already picked out what I'm going to wear and I have a bomb panty and bra set. When I get through laying it on him, he'll be asking "Sheridan who?" Laughing, I sit up, basking in my fantasy. My eyes shift to the Bible on my nightstand that Faye's father gave me when I got baptized and I get a pang of guilt. I know what I'm planning is wrong, but I can't help myself. I get out of bed and go to my dresser. I open my sock drawer and take out one of the Wine Coolers I stole from the liquor store last week. I only have four left, so I take just a sip so it'll last. I nearly drop it when I hear my mother calling me from downstairs.

"Vicky! Girl, are you still sleep? It's almost noon. Sabrina's on the phone."

I fumble with the bottle of peach Wine Cooler and shove it under my socks and close the drawer. "I'm up, Mommie! Tell her I'll be right there." I run into my restroom, use it right quick, wash my hands, and rush downstairs. My feet get tangled in the hem of my gown. I grab the rail before I trip.

"Stop running down those stairs before you fall, Vicky."

"Okay, mommie," I say, slowing my roll.

I go into the kitchen and grab the phone. I can see my two younger brothers playing basketball in the backyard. "Sabrina, what's up girl?"

"Uh…uh…hmm…hey, Vicky."

"You sound horrible," I say.

"I think I have the flu."

"The flu? That's whack."

"I'm not gonna be able to go to the party with you guys tonight."

"Dang! Are you sure?"

"Girl, I can't even move, I'm so weak."

"Aww, I'm sorry, Sabrina. Did you tell the others?"

"No, can you tell them for me."

"I will and we're gonna come and see you before we leave. Do you want us to bring you anything?"

"No, I don't want you guys to get sick, too."

"Okay, but we're gonna miss you."

"Have fun for me, okay."

"Okay, Sabrina. Feel better."

"I will. Bye."

"Bye." I hang up and the excitement I felt earlier is

gone. I hate Sabrina's not going. It's just not the same when one of us is missing.

"What's wrong?" my mother asks, entering the kitchen.

"Sabrina has the flu and can't come to Melanie's birthday party tonight."

"That's too bad," my mother says. She looks at me with her green eyes filled with sympathy. "You've practically slept the day away. You have chores young lady."

"Okay, mommie. I'll get to them."

She leaves and I go to the backyard. My brothers stop playing ball and give me a crazy look. "What do you want, V?"

"Nothing, just the ball," I say. I snatch it out of my youngest brother's hand and run. They chase me around the yard.

"Stop messin' around, V. We're gonna tell dad."

"Dad is at work! Ha! ha! You're such babies," I say, throwing the ball at them. I leave them standing there shaking their heads and go back to my room.

I take the outfit out I'm going to wear to see Gary and admire it. He's gonna love my little red and white jean skirt suit and my red bra and matching silk panties. Then I get my outfit I'm going to wear to Melanie's party and give it a kiss of approval. It's not as cute as what I'm going to wear to see Gary, but it's still the bomb. I hold the purple dress with black tassels at the bottom up to my frame and strut. I'm so glad Gary won't be there with Sheridan. The Bradshaw Bears have a game in San Jose tonight against their regional rival The Glendale Gladiators. The cheerleaders had to draw straws to see who could go. Sheridan and I didn't make the cut. I'm glad, because Melanie's parties are all that and a bag of chips and she always has booze.

I put everything away, take my shower, and do my chores. By the time I finish, eat lunch, and go to the grocery store with my mother, I'm wiped out. I know I'll get my second wind when I get dressed for the party. We all plan to get dressed at Danielle's house. Her father's going to take us to the party, bring us back to Danielle's house, and we'll spend the night there, and then in the morning we're going to Faye's father's church. It's going to be an exciting weekend.

"Be careful," my mother says. She pulls in front of Danielle's house and I start to get out of the car. "And you listen to the judge and *be* careful."

"Mommie, you said that already. I'm a big girl now. I'm eighteen with a driver's license! I'm practically grown."

"Victoria, you watch your tone of voice when you talk to me or you won't be going anywhere."

"Sorry." I grab my garment bag and small vanity case from the backseat, kiss my mother on the cheek, and head to Danielle's front door. I look over my shoulder at my mother and she just stares. I love her, but she gets on my nerves sometimes. "See you tomorrow, mommie."

"Love you, Vicky."

"Love you, too, mommie."

She finally leaves and I ring the doorbell. The door flings open and Richard, Danielle's older brother, stands there pointing a rifle at me. I knock it out of the way and rush upstairs.

"Hey, I didn't say you could come in!" he screams.

"Richard, get a life," I say.

I push the door to Danielle's room open and I catch her picking at her pubic hairs. "Find anything interesting?" I ask.

"Girl, don't you know how to knock?"

"You don't have anything I haven't seen before. What are you doing?"

"I think Danielle has a cyst. It hurts."

"Let me see. I stoop down and feel on her vagina."

"Ouch! That hurts."

"I don't feel anything I say."

"Look at the lesbos!" We look toward the door and Sheridan aka Barbie doll starts to laugh.

"I think I have a cyst," Danielle says.

"What's a cyst," Faye asks, standing behind Sheridan.

We all laugh and Faye's eyes widen and fill with tears. "Why are you guys always laughing at me? And Danielle, your crazy brother tried to shoot me with that crazy Bebe gun. I thought he got rid of that after he shot your neighbor's dog."

"It's not the same one," Danielle says, putting on her underwear.

"Where's Sabrina?" Faye asks, looking around.

"I knew there was something I needed to tell you guys. She has the flu and can't come with us."

"That's messed up," Sheridan says.

"We should go and see her," Faye says.

"She doesn't want us to. She says it's catching," I say.

"We could wear a mask. You know how they do in the hospital," Faye says.

"And where are we supposed to get masks?" Sheridan asks.

"We'll go see her after church tomorrow," Danielle says. "I think you guys better sit down because I have some messed up news, too."

We all share fearful looks and wait for the bomb to drop.

"What is it?" we all ask.

"My parents had to go out of town yesterday to see about my grandmother, and they said I couldn't go to Melanie's party."

"What the fu—freak," Sheridan says.

"Why not?" I ask.

"They don't feel comfortable with me going to a party when they're out of town."

"But Richard's here. He can handle things and he can drive us to the party. He has his license. Shoot, *you* can drive us, Danielle. You have your license and I can, too," I say. "I have my license."

"My father doesn't want us driving his car and he says Richard's a loose cannon and he says I don't have enough experience driving yet."

"We have to go. This is the party of the year," I say.

"The party of the century," Sheridan says.

"If the judge said she can't go, then she can't go," Faye says. "I have my license, too, but I wouldn't go against the judge."

"Be quiet, Faye. We're going to the party," I say.

"We can't. Richard will tell my father and I'll be grounded for life."

I stand there thinking about how cute my purple dress is and how much booze Melanie is gonna have and I try to come up with a solution. "How much money do you have?" I ask them.

"Not a lot," Sheridan says.

"I have about fifty dollars in my underwear drawer," Danielle says.

"I have the money I was gonna tithe with," Faye says.

"I have about twenty. Let's put our money together and pay Richard to take us to the party and back and to keep it a secret."

"That's not a bad idea," Sheridan says.

"He might go for it." Danielle says.

"What do we have to lose?" I ask. I go into my bag and pull out my Wine Coolers. Danielle says, "That's what I'm talkin' 'bout and Faye shakes her head so hard her weave actually moves.

"Hey, that's my jam!" Sheridan screams from the backseat of Danielle's father's Cadillac. "I wish they would have played that at the party. Turn it up!" she screams. "All I wanna do is zoom a zoom zoom zoom!"

"That's too loud. I hate that stupid Rump Shaker song," Faye says.

"That's because you've never been zoomed!" Sheridan says, laughing.

"I know that's right I say," laughing along with her.

"That party was the bomb!" Danielle says.

"It was okay," Faye says.

"Did you feel that?" I ask.

"Feel what?" the others ask.

"The street moving. Are we having an earthquake?"

"No, fool," Sheridan says.

"It feels like it," I say.

"You're drunk," Sheridan says.

"I only had one Wine Cooler...or did I have two?...maybe three...and a shot of Vodka. It seems like it's taking forever to get to your house, Danielle. I think we're lost," I say.

"Shut-up!" Faye says. "My head hurts."

"Did you have some of the punch?" I ask.

"Yeah."

"It was spiked! Psyche!" I say.

We all are quiet as we approach Danielle's street. And then Sheridan clears her throat loudly. "Ladies, you were probably wondering why I stayed away from the spiked punch and the Wine Coolers tonight. Well, I have a very good reason."

I sit at attention, waiting for Sheridan to continue. "What? What is it, Sherry?" I ask.

"You're all going to be aunties!"

"What do you mean?" Faye asks.

"I'm having a baby. Gary and I are pregnant."

I put my finger in my ear, thinking I had heard her wrong. "What did you say?"

"Gary and I are pregnant."

My throat constricts and I can't breathe. My eyes sting and tear up and my head throbs. "What the fuck do you mean you're pregnant?"

"I'm having Gary's baby."

I lunge at Sheridan and grab her by the throat. The others scream. "You're lying. You lying bitch. You can't be. You can't be!"

"Get off of me!" Sheridan screams, kicking the driver's seat in front of her. "Help me!"

"Stop, stop, you guys," Faye screams. "You're gonna make us have an accident."

"I hate you, Sheridan!" I yell.

She gets out of my grip and we tear at each other in the backseat. We scratch and kick and I push Sheridan over the driver's seat and the car speeds forward, throwing us back. The next thing I know Faye is screaming, "He has a gun" and I hear the tires burning rubber and a loud thud against the windshield and the sound of glass shattering. Then I feel the car lift and roll and then there's a squashing sound and the car comes to a sudden stop.

Shrill screams fill the inside of the car. I press my hands over my ears, but the screams and crying seep through.

"What happened? My God, what happened?" Faye asks. "What was that?"

We slowly get out of the car and gasp at the sight of blood on the windshield and ground. A piece of crumpled metal is on the ground next to what looks like a pair of legs. We can't see the rest of the person.

Faye falls to her knees and says, "Is he dead? Please don't let him be dead. Did I kill him? Lord, have mercy. No!

No! No!"

The legs start to shiver and we all scream. "Call 911! somebody call 911!" Sheridan yells. Faye runs to the nearest house and bangs on the door. The lights in all the houses start to come on. Tears stream down my face and my stomach drops when gurgling sounds come from underneath the car. We share terrified looks when we hear a whisper. "Danny, Danny," the voice calls out.

Danielle begins shaking and screaming and the voice gets louder. "Danny, help me!" Danny points to the metal that we now realize is a gun. "It's Richard, it's Richard." She dives under the car trying to get to him. I stand there unable to move. Sheridan goes under the car with her and they try to move him. The sound of a distant siren fills the cold night air, and I turn when I hear running footfalls.

"Don't touch him! Don't, because you can cause more harm than good."

We look up at the stranger, hoping he knows what he's talking about. Sheridan rises, but Danielle stays on the ground. "It's me, Richard. It's me. Take my hand," Danielle says.

Chapter 28

Danielle

"He took my hand and squeezed it, gently. 'You can't leave me, Richard. You just can't. We have to grow up. You have to graduate from college and meet 'The One' and get married and have a bunch of babies and become the FBI agent you've always wanted to become.'"

"I still remember his last words. 'Danny, I wasn't trying to hurt you guys. I was just playing. I thought you knew it was me when I jumped in front of the car and pointed my Bebe gun at the windshield. I saw you guys coming. I was trying to catch up with you to tell you Dad and Mom were on their way back home. I didn't want you to get in trouble.'"

"I said, 'Don't talk, baby.'"

"He wheezed and coughed and then said 'Who are you calling a baby? I'm the oldest.'" I squeezed his hand again and I felt cold liquid on my legs. I looked down and it was his blood. He was bleeding out. 'Where in the hell is the ambulance?' I screamed."

"Flashing lights appeared and an ambulance pulled up and paramedics jumped out and then a fire truck arrived and several police cars and the street looked like a war zone. They lifted my father's car off of Richard and I screamed at the sight of his legs. They were barely attached to his body. He was taken away in an ambulance and we were taken to the police station. Our parents showed up after spending time at the hospital. My father pulled a few strings and we were all released. My father informed us that Richard died before he had reached the hospital. I felt like I had died that night, too. I kept going over what happened in my head, blaming the others. We all blamed each other."

Dr. Hayes takes in a deep breath and says, "Faye, are you okay?"

Faye, with a face drenched in tears, says, "I'll be fine. I know God has forgiven me."

"I know it's harder for you because you drove that night," Dr. Hayes says.

"No...I didn't. I wasn't the driver," Faye says.

"Based on Vicky's account, Sheridan and Vicky were in the backseat."

"Yes, they were," Faye says.

"She didn't drive, I drove. I was the driver, Dr. Hayes," I say. "I killed my brother. I did. When we tried to bribe him he said he wouldn't take us to the party, I got so pissed that I defied him and my father. I did the unthinkable and I paid the ultimate price."

Sheridan, Faye, and Vicky come to me and hold me. "We're so glad you showed up, Danielle" Vicky says.

"Please forgive me. If I hadn't been drunk and trying to steal Gary from Sherry, I never would have reacted to Sherry's news like I did and we wouldn't have been fighting in the backseat."

"And if I had kept my legs closed, I never would have gotten pregnant with Gary's baby and I wouldn't have dropped that bomb on Vicky, knowing that she would have been hurt, and I wouldn't have fallen on you, and you wouldn't have pressed on the gas," Sheridan says.

"And if I hadn't been so quick to react, I would have seen that it was Richard and not some stranger trying to shoot at us," Faye says.

"And if I had listened to my father, we never would have gone out in the first place," I say.

"I'm sorry, forgive me," we all say together.

We hug, cry, and hold each other like our lives depend on it. Dr. Hayes, with tears in her eyes and a smile on her face joins us in a group hug.

We come out of our group hug and surround Sabrina's grave site. Seven months has passed since we bared our souls, successfully reliving the night that threatened to destroy us forever. But with a lot of prayer, strength, and courage we made it through. Sheridan had an incredible art show and she, Gary, and her mother-in-law are moving into a mini-mansion in Beverly Hills *for real*. Escrow closes in a month and Sheridan is beyond excited. She sold everything and made high six figures after New Hope took its portion. Gary and Sheridan are members of New Hope now and Gary is running the boys Rites of Passage Program and has started a junior football league. Faye is eight months pregnant with a girl and is preparing for her baby shower. Vicky is teaching again and she and Curtis have reunited and are living happily with their children in Los Feliz. Everyone is doing well. As for me, I've made some drastic changes. Frankie and I are now divorced, and I've moved back to Los Angeles. I still love her, but after several sessions with Dr. Hayes, it became apparent that Frankie was my rebound love. When I returned to New York, it was even more difficult to connect and we eventually drifted apart. I've started my own practice and am happier than I've been in a long time. I'm trying to buy my own house, but the Browns have kidnapped me and won't let me leave. I know they're trying to heal like the rest of us. Walter comes by a lot and we've gotten really close—nothing sexual—just friends. Sabrina did come to me in a dream once and told me she would give me her blessing if I decided to hook-up with Walter. I woke up in a cold sweat. I couldn't imagine being with Walter. The others tease me and tell me to never say never.

"What are you guys thinking?" Faye asks.

"About Sabrina," Vicky says.

"I'm glad she brought us together," Sheridan says.

"Me, too," I say.

Faye takes the bouquet of flowers off of the ground and sets them up against Sabrina's headstone. We read the words out loud.

"In loving memory of our daughter and member of The Fresh Five," Sabrina Louise Brown. September 5, 1975 – October 1, 2013."

"Look! Look!" Faye screams.

"What?" we ask.

"Up there," she says, pointing. "Butterflies—one, two, three, four!"

"Wow," we say, while we watch the butterflies land on top of Sabrina's headstone.

"That's a trip," Sheridan says.

"It sure is," I say. "You guys ready?"

"Yep."

"We better head out or Mother Brown is going to have our heads. You know she's been planning this barbeque for twenty years."

We laugh and leave the cemetery.

"You think everybody is having a good time?" Mrs. Brown asks, looking around at all the people in Sabrina's backyard.

My eyes zoom in on Curtis feeding Vicky potato salad and Matt chasing Tangie with a water balloon. Then I look over at Sheridan pressing on Gary's six-pack. And I'm not talking about beer. He looks almost as good as he did back at Brad. Kim, looking like a model, dances around her parents. On the other side of the yard, Faye sits in a lawn chair, massaging her stomach while Mark massages her feet. Walter and Mr. Brown fuss over the barbeque on the grill. I shut and open my eyes and take in the air filled with love and the aroma of good food and say, "Yes, everyone is having a good time."

"You girls have made me so happy," Mrs. Brown says.

"We're glad you're happy…Mother Brown I hate to say this, but I really need to get my own place and I'm ready to buy some property in California."

"I know you are, Danny." She perks up and then says, "I have a great idea!"

"What?"

"Why don't you buy this house? Sabrina's house?"

"This house?"

"Why not? It's in a great neighborhood, not far from your practice, and I'll sell it to you at a good price."

I contemplate her offer, wondering why I hadn't thought of it myself. I've always loved this neighborhood and this house. It would be like keeping Sabrina's legacy alive. I give her a curious look.

"Jerome and Mother Brown don't come with the house," she says, laughing.

"Mother Brown!"

"Jerome and Mother Brown are ready to move back home."

"Okay, Mother Brown. You have a deal."

"Oh, Danny, thank you."

"No, thank you."

"Pierre, come back here! Get back her, Pierre!"

We look toward the back gate when Mrs. Franklin runs in chasing Pierre. He heads straight for Faye's feet and we all shriek, waiting for Faye to scream and try to run. But instead of running, she giggles and reaches for Pierre. He jumps in her lap and licks her face. Shocked, we all just stare.

"Hey, Pierre, guess what...I'm having a baby." Pierre barks and jumps out of her lap into Mrs. Franklin's arms.

The yard fills with raucous laughter.

Epilogue

You're probably wondering where I am — heaven, purgatory, hell, my grave? Where I am depends solely on your belief or disbelief. I can tell you this, I'm not in pain and I'm at peace. As you witnessed, God answered my prayers and brought my friends together. But he did more than that. He helped them discover, discard, and grow into the beautiful women they are today and for that I am truly grateful.

I oftentimes wonder how things would have been different if I had not fallen ill the day of the party. What would have happened if I had been there? I probably would have been in the backseat with Vicky and Sheridan, sitting between them, so they never would have been able to attack each other. On second thought, we never would have gone to the party, because I wouldn't have gone against the judge's wishes. We would have stayed at Danielle's house and had a party there. Then again, maybe we would have gone. No one knows how decisions and actions in life will impact us and those we love.

Thank you for going on this journey and many blessing to you and yours. Love always, Sabrina Brown.

The End

BOOK CLUB QUESTIONS

1. Do you think Sabrina was wrong for keeping her illness a secret?

2. Do you think Sabrina should have given up on trying to reunite the Fresh Five?

3. Do you think Mrs. Brown should have gone against Sabrina's wishes and told the others about Sabrina's illness?

4. Do you think Sabrina should have forgiven Walter?

5. Do you think Sabrina should have let Walter attend her funeral?

6. Upon being introduced to Sheridan, did you think she was African-American and why?

7. Do you think Mark should have forgiven Faye?

8. Were you surprised to find out what Faye did and who she did it with?

9. Do you think Vicky is a bad mother?

10. What did you think Vicky had done to her kids?

11. Do you think Danielle is gay?

12. Were you surprised to find out who Danielle is married to?

13. What or who did you think broke the Fresh Five up?"

6251860R00161

Printed in Great Britain
by Amazon.co.uk, Ltd.,
Marston Gate.